The Forget-Me-Not Girl

Sheila Newberry was born in Suffolk and spent a lot of time there both before and during the war. She wrote her first 'book' before she was ten – all sixty pages of it – in purple ink. Her family has certainly been her inspiration and she has been published for most of her adult life. She spent forty years living in Kent on a smallholding with her husband, John, and has nine children, twenty-two grandchildren and six great-grandchildren. Sheila retired back to Suffolk where she still lives today.

Also by Sheila Newberry

Angel's Secret
Bicycles and Blackberries
The Canal Girl
The Daughter's Choice
The Family at Number Five
Far From Home
The Gingerbread Girl
The Girl With No Home
Hay Bales and Hollyhocks
Hot Pies on the Tram Car
Molly's Journey
The Nursemaid's Secret
The Poplar Penny Whistlers
The Punch and Judy Girl
The Watercress Girls
The Winter Baby

Sheila Newberry

The Forget-Me-Not Girl

ZAFFRE

First published in Great Britain in 2019 by
ZAFFRE
80–81 Wimpole St, London W1G 9RE

A CIP catalogue record for this book is
available from the British Library.

ISBN: 978-1-78576-539-1

Also available as an ebook

1 3 5 7 9 10 8 6 4 2

Typeset by IDSUK (Data Connection) Ltd
Printed and bound in Great Britain by Clays Ltd, Elcograf S.p.A.

Zaffre is an imprint of Bonnier Books UK
www.bonnierbooks.co.uk

To an inspiring great-grandmother, Emma Meehan,
née Wright, the Forget-Me-Not Girl
She was born in Wymondham, Norfolk in 1840
This is the first part of her story, alongside the sadly shorter
one of her beloved Thomas Frederick (TF)

If I were a blackbird, I'd whistle and sing
I'd follow the ship that my true love sails in
And on the top rigging, I'd there build my nest
And I'd pillow my head on his lily-white breast

Traditional

PROLOGUE

Boxing Day, 1936

'Shall I brush your hair for you, Grandma Emma?' the small girl asked. She sat beside the bed where the old lady lay, propped up by plump pillows with her eyes closed. At times like this Emma felt her husband's presence, which comforted her. Her bed had been moved downstairs to the sitting room and placed so that she could see out of the big window. The Christmas decorations were still up and a Yule log was blazing in the fireplace, for this was the wedding day of her youngest granddaughter, Myrtle. Emma was now very frail and unable to walk from the Old Swan Inn, where she lived with her son Ernest and his wife Bel, to the church opposite as she had a year ago when Myrtle's sister, Nell, was married. Later, the room would be full of happy chatter when the wedding party and guests returned after the service. Emma would be at the centre of this, as always.

Emma's eyes opened; she couldn't see very well, but she wouldn't admit it. She gazed at the little girl thoughtfully.

Shummy, as the family called her, was awaiting the arrival of her fellow bridesmaids. Emma had chosen their outfits. She herself had worn a ruby-red velvet gown when she married her beloved TF on 26 January 1863 in St Stephen's Church in London, and her great-granddaughter, four years old, was dressed in red velvet today. She had a little silver Dutch bonnet and she clutched a beautiful white muff. Emma had borrowed a muff like that on her wedding day, she recalled. It had been snowing that day and seemed likely to do so today.

'You may brush my hair, but very gently, dear.' She indicated the brush on her bedside table and closed her eyes as Shummy knelt beside her to brush the long silver locks, which still had a curl at the ends.

'Did you have black hair once, Grandma?' Shummy asked.

'I did,' Emma said. 'Black as a raven's wing, my mother said. TF, my dear husband, had very fair hair, Ernie was red-haired like his Irish grandfather. I looked after his and Bel's children when they took on the Buck Inn at Uggeshall. I used to brush the little girls' hair before they went to school. The Boy Hedley was at work, of course. Bella, your mother, was blonde like Myrtle and you; Nell had red hair like her father and Little Ernie . . .' Emma paused, then added, 'That's enough brushing, dear, thank you.'

Shummy put the brush down. 'Grandma, where is Little Ernie?'

'He's with the angels. He was seven years old when they laid him to rest.'

'Mummy said when Nanna and Grandad went out on Christmas morning, they were going to Uggeshall Church to visit Little Ernie.' They'd carried a wreath, which Shummy had watched Nanna make.

Bel put her head round the door, and said, 'Shummy, the bridesmaids are here, come and join them in the kitchen. I must help Myrtle with her flowers. Mother, I took a sprig from the myrtle bush you planted long ago in the Buck garden, as you suggested.' She noticed the empty cup and saucer on the bedside table and picked it up. 'Oh, your forget-me-not cup. Best not leave it here in case it gets broken, I know how you love your mother's old cup.' Then she bustled away, followed by Shummy.

The bone china cup had been hand-painted with the delicate little flowers, which had faded over many years. It was the only thing belonging to her mother that Emma had been given.

Emma's eyes closed again. She wasn't asleep, but remembering her dear mother who had been her inspiration, and her wonderful husband – how happy she had been on her wedding day . . . Emma smiled to herself, recalling their first meeting. It was love at first sight for them both.

Another vivid memory surfaced: TF visited her one day when she was on holiday with the Summers family by the sea. As the sun was setting the two of them went on the last boat trip of the day and the red sky was reflected in the water. The colour of my wedding dress, she mused . . .

Gladys came into the room, dressed in the outfit she had worn for her own wedding but with a new hat. She was the mother of five children herself, and she was particularly close to her grandma, who had lived with her for a time, and helped with the children while her husband was away in the navy. Gladys pinned Emma's hair into place. 'I have to go now, Grandma – we are just about to go out of the door and you must wave to the bride! The bridegroom and best man are waiting in the church. Your children have come from far and wide. Tom, Ted, and Alice – and Frank in Canada sent a cable. Can you hear the bells – Hedley is ringing as usual!'

'Yes, I hear the bells,' Emma said. 'Is it snowing?'

'It's stopped now, but it's a white world, Grandma.'

As it was in Marylebone Terrace, in London, Emma thought, when TF and I arrived at our first little home after the wedding feast. We were warm that night, despite the weather – two young people passionately in love, as we were to the end.

ONE

Emma

Browick Bottom Farm, Wymondham, Norfolk, 1840

The lantern hooked on the cowshed door shed a patch of yellow light onto the growing pile of snow in the yard. There had been a heavy fall during the night and two young men with shovels, Edward and twelve-year-old Samuel, their faces muffled by woollen scarves against the freezing cold, worked without conversing to clear a pathway to the farmhouse, where another light gleamed through a gap in the curtains of an upstairs window. There was an intermittent lowing from the small herd of dairy cows inside the shed, for it was time for the early milking. Then the horse, pigs and fowl must be tended to, and then many buckets of water needed to be hauled up from the well before the lads could pause for breakfast.

The workers looked up as they heard the crunch of footsteps in the snow that had not yet been cleared, and William made his way up the path. The wooden sails of the small drainage mill were motionless, festooned with icicles, but when the thaw came, the stream would flow and William would be in charge of the irrigation, for he had a keen interest in farm machinery. The middle son of the three, he was his father's right-hand man.

William, a strong, cheerful chap of eighteen, had been despatched half an hour earlier to fetch the midwife. Sophia, his young stepmother, was in labour with her third child. The back door of the house opened at their approach and – with oil lamp in hand – his father, Tobias, observed mildly to the stout little woman that William was helping up the steps, 'You took your time, missus.'

The midwife soon divested herself of several heavy shawls, and then rubbed her hands together to warm them. Her fingers were bone-white from the cold. She removed her bonnet, but not the little cotton cap beneath that covered her hair. 'Everything ready?' she asked sharply. Tobias nodded. 'Then I'll goo straight up. William can bring my bag. Is there aplenty hot water in the jug? Where's the little one – not with her mother, I hope?' At three years old, Martha still slept in her parents' room.

'She's in the kitchen with her sister. It's the warmest room in the house; the new range do give out a good heat. Lizzie made her a bowl of bread and milk and will cook the lads' breakfast. I lit the fire in the bedroom first thing.'

'Young Sophie's not here to help?' the midwife turned her head as she grasped the polished banister. Lizzie was, after all, only seven years old herself. She hadn't known her own mother, who had died soon after her birth. She was a quiet girl and devoted to her small half-sister Martha, but was somewhat overshadowed by her strong-minded older sister, Sophie, who was fifteen.

'The gal went to her first job after Christmas. It was time. You can't have two grown women in the kitchen,' Tobias replied. There was a piercing scream from upstairs. 'You'd better git up there quick, missus,' he added.

Sophia, who coincidentally bore the same name as her predecessor, had thrown back the covers on the bed. She was nothing like the first Sophia, who had borne seven children, but lost two in infancy. She had been a tall, well-made woman with red cheeks – not always a sign of good health – and a placid nature. There had invariably been one of her family in attendance when her babies were born. In contrast, this young woman was small in stature with glossy, centre-parted dark hair pulled back and knotted at the nape of her neck. Her high cheekbones gave her an exotic look, unlike the strapping local girls with their flaxen hair. This second Sophia had just her husband for support. Tobias was middle-aged and grey-bearded, but didn't panic like a young father, and never had, since he'd grown up with pigs farrowing and later, calving cows. He'd taken on the tenancy of the family farm when his father retired.

The midwife knew why Sophia had no close relatives with her, of course. The second Sophia came from a family of Dissenters – Protestant Christians who had separated from the Church of England during the past three centuries. Sophia's father was politically ambitious, like so many of his fellow dissenters who were keen on education and had founded several local schools. They said they were directed by God alone, and they followed the scriptures devoutly.

The Wrights, on the other hand, attended services in Wymondham Abbey, their parish church. Sophia, a bright, intelligent girl who had learned to read and write by studying the Bible, had been employed to look after Tobias and his family when he was widowed after the death of the first Sophia. She was not only a competent house-keeper, but she also cared for baby Lizzie and carried on teaching the younger children at home, as their mother had done. Wisely, she did not try to replace her. However, the children were soon captivated by her lively storytelling and succulent cooking.

Tobias saw how she cared for his children and she was accepted as one of the family and realised that he was starting to feel something for her himself. One evening, when he came in weary after a heavy day on the farm, his boots muddy, he had slumped into his chair by the stove in the kitchen and heaved a sigh. He could smell his dinner, rabbit stew, warming in the oven, but was too weary to get himself cleaned up before he ate.

Sophia came into the room, with a bowl of hot water, soap and a towel. She knelt beside the chair and pulled off his soiled boots. 'Don't worry, let them dry by the fire, then I'll clean them for you,' she said. She passed him a flannel to dip in the water and clean his face and hands. 'Soak your poor old feet, Tobias, and I'll dry them for you.'

He looked at her concerned face and said simply, 'I think I should marry you, Sophia, if you will hev me, because like the children, I can't do without you.'

Her face had lit up. 'Of course I will, Tobias. I feel like one of the family already; but I don't think my father will allow it—'

'He can't say no, once you're of age,' he told her.

She held out the big towel and said, 'Right foot first.'

He looked down at her dark head, with tendrils of hair curling in the steam from the bowl of water. He guessed she was waiting for him to say he loved her. Then, on impulse he said, 'It's lonely, you know, to lie by myself in that big bed. Would – you mind that?'

She looked up, and she was smiling. 'Of course I wouldn't – but we must be married first, Tobias! I didn't realise I loved you – and your family – until you said what you did.'

He could say no more then. 'I meant it; I promise to love and cherish you all my days.'

Later, when she came of age, Tobias and Sophia had married secretly in Norwich, knowing her parents would disapprove. He was nearly twenty years her senior, but it was certainly a love match. Tobias was tolerant and kind, unlike her stern, unrelenting preacher father.

A year later, Sophia had given birth to a tiny son, and as was the custom with her kin, she gave him a biblical name – Urim. One meaning of this was *innocence*. Sadly, the baby, like so many at that time, died shortly afterwards.

Although Tobias assured her that he didn't mind at all if the next baby after Martha was also a girl – he had three sons already, after all, who had followed him into farming – Sophia prayed for another son, to replace the lost baby.

The midwife tidied the rumpled bed, eased Sophia up so that her shoulders rested against the pillows piled high behind her. 'Stretch your arms up, my dear, pull on the rope,' she coaxed the exhausted woman. This was a cord fashioned from torn sheeting tied to the bed rail. Sophia closed her eyes and did as she was told, as the midwife examined her. She knew she was in safe hands.

Tobias arrived with a tray of teacups and was in time to see the baby caught in the midwife's capable grasp and the cutting of the umbilical cord. The baby was wrapped swiftly in a towel and placed in the waiting crib, the same one Tobias had made for his firstborn with the first Sophia. It was made of wood and set on rockers. He set the tray down with a clatter on a small table and rushed to Sophia's side. After all her efforts, sweat streamed down her face, and she lay there looking up at him, her body racked with more pain, as the placenta was expelled.

'You – shouldn't be here – to see all this,' she murmured faintly.

'My dear gal, course I should,' he said robustly, sponging her face with a wet flannel handed to him by the nurse. Then he supported Sophia while she sipped her tea. She grimaced. 'Too sweet!'

'You need the sugar to git your strength back,' Tobias insisted.

'The baby – is he – all right?'

The midwife gave Tobias a nod. Her lips formed a word. He nodded in return. 'Sophia, us hev a baby daughter. All is well.'

'A daughter,' she repeated.

'Yes, dark-haired, like you. What shall us call her?'

'I am too tired to think,' she said, turning her face to the pillow.

'Us'll let the children decide.'

The baby had cried lustily when she was born but had been quiet since. Now there was a different cry. At this sound, tears trickled silently down Sophia's cheeks.

'She need her mother,' Tobias said to the midwife. He was referring to Sophia as well as to the baby.

The midwife scooped the little bundle up and passed the baby to Tobias. He cradled her for a moment, then carefully placed the baby in the crook of Sophia's arm, and adjusted the bedcovers over them both. 'She is *bootiful,*' he said huskily in his soft, Norfolk burr. 'Yes, she do take after you, my dear.' He cleared his throat, having seen Sophia kiss the top of the baby's dark, downy head, before gently turning it to her breast. 'I will leave you now, I must give the family the good news. Will you, missus, kindly tell those who might care to know?'

'I will,' the midwife promised. 'Give me time to bath the baby afore the children rush in here,' she indicated the bowl patterned with bright-blue cornflowers on the washstand. 'The water in the jug should be cool enough by now. Your good wife needs a clean nightgown, too. Stir up the fire afore you goo, Tobias.'

The new baby was registered as Emily, but on 5 March 1840, she was baptised Emma in Wymondham Abbey. William stood as her godfather. The rift between Sophia and her family was irrevocable, it seemed. The Penny Post was at last a reality, putting people in touch all over the country, but Sophia's father would, she knew, open any letter addressed to her mother. He was a pious man but implacable. She could never return to the fold, but her steadfast faith endured.

TWO

TF and Isabella

Newcastle to Glanton, Northumberland, 1836

Isabella travelled for the last time in the family carriage, accompanied by her maid, who would bravely return to face the music without her once the wedding was over. This loyal woman had packed Isabella's leather-bound trunk, tucking several pieces of jewellery among her clothes. These included an extravagantly ruffled black satin opera cloak lined with scarlet, which Isabella had worn on her twenty-first birthday outing to the theatre with her father, together with an ostrich fan and elegant opera glasses. At the last minute, she added a few favourite books, a family portrait in an ornate silver frame and a small sewing basket, which held her embroidery silks and reels of cotton. Hidden in the basket was a tiny japanned box inside which was a golden guinea, a birthday gift from a favourite great-aunt, Eliza Nesbit. Apart from this, Isabella had only ten shillings left from her monthly allowance in her purse, but this would enable the young couple to stay a few days in a cheap lodging house once married.

Isabella's companion looked at her mistress and felt compelled to ask her, 'Are you sure, Miss Isabella, you want to go through with this? If you want the driver to turn and take us back home, I won't say anything, if I should be asked . . .'

'Thank you, Milly,' Isabella said. 'I'm afraid my father will never forgive me for a runaway marriage, but if I don't go through with it, I will forever regret it . . . Have you ever been in love?'

Milly shook her head. 'I never had no chance of that, Miss Isabella. Never!' She dabbed at her eyes, then added, 'I just want you to be happy, that's all.'

'I know you do. I wish you could come with me wherever I am going, but I will have to learn to do things for myself now. Here we are, and there's my Irish Tom waiting by the church gate. Please ask the driver to leave my trunk in the porch. Well, goodbye, Milly, and good luck!'

Isabella had been born in Ashton-under-Lyne to a wealthy family, was educated privately at home, where she also had three younger sisters and a small brother, and enjoyed a lively social life when she stayed with her father, Abraham, in his city apartment. She had met her 'Irish Tom' when he was employed by her father as a skilled painter in a team of maintenance men who refurbished the fleet of cargo ships which delivered coals from Newcastle. Tom was born in 1812 in London, Middlesex when his parents had come over for the summer harvest, but he was brought up in County Clare on the family smallholding. He had a lively mind and a cheerful disposition, but his education was patchy, and as a youth he became an apprentice house painter. Like many young men, before and after the potato famine, he had ventured first to Liverpool to find work, and then to Newcastle. The two were an unlikely match, but fell in love immediately, despite her family's disapproval at Irish Tom's lowly status.

Isabella had always known she was her father's favourite child and that he had hoped she would eventually be involved with the family business. He had confided to her once that 'Marriage is not the be-all and end-all for an intelligent young woman like you. This fellow you appear infatuated with is never going to rise above his humble beginnings. Don't do something you will regret.'

Despite this, and against her father's wishes, Isabella and Irish Tom married in a quiet ceremony with only two witnesses and later made their way to a lodging house in a not very salubrious area for the night. Their landlady, a grim-faced woman, looked at them suspiciously and scrutinised the new wedding ring on Isabella's finger. 'This is a respectable house,' she said curtly as she escorted them up some rickety stairs to an attic room. 'I'll bring you up some supper, that's an extra sixpence, mind, and you can boil a kettle on the fire. The privy is out in the yard.'

When she had gone, Isabella sat down on the bed and said through her tears, 'I thought this was to be our honeymoon.'

Tom sank down beside her to a twanging of broken springs. 'The mattress is all lumpy,' he said, 'and there's no window apart from the skylight, but we're together at last, and things will get better – the first thing I must do tomorrow is find another job.' He looked round at the walls. 'Can't see any bugs,' he said reassuringly.

Isabella gave a shriek, 'Bugs!' She was horrified at the thought.

Supper was hard bread and lumps of cheese, but they ate it all because they were hungry. Then they went to bed. It was a honeymoon night after all, despite the drawbacks. He respected her innocence and she responded to him accordingly. 'I love you so much, Tom!' she whispered. She would always blush when she remembered what happened that night, when her life changed forever.

Tom whispered, 'I never dreamt I would marry a wonderful girl like you, Isabella. Life will be good from now on, I'm sure.'

Tom went out early next morning to look for work. He knocked on doors but had no luck. After almost a week, they heard of a farm cottage in the parish of Glanton in Northumberland. And when the man in the local shop who passed on this information mentioned that he was visiting his grandmother in Glanton the following weekend, and offered to take them along to introduce them to the farmer who owned the cottage, they took a chance and travelled there.

They could move in right away, as it had been unoccupied since the summer, the farmer told them. 'Too quiet and cut off for most people,' he observed. There were wonderful views over the valleys of the rivers Aln and Breamish. 'How beautiful!' Isabella cried out in her excitement from the cart where they sat in the back among packages and swathed in horse blankets to keep warm.

When they saw Field Cottage, which was down a long track from the farmhouse and opposite a ploughed field, it wasn't quite what they'd expected. It was a large single-storey, wooden hut, obviously erected some time ago, though it was well-made. Inside, the walls were lined with sacking, to keep the rooms warm and draughtproof. There was a tiled roof, however, which would keep the place dry. There were no curtains at the windows, and Isabella immediately thought, *My first sewing job!* She was pleasantly surprised to discover how big the rooms were: two bedrooms, a large living room with a fireplace, a kitchen with a stove and a small scullery with two tin baths hanging on the wall.

'One each,' Tom said with a wink. He pointed out the copper. 'You can boil all the linen, Isabella,' he said.

'You'll have to help with that,' she told him.

Outside was the privy, which was festooned with cobwebs and needed a good clean. Nearby was the pump, with a bucket ready to fill with water. Tom spotted an overgrown vegetable patch at the rear of the house, and he wondered if they could keep a few chickens there as well.

The previous tenant had left a few sticks of furniture, including a double bed. The farmer's wife had provided a bundle of bedding and a clean mattress. She had also put pots and pans in the kitchen, and her husband had left a large box of chopped wood for the fire. It was a chilly November day and Irish Tom's first task was to light the fire in the living room. The chimney had obviously not been swept, for they were soon choking from billowing smoke, and Tom had to force open the windows, despite the cold air rushing in. Isabella huddled in a blanket. She couldn't wait to get into that comfortable bed. Still, she felt happy and relieved – they had a place they could call home, and their love would help to keep them warm.

The kindly farmer's wife, suspecting that the delicate-looking girl might be pregnant, provided them with home-made bread, vegetables, eggs, a round cheese wrapped in muslin, a flitch of streaky bacon a crock of flour, and buttermilk. Tom, she said, could repay her by whitewashing the farm kitchen in the spring. She would also enquire among the farming fraternity who might need a house painter. It was a thriving community, thanks to the road links to Newcastle.

But there was a downside. In the larder Isabella discovered, to her horror, a rabbit hanging stiffly by its heels on the back of the door, which she was expected to skin and joint for a stew or pie. As a girl from a wealthy background, she had never learned to cook, to sweep and dust a room, wash clothes and linen, or even make up a bed. Tom had done that chore in the lodging house. She sat down on the one easy chair and wept. 'Oh, Tom, you have married a useless woman – I know *nothing* about running a house – I was spoiled by my father and ignored by my mother!'

Tom knelt by the chair and put his arms round her. 'I'm sorry mavourneen,' he said simply, 'but you will get used to it. I will help you all I can.' He gave her a long and lingering kiss. 'I never imagined I would marry a lovely girl like you because I'm just a labourer, and you're a lady.'

Before long Isabella was smiling again as the cottage was becoming a home to them both. Their love life was also blissful, and Tom was an ardent lover. She was learning to cook and she was an accomplished needlewoman. She even darned Tom's socks, and that wasn't fancy needlework, she thought ruefully.

'I am putting on weight,' Isabella mentioned to Tom one evening.

He looked at her speculatively. 'Do you think,' he said slowly, 'a baby could be on the way?'

'Oh, Tom, I never thought of that!' she looked alarmed.

'Well, you have felt sick several mornings, haven't you? And . . .' he hesitated, for she didn't like to discuss certain things. 'I believe you have missed something these past two months . . .' He wasn't sure how to put it. 'That could be a sign,' he added awkwardly.

'I know nothing about babies. My mother always went away for a while before my brothers and sisters were born, and I was never told why. Mother would return with the babies, but I had no idea where they came from. We have been so happy, just the two of us, my parents quarrelled all the time until my father left home. I'm not sure I can care for a baby.'

Tom put his arms round her. 'I'll look after you, Isabella. I am used to these things.' Her reaction worried him, but he was excited at the thought of being a father. *I must encourage her*, he thought, *she didn't have a normal childhood like me.*

Isabella was heavily pregnant during the long, hot, dry summer. In July, she wore a coarse sacking pinafore over her dress like the other women on the farm, and a large hat, tied round with a scarf, which she knotted under her chin. Being fair-skinned, with fine, light-brown hair, she needed protection from the sun. Even at this late stage in her pregnancy, she could help a little with the work in the fields. Besides, they needed her earnings and she actually preferred being out of the house, for what was there to do in such a small space? Her only domestic skill was sewing, but she had already made a pile of flannel garments for the baby. As for cooking, she had learned to throw everything in the stock pot, including marrow bones, and Tom had showed her how to make dumplings, and to call potatoes 'tatties'.

When she clutched at her back, a fellow toiler paused in her hay-raking. 'Is it time, hinny?' She had a small child clinging to her skirts, but Isabella was aware she wasn't married. There were also four widows in the workforce.

'I – I'm not sure . . .' Isabella managed, before she sat down abruptly among the stubble, doubling-up with the pain in her middle.

'What does the midwife say?'

'I . . . haven't seen her yet.'

The women, having observed the damp patch spreading on Isabella's skirts, provided a protective circle around the girl, to screen her from the gaze of the male workers. A large matron, who was in charge of the women, called out sternly to the men, 'Dinna keek, mind!' She turned to Isabella. 'Your waters have broke, hinny. Where is Irish Tom? The laddie will need to fetch him.' She indicated the youngest worker who could run fast and was usually sent on errands.

'He is painting at the doctor's house,' Isabella gasped, as another pain gripped her.

The doctor, an elderly man, had just arrived home in his gig, intending to have some lunch before his afternoon calls, when the lad ran up the drive to the house.

'Sir,' he panted, 'the painter's wife – the bairn is comin'.'

'Tom!' the doctor shouted. 'You are needed at home. I'll turn the horse round and take you there – you too, boy.'

'Hurry, sir, She's in the field. They canna move her!'

Irish Tom had been painting the top windows of the house and came down the ladder. He wiped his hands on his painter's smock and climbed aboard the conveyance. They set off at a fast trot and reached the field in a few minutes.

Isabella was lifted up and carried across to the cottage in her husband's strong arms. The doctor, concerned for her well-being, followed them indoors, carrying his bag. 'Is there no woman who can help?' he asked.

Tom shook his head. 'I will make her ready. There is hot water in the fire kettle, and clean linen in the bedroom chest. *I must top up the stockpot and put tatties to bake in the wall oven*, he thought to himself. *We will need our supper when this is all over.* Had she remembered to fetch cheese and butter? he wondered.

'We must hurry. The patient is in distress . . .' The doctor looked Tom in the eye. 'What does this young lady know of childbirth?' He deduced that Isabella had 'married beneath her' and that like most of her contemporaries she would probably be ignorant of the basic facts of life.

'Nothing,' Tom said. He coloured up, recalling that Isabella had not even been aware what would happen when they first made love. However, her passion had soon matched his own.

'You have some knowledge, I take it? You are from a large family in Ireland?'

'Yes, but I have never witnessed a birthing, sir . . .'

'Well, you are about to, and your wife will need your comfort and support. Just do as I say.'

Two long hours later, the baby arrived, a boy, crying lustily. The doctor was impressed by Isabella's fortitude. She hadn't become hysterical like some well-bred young ladies, even though it was not an easy labour. The doctor estimated the baby's weight at more than nine pounds. Seeing him, Tom marvelled at his size and wondered if he would fit into the tiny garments his mother had sewn. The baby had not inherited his red hair, but was so fair, he appeared to have none at all. Tom glimpsed blue eyes, before the baby closed them again.

'I will fetch the midwife,' the doctor decided. He hesitated, 'Don't worry about paying my fee, but the nurse will need her money. She has a family of her own to feed. Will this be a problem?'

They turned at the door at the sound of Isabella's voice, loud and clear, from the bed. 'We have a guinea – will that be sufficient? We must pay our way. Thank you, doctor, for your kind attention. I could not have got through all this without your help – or without Tom at my side.'

'You have a healthy son – I am glad to have been of help. What is his name?'

'Thomas Frederick, after his father,' Isabella said. They had not discussed baby names, but she was determined to name the baby after her beloved Tom.

After the doctor left, Tom held out his arms for the baby and stood by the bed, gently rocking him in his arms. 'Thank you for our wonderful son, Isabella,' he said huskily. 'I am the proudest man in Ireland tonight!'

'You aren't in Ireland, my darling,' Isabella reminded him with a smile, looking up at him cuddling his newborn son. 'We're here, and now we are a family. I'm glad I married you, Tom'

'So am I,' he said. The baby began to whimper. 'Do you think he needs, you know, his mother's milk – you should put him to your breast—'

Isabella gave a shriek, 'No! I thought we could give him a bottle of cow's milk!'

'Didn't you see your mother nurse the babies who came after you?' he asked.

'Of course not, she had a wet nurse, but we weren't allowed to watch her feed them. Mother was always out and about, a social butterfly, my father called her.'

Tom looked at his wife, who was weeping now with her face pressed against her pillow. He wouldn't tell her that he was hungry and needed his supper, he decided. 'I should make you comfortable – wash you and change the bed; the nurse will expect that to have been done. I'll put the baby in the cradle while I'm busy.'

Tom put the linen to soak in cold water in a tin bath and washed his wife tenderly, before slipping a clean nightgown over her head. He tentatively touched her swollen breasts. He said to himself, *I must encourage her to nurse the baby. It's not something well-bred ladies do, I think.*

When the nurse arrived, she saw the new mother clasping the baby in her arms while Tom coaxed her to feed him.

'You've done well,' she said to them. 'Now, you both need a rest. Tomorrow is another day, as they say.'

Their son was baptised in the nearest Catholic church. He was soon known as TF to differentiate him from his father. Irish Tom's brother Pat, who was in Woolwich, passed on the good news to their family in County Clare, but Isabella did not tell her parents of the happy event because there had been no contact with them since her marriage. She wrote instead to her Aunt Nesbit, secretly hoping that she might inform her nephew Abraham in Newcastle. *Surely*, she thought, *Papa will forgive me now?* But the silence continued.

In 1840, the same year Emma Wright was born, Irish Tom and Isabella, who were expecting their second child, moved to Harbottle, an historic village on the border with Scotland, at Aunt Nesbit's invitation. Mrs Nesbit was eighty and a widow. Like Isabella, she had been rejected by her own family when she married 'into trade'. She and her late husband were childless, but had a working partnership as well as a happy marriage, and she was eventually reconciled with her parents and extended family. The local Nesbits, who were numerous, had taken her to their hearts without reservation.

Eliza Nesbit now existed on a modest income, boosted by the rent from a nearby property, in which she had invested. This house she generously offered to Isabella and Tom with their growing family. In return for a modest rent she said she would be glad of their support and company, for she was not able to get out and about because of her painful 'rheumatics'.

The young couple and their small son travelled to Harbottle with their few possessions in the carrier's cart. 'Aunt Nesbit was right,' Isabella exclaimed, as they rattled along the cobbled street to their new home. 'This is obviously a respectable place! Most of our new neighbours are retired like her, she says, with private means . . . Oh, there's the parade of shops she mentioned – a butcher, a baker, an ironmonger, and a general store, and somewhere along here lives a Methodist minister and a judge!'

'What about the candlestick maker?' Tom quipped.

'Perhaps not, but now there will be a house-painter!' she returned.

They arrived at their journey's end. The villa would be their first real home. Inside they found the furniture was second-hand but well-polished, there were good curtains at the windows and, best of all, a new feather bed.

'I wonder if Queen Margaret had such a bed when she retired here in 1518,' Isabella said when they snuggled down on the soft mattress that night.

'Why did she choose Harbottle, I wonder?'

'She lived in the castle, which the Granville family built in 1075 to protect against invasion from Scotland, but it was twice taken by the Scots, the last time after Bannockburn. And the Drake stone is near Harbottle . . .' Isabella was an avid reader of local history books.

'That's enough of the history lesson,' he teased. 'Let's get some sleep before TF wakes us up.'

Over the next few weeks, the family settled well into their new home, with Irish Tom happily painting houses up and down the street. And soon their second child, another big, blond boy, was born with the help of a midwife paid for by Aunt Nesbit. They named him Robert Nesbit in her honour.

THREE

Emma, Spring, 1843

Emma was three years old, a determined little girl who had a mind of her own. She loved living on the farm and often spent time outside with her brother William, who hoisted her on his shoulders and introduced her to all the animals on the farm. 'Don't spoil her, Will,' Sophia counselled him, but she was glad her second daughter was having a freer childhood than she had had.

Martha was six and had daily lessons with her mother in reading and writing. She already helped with minor household chores, like her half-sister, Lizzie, who seemed very grown up at almost ten years old. Martha would pause in poring over the Bible on the kitchen table and glance enviously out of the window when she heard her little sister exploring outside in the yard.

One afternoon Martha was supposed to be keeping an eye on Emma but didn't notice when the little girl toddled off outside following William. He was on his way to the milking parlour, so turned and told her, 'You can't come with me this morning. Perhaps later on, eh?'

Martha came and stood at the back door now. 'Come back *now*, Emma!'

'Off you go,' William said, giving her a little push in the right direction.

Emma already had a mind of her own, as her mother often said. She appeared to be obeying Martha's call, but climbed into the dog's kennel instead. He wasn't there because he always accompanied William or Tobias as he was useful when it came to rounding up the pigs when they slipped out from the enclosure and went to investigate the vegetable patch. The pigs were easily spotted, but hard to catch.

Martha was cross and decided to ignore her. Emma will come crawling out of there directly; I can spot her from the window while I'm doing my arithmetic, she thought to herself.

Half an hour later she suddenly became aware that she had not spotted Emma for some time. Realising in a panic that she had not shut the gate, she rushed outside to the kennel. It was empty. Her mother's words echoed in her mind, 'Remember she's only young, not old enough to be sensible like you, Martha.' Martha looked round frantically: the washing was blowing on the line, high up because of the big prop. The pushcart William had made for his little sister on her last birthday was there, with her rag doll inside. She looked to the left of the enclosed yard at her mother's vegetable garden, and then to the flowerbeds on the other side. There was a mass of lavender there, and the honeybees would be busy in the summer. Emma, when she was two, had stroked a furry little bee buzzing on the lavender, causing her mother to panic, but she hadn't been stung. However, Emma was nowhere to be seen.

Just then, her mother came into the kitchen, looking weary after making the beds. 'Where's Emma?' she asked immediately.

'She's outside, she was in the kennel, but—' Martha floundered, her face red as she attempted to hold back the tears. 'Mother – the gate was left open!'

'Come on then, we must find her. Suppose she went down to the pond . . .' Sophia desperately needed a cup of tea, but she was panicking now.

They met William on his way back to the house, and he joined them in the search. After some frantic searching, it was the dog who found her. She was not far away, under a big bush, which had concealed her. She was talking to herself as she watched a caterpillar balancing on a large leaf.

'Bring her out – now! I can't bend to get under there,' Sophia cried to Martha.

Martha crawled under the bush, getting scratched in the process, and seized her sister. 'Come out, you bad girl!'

'It's you who are the bad girl, not keeping an eye on her as I asked you to,' Sophia told Martha. She held firmly on to Emma's hand. Martha walked behind them. It's unfair, she thought, I am supposed to be doing my sums, and watching Emma at the same time.

'The child is fearless,' said Tobias when Sophia told him about the events that night. 'And growing up so fast.'

'Well, soon Emma will not be the baby of the family. You may have a new little son to spoil,' Sophia said hopefully, patting the bulge hidden by her capacious apron. Martha, she suspected, might have guessed that her mother was expecting another baby, but she was not old enough to become Sophia's confidante yet. Lizzie had guessed, of course, and helped Sophia as much as she could. She always thought of Sophia as her mother, not a stepmother.

Emma had until now slept in a cot in her parent's bedroom. But everything changed for her one day a few months later when she was taken upstairs to bed and discovered that she was now in a corner of Lizzie and Martha's room. Instead of the cot, she had a little single bed and the only familiar thing was that her rag doll, Rosy, lay on her pillow as she did every night.

It was Martha who tucked her firmly into bed, not her mother, saying, 'Don't call out to Mother, she is not well, and has gone to bed herself. Goodnight. You aren't a baby now.' And she closed the bedroom door firmly. Emma cried herself to sleep.

Much later, Lizzie tiptoed into the bedroom, candle in hand, and looked down at Emma. 'Don't cry, Emma,' she said softly, 'I have something nice to tell you . . .'

'Where's Martha?' Emma sat up, peering over at the big bed opposite, shared by the two big girls. 'Mother din't kiss me goodnight, cos I was a bad girl.'

'Martha is having her cocoa in the kitchen. Emma, we have a new baby sister, and Mother is looking after her, so she can't come to say goodnight. Would you like to see the baby for a few minutes? She is only an hour old.'

Lizzie was tired; it had been a long day for her too. She was glad she had been able to help her mother, and she was now aware of the true facts of giving birth. 'I shan't get married, because I couldn't go through all that – Mother is so brave!' she thought to herself.

Emma scrambled out of bed and followed her sister out of the room. There was more light in the big bedroom from the large oil lamp, and Emma moved cautiously toward the bed. There was a little bundle, wrapped in a white shawl, cradled in her mother's arms. Sophia was propped up with pillows behind her.

She managed a smile when she saw Emma. 'Oh, Emma, my darling, this is Jerusha, your special little sister.'

'Rusha,' Emma repeated. 'Ru,' she added firmly.

Jerusha would indeed be a very special sister to Emma, who would always call her Ru.

FOUR

Abraham

Newcastle, 1842

Isabella's father, Abraham, who appeared grey and elderly like his biblical namesake, was in fact only in his early fifties. Living apart from his wife for many years, by mutual consent, he had thrown himself into his work and built up his business, but he was a lonely man. He missed Isabella. He had indeed hoped she would join him permanently in Newcastle and take over the business in due course. Perhaps, he thought, he had been too indulgent with her. It had been a bitter blow when she left home as she did and his obstinate pride prevented him from attempting a reconciliation.

He now pinned his hopes on his only son, Charles, who was fifteen, only to be disappointed again when the boy declared he had no interest in working in an office after boarding school, where his scholastic prowess had disappointed, but instead intended to go to sea. Charlie was at present staying with his father while he waited to join the naval training ship in the harbour. Like Isabella and his youngest sister, Anna, he rebelled against his mother's strictures. When Anna had earlier appealed to her father for help, he'd arranged for her to be employed as a parlourmaid in the grand house of an old friend, a prosperous mill owner in York. She kept in touch with her brother as they had always been close.

Charlie was out and about and somewhat bored when he called in at the office to see Abraham on a balmy autumn afternoon. He was surprised to find his father sitting motionless at his desk, with his head in his hands. 'What's wrong, Pa?' he exclaimed, concerned.

'Headache . . .' was the tetchy reply. 'Letter here addressed to you. Your orders.'

Charlie saw that the envelope had been opened. He suppressed his indignation, for he could see that his father looked drawn and ill.

'Brandy, boy – fetch me a glass, will you?' Charlie noticed that the bottle was almost empty.

'Medicinal,' his father said, seeing his concern. 'Only thing that helps.'

The clerk at his desk in the corner had his back to them, ostensibly concentrating on his ledger. 'Don't worry,' Abraham told his son, as the man must obviously be able to hear their conversation. 'Nothing goes beyond these walls. There is something I need you to do for me before you go away. I heard from my Aunt Nesbit some time ago that Isabella, the Irishman and their children are living near her. I replied today that I have booked you a seat on the first stage coach to Harbottle tomorrow and have asked her to arrange that your sister and her children will be with her when you arrive. You will return the same night.'

'But Pa – won't you visit them yourself? Why don't you come with me?'

Abraham shook his head. 'I don't wish Isabella to see me like this. You can deliver a letter.'

TF and Isabella, Harbottle 1842

Isabella was happy living in Harbottle, and to be wearing smart clothes again. She had no worries about money now, for Tom was busy working. She liked keeping Aunt Nesbit company each afternoon when she would visit with her two little boys.

One afternoon, Isabella was unaware, as she ushered her children along the path to Aunt Nesbit's house after dinner, that she was about to have a pleasant surprise. TF followed after his mother, holding on to his small brother's chubby hand. Robbie was eighteen months and a determined toddler. 'Stay on the cobbles, Robbie,' TF warned, 'or you'll be runned over!' A large cart, drawn by a dray horse, clattered past.

Robbie held out his arms to his mother as they arrived at Aunt Nesbit's front door. 'Up!' he commanded, eager to bang the knocker. He was a boy of action, but few words.

The door opened almost immediately and when she realised who was smiling and welcoming them in, Isabella exclaimed, 'Charlie! Is it really you? What on earth are *you* doing here?'

'I came to see you! I hope you're glad to see me?'

'Of course I am! But you've grown so much – you were just a little boy when I saw you last!'

'I was bigger than these two – aren't you going to introduce us?'

Isabella hung her cloak on the hall stand. 'Charlie, this is Thomas Frederick, known as TF, and this is Robert Nesbit, who is known as Robbie. Boys, this is your Uncle Charlie!'

'Pleased to meet you,' Charlie said politely as he bent to shake their hands.

'You're winking, Uncle Charlie,' TF said, trying to wink back.

'Well, you are the first to call me that, and I must say I approve!'

'You don't look like an uncle; you haven't any whiskers on your face!'

'When are you coming in to include me in the conversation?' called Aunt Nesbit.

She was a small lady, wrapped around with blankets and sitting in a chair with a footrest. Her snow-white hair was covered by a frilly cap, which was tied with ribbons under her chin. She wore a black dress with a shawl round her bowed shoulders fastened at the front with a sparkling brooch. Tiny diamonds surrounded a lovely blue stone, which she told a curious TF was lapis lazuli. It had been left to her by her grandmother. 'They say it aids the memory,' she added. 'I suppose you could say I am of an age to need it now.' She was actually very perceptive still, and had a lively interest in the world at large, even though she never stepped outside her house nowadays.

TF and Robbie were patted on the head in turn and Robbie said hopefully, while trying to dodge this attention, 'Pep'mint?'

'TF, fetch the tin, please, let's see if I have any left,' Aunt Nesbit said indulgently.

'Rob is Aunt Nesbit's favourite,' TF said to Charlie without rancour. The two of them were already inseparable.

Her gnarled fingers opened the tin with some difficulty. 'Ah, here you are, one each for you and one for me.' The peppermints were soft as they were left over from last Christmas, but the boys sucked them without complaint. Robbie climbed on Aunt Nesbit's lap for a cuddle, but TF joined his mother and uncle on the couch. He was eager to find out more about Charlie.

'What do you do, Uncle Charlie? My dada is a house-painter,' he said proudly.

'Have you left school?' Isabella asked, she'd noticed that his boyish mop of hair brushed his stiff collar and his voice lapsed on occasion into a squeak. Charlie is not yet a man, she thought.

'Yes, and I am about to become a mariner,' he said proudly.

'What's that?' TF wiped a dribble of peppermint from his chin with his sleeve, hoping his mother wouldn't notice.

'A sailor – and you must know what sailors do—'

'They go to sea in a big ship. Mama sings about them climbing the top rigging – what's that?'

'Rigging is what sailors do with the sails. I haven't practiced that yet. I join the training ship next week. I can't wait to go to sea and sail to faraway places – my ambition is to go to New Zealand, a newly discovered island on the other side of the world. Who knows, I might encounter pirates or cannibals on the journey.' Charlie ignored Isabella's warning glance.

'You might have to fight the – cannonballs,' TF said. He wasn't sure what they were, but he seemed to have said something funny, for they were all laughing, so he giggled too.

'Dada came over from Ireland on a big ship – he was very sick because the sea was so rough. He said you need bow legs to walk on the ship's deck in a storm. Have you got bow legs, Uncle?'

Even as Isabella was about to reprove her son for asking such a personal question, Charlie cheerfully rolled up his trouser legs, with some difficulty, because they were tapered elegantly to fit his high boots. 'See for yourself. They are, I'm afraid, unbowed.'

'Your legs are not like my dada's; he's got ginger hair on his. He can whistle – can you?'

Charlie obliged, putting two fingers in his mouth to produce a shrill whistle. Aunt Nesbit clapped her hands over her ears in protest.

Isabella was saved from more embarrassment by the arrival of the maid, pulling a little cart with refreshments for them all. Lemonade in special little glasses for the boys. 'Be careful with those,' Aunt Nesbit warned them. 'They are the last two of my wedding set.' There was tea for herself, Isabella and Charlie and a plate of small hard-baked biscuits.

'We must go soon, Tom will be home and I haven't made him any supper,' Isabella said.

'It's getting dark, the days are drawing in.' Aunt Nesbit caught Charlie's eye. 'You'll walk them home, won't you, Charlie? You ought to say hello to Tom, he's a very nice fellow. Be back here in good time to catch the coach. Remember it will be along here at seven thirty.'

Tom was indeed home, and in the kitchen. 'I got some kippers in the market – there's enough for one more,' he said, after Isabella had introduced them.

'I will be eating tonight with my father, thank you.' He held out his hand to Tom. 'It's good to meet you at last.'

'I'm glad that you can tell your father that we are well and happy living here,' Tom said. 'I'll see to the boys, Isabella – take your brother in the parlour, you can talk privately there.'

The lamp was lit, the fire flickering into life in the grate, and Isabella and Charlie were alone. 'Has Papa forgiven me?' she asked.

'I believe he has, but he is far from well, Isabella. I don't think he will be able to visit you. But he gave me a letter for you. Here you are.'

The letter was written in a shaky hand.

My dear Isabella,

I so often think of you. Please accept this gift from your loving Papa, Abraham.

Tears rolled down her cheeks.

'He doesn't say much, but he has enclosed a five-pound note.'

Charlie took another piece of paper from his pocket. 'This is Anna's address. She would be happy to have a letter from you and promises to write back. And I will keep in touch from now on.'

Later, in their room, Isabella showed Irish Tom the brief note from her father. 'Look, we are rich!'

'Come to bed,' he whispered. He wrapped his arms around her and hugged her close. 'You are too thin, Isabella. You need a little more flesh for me to squeeze.' She smiled, knowing what this was leading up to.

'Ah, you'd like me to *fall* again, I know – you'd love a little daughter! So would I, but not yet.'

'Spend that money on yourself, I'm sure that's what your pa intended.'

'No, I'll keep it in the trunk for a rainy day.'

It would be a year before they saw Charlie again, although he wrote to them when he was in port. There was no further communication from her father, but Isabella exchanged letters regularly with Anna, who sounded happy in her situation. She was coming up to her twenty-first birthday, Isabella realised, but there was no mention of a young man in her life.

TF was not yet at school, but he had already learned to read and write, encouraged by his mother, and one day, when Robbie picked up one of his brother's books, she discovered that he could read too, having listened to TF reading aloud and watching his finger move along the printed words. Aunt Nesbit urged caution, 'Too much learning too early addles the brain . . .' Isabella didn't agree, but she would never argue with dear Aunt Nesbit.

They continued with their regular visits, but Aunt Nesbit was much frailer, and now bedridden. Isabella found herself in the role of nurse, administering medicine from the doctor and assisting with bed baths when required. 'Send the boys out in the garden,' Aunt Nesbit said, 'they shouldn't be in a sick room.' Isabella warned them not to play ball near the house. She looked out on them from her aunt's bedroom window, happy to see them enjoying their games. She tapped on the glass if they were doing something they shouldn't. They looked up, saw her face, and stopped in their tracks.

'Charlie is home from his latest voyage,' Aunt Nesbit said. 'He is coming tomorrow with Anna. Will you ask Tom to carry me downstairs in the morning? I don't wish Charlie to see me like this. He wants you and the boys to be here, of course. I thought you might care to cook a meal for us all.' She reached under the pillow for her purse. 'Buy whatever you fancy!'

Fillets of steak, Isabella thought. I can manage to fry them. 'Is Tom invited to join us?'

'Of course!'

'I'm so happy Anna is coming, too!' Isabella said.

Anna had changed from a skinny fourteen-year-old into a comely young woman. Charlie had matured too. He had grown several inches taller, had the beginnings of a beard and a downy upper lip. He also smoked a foul clay pipe. Even out of uniform he looked like a sailor, down to the rolling gait.

Later, as Anna joined Isabella in the kitchen to help serve up the dinner, she said, 'I'm glad things have worked out well for you, Izzy. Your Irish Tom is so handsome and jolly, how could Pa disapprove of him as he did? And your boys are beautiful!' She sounded wistful.

'Oh, you'll get married one day and have some of your own, I'm sure!'

'Mama often said no one would marry me because of my large nose – she said I took after Pa in that respect!'

'She always had a sharp tongue. Your nose is – well – distinguished – shows character!'

'Thank you! I am ambitious, and that's something I admit I inherited from Pa! And I'm proud to have Eliza as my second name, after Aunt Nesbit! I hope to move on to better things, maybe go to London eventually.' Anna hugged her sister. 'We mustn't lose touch. I missed you so much.'

'As I did you, my favourite sister, Anna Eliza.'

In 1844 Abraham died. His widow inherited the family home, the business – and the debts. Due to Abraham's health problems the company had gone downhill and would have to be sold. Anna and Isabella's two other sisters received a modest sum each and Charles was left the lease of the apartment in Newcastle. Perhaps Abraham had intended to reinstate Isabella, but there was no mention of her in the will.

This concerned Anna and Charles, but as Anna said, 'I imagine Aunt Nesbit will make sure Isabella is well provided for when she is gone.'

FIVE

Emma,

Wymondham, 1846

The Swing Riots of the 1830s had affected rural life considerably. Farm labourers had faced unemployment due to the advent of the threshing machine, which cut down the numbers of men required to labour on the land. Wages were already at rock bottom. The rioters smashed these machines all over the country and there was an outcry in Parliament. The Whigs urged strict measures to curb the unrest. The ringleaders were hanged and many of the rioters were transported to Australia, most never to be heard from again by their families, who were left destitute.

The cottagers who for generations had produced woollen cloth on looms at home, also saw their industry in decline, due to the import of cheap material from abroad. There was trouble from those out of work, and vigilantes banded together to restore law and order. While Emma's brother, William, favoured farm mechanisation, he deplored the violence. Wymondham was a pioneer in setting up an early police force, known as Vestries, who employed watchmen to 'check theft, implement the new Poor Law and keep an eye on alehouses'.

Browick Bottom Farm had lost half its workforce. William took on the brunt of the work and kept things going, along with his father. His elder brother Edward was now the father of a son. The farm could not support another family, especially as Sophia and Tobias had added to their own, so Edward became a drill man on another farm. The drill, invented by Jethro Tull, was now widely used and proved its worth at sowing time. One man could do the work of many. Samuel, the youngest of the three sons, had been offered the opportunity to join an uncle on his fishing boat at Lowestoft. He never returned home, as his father hoped, because he met Thomasina, one of a group of fishwives who came to work there when there was a glut of fish. They fell in love and he followed her back to Scarborough, where they married, and eventually bought a fishing boat.

Emma, now six and a half years old, was not aware of all this. She was as happy as the day was long. While Lizzie was still at home not much was expected of her and she was free to accompany William around the farm as she had always done.

'Us need help to feed the animals and fowl and you, dear gal, do need a good blow o' fresh air!' he'd say, and Emma would follow along behind him with the new family dog at her heels. He was a liver-and-white spaniel named

Fly, who was as devoted to her as she was to him. William smiled to himself but didn't comment when he overheard Emma telling stories to the dog. Once she said earnestly to Fly, 'Do you know why your nose is always damp? It's cos you poke it in muddy puddles.'

Out in the yard, Emma would first attend to the hens. She didn't mind putting her hand in a nesting box under a sitting hen and was excited if she found a warm, speckled egg, with a feather or two clinging to it. She'd put the collected eggs in her apron pocket and take a dipper of corn from the sack, praying she wouldn't see a mouse, and scatter it to the scratching hens. The animal feed was kept in the cobwebby barn and Emma longed to stroke the kittens she saw in there playing and rolling in the hay, but they arched their small backs and spat furiously if she came near. She was rather afraid of the two pigs, although they nuzzled her through the bars of their pen. Also she knew that she couldn't make pets of them, because they would eventually be slaughtered and end up on the family table. As her father said, 'You can use every part of a pig except its oink.' The cows she was not so familiar with, but the farm horse was her favourite, after Fly. She loved the way he blew gently into her palm when he was nosing for a treat. After feeding all the animals, she returned to the house where the reward for her work was a glass of fresh, frothy milk.

But these carefree days didn't last. Lizzie left home to go into service when she turned fourteen and Emma missed her, especially as she didn't get on so well with Martha, who was now the eldest of five girls for, after Emma, there was Jerusha, Keturah and a new baby, Rebecca, a few months old. Jerusha was sickly and suffered from asthma, she was what her father called a 'poor doer' and Emma loved her dearly. They shared a bed while Martha had one to herself now that Lizzie had left home. Keturah was sturdier and energetic, while Rebecca was a happy, gurgling baby whom they all adored. The two little ones still slept in their parents' room.

'Surely the next one will be a boy,' Sophia had sighed.

Martha's schooling was virtually over and she no longer joined Emma at the kitchen table for lessons with their mother, for she was needed to help out with chores, though her religious instruction continued. She attended church twice every Sunday and was expected to allow Emma to tag along. Martha also helped her mother in the dairy, while Emma kept an eye on the little ones indoors. The ten-year-old hung out the washing between two old apple trees after she'd spent a steamy morning in the wash 'us, turning the mangle after the clothes and linen had been boiled.

William lit the fire under the copper first thing on wash-days, and for the monthly baths in the tin tub placed before the range. They bathed in pairs: Emma with Jerusha, Keturah with Rebecca. Martha was privileged to bathe alone. William ferried water from the copper and later he emptied the bath and mopped the kitchen floor. Then Emma enjoyed brushing Jerusha and Keturah's damp curly hair round her finger into ringlets. 'Just a few more strokes to one hundred – please keep still!' she coaxed the small, wriggling girls. Sophia sat alongside, smiling, while she nursed the baby. Sometimes Keturah plucked at her mother's sleeve, wanting the same comfort, and she was lifted up as well.

Martha was understandably envious of Emma's relative freedom and determined to involve her in the cooking, particularly the weekly bread-making, which Emma didn't mind at all. While the bread oven in the kitchen wall was getting hot, Emma was given pieces of the elastic sour dough, which her sister had pummelled and left to rise earlier and was instructed to 'make some shapes for the little ones'. Keturah, who scrambled up on the chair next to Emma, demanded a piece to play with, too.

'You can roll little balls for the birds, so they won't pinch the fowls' feed,' Emma suggested.

The loaves Martha made were placed in the oven on a long shovel by William when he came in for his elevenses. One day when Emma was seven, he came in bursting to tell them some news. 'The new church school hev opened today – I think our Emma should goo!'

Sophia wasn't so sure. 'She's reading and writing well with me at home, Will. Can we afford—' 'Course us can! Tis thrupence a week. She be a bright lass; she do need her chance!'

Martha, who was now as tall as her petite mother and could wear her passed-down clothes and boots, was to take Emma along on her first morning to enrol her at school.

She asked Sophia if she might borrow her Norwich shawl, which Tobias had bought his bride on their wedding day. Sophia agreed. 'Try not to pull any more threads, though, I meant to darn it.'

Dressed in Sophia's clothes and shawl, Martha looked quite grown up from the front, but the long hair, which hung in a plait down her back, was a giveaway as to her real age.

Emma wore a plain brown Holland dress, with a straight, calf-length skirt over black hand-knitted stockings and well-polished boots. The frock was protected by the regulation pinafore, starched white with no frills and with a clean white handkerchief in the pocket. Her curly hair was tied back with a stiff bow of Petersham ribbon. Her mother had crocheted her a new shawl from the same black wool she had knitted the stockings. She felt nervous; would any of her friends from church be there? She had never been apart from her family or away from the farm on her own before. Martha took her to the reception class, and watched while the children were settled onto the hard benches behind the long tables – desks were for the older pupils in the other class behind the partition. There was only a single large room.

'Got your rag to clean your slate?' Martha whispered, as two girls moved along to make room for her sister.

'Yes.'

'See you at dinnertime, then. Can you find your way back on your own?'

'Course I can!' said Emma, and then Martha was gone.

Emma looked over at the teacher, seated on a high chair behind a tall desk, while the register was called. She had to wait almost to the last to hear her name, as it began with a W. No daydreaming allowed here, the windows were too high to gaze through, but she could hear traffic going by, for the school was near the Abbey, with the schoolhouse next door.

The class was being taught by a pupil teacher called Anne, whom they all knew well from church, but they must now call 'Miss'. Pupil teachers were boys and girls of thirteen years of age and over who were apprenticed as teachers. It was a five-year apprenticeship before they became qualified. Anne smiled at the thirty-five children in this class reassuringly as she gave out the slates and pencils. Paper and dip pens were for the class they could hear reciting in the other half of the room. Reading books were shared by two and sometimes three children. Texts hung on the wall, which were changed daily. *It is rainy*, or *Sunny*, or *Snowing today*. A globe of the world, much of it coloured pink, was a temptation for the bolder children, who set it spinning if they arrived before the teacher in the morning. There was also a blackboard, not yet dusty with chalk, from which they copied the teacher's letters or numbers.

Emma looked with interest at the conical paper hat on the teacher's desk. Whatever could that be for? she wondered. It had a large D marked on it. There was also a whippy looking cane and Emma's neighbour whispered, 'You need to wear thick drawers in case you git it.'

The morning's lessons began with a passage from the Bible read by Miss Anne and then the questions began. 'Hands up if you know the answer!' Anne said. Emma's hand shot up every time, but she was not chosen. Then the class recited a poem, which Anne tapped out on the board. Those who had not learned to read at home made the tempo uneven as they copied desperately what others said. Anne did not miss much and she returned to her perch and made notes in a little book.

Emma enjoyed the drill at mid-morning, although it was difficult to jump about in the gaps between the tables, while wearing a narrow skirt, but in summer, she was told, they would exercise on the grass outside, near the hut which housed the bucket for if you needed to be excused. Emma made her mind up never to venture in there because a boy told her there was a rat hiding inside.

She had learned simple adding up from her mother, but multiplication and division were puzzling to Emma. She was handed an abacus and told how to use it. However, she could pronounce most of the names in the Bible reading, for weren't some of them in use in her family?

At noon, some of the children opened their lunch pails on the tables before being released outside. Emma had not far to go, but she ran all the way home. Martha was laying the table and Sophia was spooning delicious, bubbling stew, with light Norfolk dumplings, onto plates. Emma's favourite. The dog sat under the long pine table and waited for her to drop him a morsel or two. 'Not too much,' her mother said, 'he's got a juicy marrow bone of his own. How did you get on this morning?'

'Oh, all right. I put my hand up, and I waved it, but Teacher didn't pick me, and I knew all the answers—'

'You would!' Martha said. 'She didn't pick you cos you waved your arm – that's rude!'

'Jam roly-poly – or are you full?' Sophia asked quickly. She'd spotted a tear in Emma's eye at Martha's remark. Tobias and William kept quiet – they knew this was the best way.

'Yes please! 'Emma said. She would have to pay a visit to their privy outside before she went back to school, she thought. I know Martha will laugh at me if I tell them about the rat.

A year later William married his childhood sweetheart, Sarah, whose sister was married to his brother Edward. Emma and Jerusha were to be bridesmaids, but Martha said firmly, 'I'm too old.' Keturah and Rebecca were too young – their turn would come, Sophia told them.

The bride was married in the shiny, plum-coloured frock she wore to church on Sundays. She was a practical young woman and this frock would be around for many years. At some point it would become an everyday dress, then unpicked to make small garments and, lastly, it would be a splash of bright colour in a rag rug. She wore a bonnet trimmed with a matching ribbon and a silk rose, fashioned by her grandmother, who also made the posies from garden flowers and asparagus fern.

Sarah was the prettiest gal around, her proud bridegroom thought, with her golden hair and big blue eyes. She was nicely rounded – who wanted a skinny gal? She was strong, too, having worked on her father's farm. The best man was Edward, a reversal of their roles from when William had stood side by side with his brother. The bridesmaids wore matching frocks made from white muslin bought at the market. Sophia had embroidered French knots on each bodice and added pink satin sashes. There was no money to spare for shoes that would be worn only once, but early that morning William had polished the bridesmaids' everyday boots to a mirror shine. As it was summer, they wore little caps and it was Martha who wielded the brush and divided their long hair into a mass of ringlets.

The church was packed with family and friends. Lizzie was home for the weekend and sat between Keturah and Rebecca in the front pew. Martha sat on the aisle end to prevent the young ones from escaping. Keturah had already dropped her penny for the collection and was anxious to retrieve it. Sophia's hands were clasped in her lap, and Tobias guessed she was saying a silent little prayer that their next baby would be a boy. He stifled a little sigh at the thought as he covered her hands with his big ones and gave them a squeeze. He was sad there had been no word from Samuel in Scarborough, or from Sophie, who was now in Norwich.

In the pew opposite were Sarah's family and at the front of the church, with their backs to the congregation, stood William and Edward looking very presentable in their smart waistcoats, jackets and trousers. The rector stood on the dais facing them, prayer book in hand. At eleven a.m. precisely, the bride and her father were ready to walk down the aisle.

Heads turned to watch the little procession. Emma clasped Jerusha's hand. 'Don't drop your flowers, Ru,' she whispered. 'We are to sit down next to Mother when we get there.'

'Dearly beloved, we are gathered here together,' the rector announced loud and clear.

The reception was held in a big barn at Sarah's family's home. It had been swept clean of cobwebs and emptied of its usual contents. There were fresh bales of straw to sit on and plank tables covered with clean white sheets. Waiting for the company to arrive were the music makers: a fiddler, a flautist and a lad with a kettle drum. They struck up the minute the door opened and the guests filed in. The only people missing were William and Edward who were tending to the animals at Borwick Bottom and would rejoin the party as soon as they were finished.

Sarah's father welcomed them one by one with a handshake. His grandson, also called Edward, soon lost his shyness and joined the other children, including Keturah,

Rebecca, Jerusha and Emma. Sophia gave Martha an encouraging push. 'Go and join them, have fun for once! Get them dancing!' Once William arrived back, chairs were brought forward for the bride and groom to hold court and to greet the guests in turn.

When the food was uncovered there were gasps of appreciation. It was actually simple fare, mostly home-made. A baron of beef, fresh-picked vegetables, including waxy new potatoes, great crusty loaves with dishes of pale-yellow butter; a round of cheese; jars of dark brown pickles; dishes of raspberries and thick farm cream. And to drink they had elderberry wine and lemonade, with slices of lemon floating in the jug. The musicians drank their beer in a corner; they had an energetic evening ahead.

Finally, long after the children had been taken home to bed and the moon was riding high, the party ended and William and Sarah retired to their first home, a cottage near both family farms.

William lit the lamp in the living room. It looked rather bare, with just a table and two chairs and a blanket chest by the window, which was as yet not curtained. The trees in the small garden beyond were silvered in the moonlight. 'I'll fetch Grandma's chairs tomorrow,' William said. These were the seats from the wedding feast, which came to Sarah on her marriage. They were low, spoon-back chairs covered in faded pink material and over a century old. Sarah planned to make cushions and embroider back covers.

Someone had pumped up water in a pair of buckets in the kitchen and lit the fire in the grate. The shiny kettle Sarah had bought from the travelling tinker was on the hob. She'd collected pots and pans, crockery and linen for her 'bottom drawer' for the past five years. 'We have everything we need,' she told William. 'We can make a cup of tea before we go to bed.'

There were two bedrooms upstairs and they climbed the steep stairs where William placed his candle in its stand in the niche outside the first door. 'Do give me the other candle and I'll put it on the washstand, us won't be quite in the dark.'

'Us must get curtains up in here, too,' she said, sitting on the side of the bed, the only other item of furniture in the room, and easing her feet out of her new boots. She rolled down her stockings and William averted his eyes. Unlike many of the local girls, Sarah was not pregnant on her wedding day. They did not presume to judge others in this respect, but they shared a dream which they were determined to fulfil. They must work hard now, but both hoped for a family in due course.

As Sarah reached for her nightgown, William nipped out the candle and said urgently, 'Don't bother with that, my dear gal, us do need to git into our bed.'

SIX

TF

Harbottle, 1846

Isabella and Irish Tom's first daughter, Mary, was born in Harbottle in February 1846, when her brothers were nine and six years old respectively. The baby inherited her father's bright hair and Irish eyes. Aunt Nesbit was propped up in her bed when little Mary was placed carefully in her arms for the first time. 'Her eyes are the same colour as my lapis lazuli brooch – she shall have it when I'm gone,' she said.

'Aunt Nesbit, you aren't going yet!' Isabella told her, alarmed.

The old lady just smiled. She knew something they did not. She was aware she was dying, but she was content, for she had managed to hold on a little longer so as to see the baby.

When Eliza Nesbit passed peacefully away a few months later the young family, who had been as devoted to her as she was to them, discovered that although she had been well provided for during her lifetime, because she had no children, under the terms of her late husband's will, drawn up long before they came to Harbottle, the estate was to pass to his younger brother and thence to his family. As the brother had also died in the meantime, his children would have equal shares.

All of this meant that the house they lived in would have to be sold, along with Eliza's villa, and Isabella, Irish Tom and their three children would have to leave Harbottle, where they had been so happy. They were allowed a month's grace before the move.

'We'll go back to Newcastle,' Tom decided. 'There should be plenty of work there,' he added optimistically, remembering his days there in his early twenties.

Once more, they travelled by carrier's cart with their personal possessions, which included Isabella's precious trunk. They left behind their comfortable home and the furnishings, which had been provided by Aunt Nesbit, but they were allowed to roll up and take their feather mattress and the baby's rush basket she had given them. Jane, a Nesbit niece, who inherited her aunt's jewellery, gave Isabella the lapis lazuli brooch, wrapped in paper and marked by Aunt Nesbit: *For my beloved Mary*. The two boys each received a small crystal glass, the only ones left from her wedding set.

Tyne Street, 1847

The multi-tenanted house was in a mean street, one of many which led down to the River Tyne, where the docks and shipyards along its wide snake-like coils were besieged daily by the unemployed, desperately seeking work of any kind. The stench from the river was overpowering. In the city itself there was regeneration, with new buildings and restoration of old ones, but this area reeked of decay.

The family were living in one room and at night they would unroll their mattress and sleep top to toe on it – the boys at one end, Isabella and Irish Tom at the other. In the winter they sometimes slept in their clothes or spread them out on top of the thin blankets. Once Mary could crawl, she would climb out of her basket and join them, seeking the warmth and comfort of her mother. In the dark they were aware of scratching and scuttling, which Isabella tried to tell herself were mice, rather than rats. They had little food themselves, but they had to ensure nothing was left out on the table, with cockroaches around as well as vermin. There were only two rickety chairs, and Isabella's trunk had to double as a seat for the children. They cooked on the fire, but soon ran out of coal and the boys would go scavenging for old wood to burn.

The house was never quiet. Wooden clogs pounded on the stairs day and night and there were screams and audible arguments from the other tenants. Ominous coughing came from some rooms of the damp and draughty building.

Outside there was a communal area with a tap where they had to queue for water each morning, and a hut containing a bucket, the only one provided. Slops were tipped down the single drain and effluent often overflowed into the street. This was also where the women hung dripping washing, hoping it would dry, and the men had to dodge as they made their way down to the docks to look for work. Irish Tom was one of these men, but his hopes were soon dashed: there was no work for painters, despite the number of rusting boats.

Isabella made her first friend in that awful place, a young woman called Dorrie who lived with her elderly, but still spry, grandmother in a nearby room. 'When my father died, Ma took in a lodger. I had a little baby,' the girl confided, 'Ma turned me out – and him – but she kept the baby and passed it off as her bairn. I never saw them since . . .'

Dorrie had work of sorts – she was a barmaid in the local pub. Sometimes she wouldn't come home until the following morning. She was good with Mary, though. 'You could be a nursemaid,' Isabella suggested.

'Lookin' like this?' Dorrie asked. She glanced down at her ragged skirt. Isabella had no answer to that. She tried to keep clean and tidy herself, but it was hard. When she went out, she covered her head and shoulders with an old shawl, like the local women.

TF and Robbie were being educated at least. They were accepted by the local Catholic school, which took a percentage of boys from poor homes. Their teacher was a strict disciplinarian but could see they had been properly brought up in the past and was determined that they should do well in future life. The boys also received a free meal at midday. In return they attended Mass on Sunday mornings. Their father had long ago lapsed in this respect.

'They are learning Latin,' Isabella told Tom proudly.

He sighed heavily. 'What good will that do them? I was working at TF's age.' Tom had given up early today, arriving home to sit around while Isabella busily tried to make a meal from scraps.

She bit back a bitter response: *Look where it got you . . .* saying instead, 'You have to turn around, not follow the crowd – go into the city, and find work there!'

He had almost the same reply as Dorrie. 'How can I, looking like this?'

She went to her trunk, lifted the lid and from the folds of the opera cloak she had worn on her twenty-first birthday, pulled out a small package.

'It's a shame you never get to wear any of your treasures,' he said, then suddenly realised what this could mean. 'You're not going to sell your jewellery, are you?' Have we come this low? he thought, distressed.

'No, I'm going to pawn it. Dorrie will take me to the pawnbrokers and introduce me. You'll be able to get a job once you're wearing decent clothes and boots, and then we can redeem my pearls. Not that I'll ever get a chance to wear them again!' She'd never sounded bitter like that before.

Tom felt sad and ashamed. It's all my fault, he thought, bringing her to this place – but where else could we go? She's been so good about it, until now. God alone knows how we will survive.

'What does your friend have to pawn, I wonder?' he said, instantly regretting the remark.

Isabella flushed. 'She receives gifts from grateful customers.' Isabella was no longer naive and understood where Dorrie had got the gold watch dangling from a chain with which she had amused Mary earlier in the week.

Irish Tom did find employment in the city, although it was casual labour so he didn't have a regular wage. The pearls remained at the pawnbrokers, but the boys had new boots as well. Isabella's hopes of moving from Tyne Street were dashed once she found out that she was pregnant again. As normal married life was not possible when they shared their bed, she could only recall one occasion when they'd been undisturbed, when the boys were at school and Mary was with Dorrie.

At this worrying time, when she was often in tears over her predicament, another friend came into her life. This was one of the Sisters of Mercy, who went into the slum areas and visited the poor, bringing food, comfort, prayers and nursing skills. In years to come, some of these sisters would go out to the Crimea with Florence Nightingale. Sister Ursula had heard of the family through the boys' school and the church. 'I am not a Catholic,' Isabella told her on her first visit, thinking this might make a difference.

'We care for those in need, whatever their religion, Mrs Meehan. Now, tell me about yourself.'

The story of her life poured out, and at the end Isabella felt a great relief. Sister Ursula had listened patiently. Now she stood up. 'I must go, but I will be back. You will receive a share of the food kind folk give us. Your daily bread and milk for the little one is assured! The market traders let us take what is left at the end of the day, you can find a good cabbage thrown in the gutter, the butcher saves soup bones, the fishmonger gives away odd bits, like cod cheeks and tails, and the ladies of the church bake cakes! We have bundles of clothes, second-hand but clean and good. Tell your husband that he and I come from the same place, though I haven't been back in forty years.'

When Sister Ursula returned, as promised, pushing a box on wheels, with provisions piled high inside, the boys were there to unpack the contents in great excitement. Tom had discovered an old cupboard on the city dump, scrubbed and painted it, and so they had somewhere to store the food.

Sister Ursula had already deduced that Isabella was pregnant, and while the boys were outside kicking a ball with the neighbouring children, she waited discreetly to be told the news.

Isabella poured them both a cup of weak tea. Tea leaves were dried out and reused until they no longer coloured the hot water, but at least she now had milk to add, if no sugar. Sister Ursula sipped her tea. Then she said, 'I must be getting on, but I believe you might wish to tell me something, my dear?'

Tears rolled down Isabella's pale, drawn face. 'Oh, Sister Ursula, there will soon be another mouth to feed – I am expecting a baby!'

'I guessed that – do you know when?'

'I must be six months. I don't know how we will manage!'

'We will help, as we have today. Would you like one of us to deliver your baby when the time comes? We make no charge for this. Again, we are helped by the good citizens of Newcastle. Would you permit me to examine you, while the children are not around, to see how things are? I will just need some hot water to wash my hands.'

'Thank you,' Isabella said gratefully. 'Please don't think we won't love the baby when it comes, sister, and maybe it will be a little sister for Mary. She is with my friend Dorrie today, who helps me all she can.'

The examination was done discreetly, Isabella just lifted her skirt as it was not the time of day to be undressed. Sister

Ursula straightened up and was smiling. 'All appears to be normal; you must drink some of this milk yourself and I will bring more provisions soon. Goodbye for now.'

The boys came helter-skelter into the room after she had gone. 'There'll be a good supper for us all tonight,' their mother said. 'One of you, go and fetch Mary back to share the feast!'

Sister Ursula was in attendance when Isabella's last child was born. It was another girl, whom they named in memory of dear Aunt Nesbit – Ann Eliza. She was a tiny baby and it seemed likely she might not survive, especially as Isabella was unable to feed her. She had been unwell for some time before the birth with a recurring fever and cough and Sister Ursula was worried, because her patient was developing the well-known symptoms of consumption. Dorrie, who had given birth herself a few weeks previously, offered to be a wet nurse. Dorrie's baby, like her relationship, did not survive, but tiny Ann Eliza struggled to stay alive and brought comfort to the bereaved mother. Dorrie was already caring for Mary most days, too, and, thanks to her devotion to her friend's children, she was now also a recipient of Sister Ursula's food cart.

Tom was feeling desperate; he was torn between looking after his sick wife and earning money to keep them going. He felt guilty when he spent a few pence on a bottle of beer, but it stopped him from dwelling too much on their predicament.

The two boys were bewildered by events at home and were far more subdued than they used to be. Robbie confided to TF, 'Mary doesn't seem like our sister now, she's with Dorrie most of the day.'

'Mama is very ill, I think, though we are not told anything, are we?' TF said.

'Do you think the new baby caused this?' Robbie asked. But his brother didn't have an answer for that. He wished they were back in the days before they came here, and their Great Aunt Nesbit was still alive.

When Mary was four years old, Sister Ursula found a place for her in the infants' class at a school run by the nuns. TF and Robbie gave her breakfast in their family room and made sure she was clean and tidy. Like them, she had a nourishing midday meal with her fellow pupils. Robbie, first out from the boys' school, collected his sister and took her home to have supper and to see her mother, before she went next door to Dorrie.

The room had been rearranged to keep Isabella comfortable. The sick woman lay all day on her mattress close to the fire and slept alone at night. She could not hug her children close or kiss them, and Mary knew to keep her distance and sat at the table by the window when she was there. At bedtime the little girl would say goodnight and go to her foster mother whom she called Auntie, and to Granny, who looked after little Ann Eliza in the evenings, for Dorrie had returned to work. Granny had a proper bed and retired at the same time as Mary. The old lady told her stories until they fell asleep, with Ann Eliza in her cot beside the bed. They didn't hear Dorrie tiptoe into the room in the early hours, but Mary was reassured to wake and find her in bed beside her. 'Auntie,' she whispered, for Granny was snoring. 'The baby needs you.'

Sister Ursula called in twice a day to check on her patient. When she mentioned to Irish Tom that she thought it would be less stressful for them all if Isabella were taken to the infirmary, he refused. 'We can't be parted from her.' She smelled the alcohol on his breath. Poor man, she thought, it is the only way he can cope. She suspected that although he went out each day, he was not working much. In the colder weather, Sister Ursula brought them extra blankets, for the boys and their father had to sleep on the floor, rolled in their covers.

TF prepared the usual supper of bread and cheese and dipped a ladle in the cooking pot for a bowl of broth for his mother. He lifted her head from the pillow, supporting her with a strong arm round her shoulders, and gently spooned the broth into her mouth. The effort exhausted her, but she swallowed as much as she could to please him.

Later, after Mary departed, and his father was not yet back, he and Robbie spread their books on the table and began their evening studies. TF guessed that, at thirteen, he would soon have to leave school and go to work as his father's apprentice. When he was younger, he had dreamed of joining the navy like his Uncle Charlie. They had not seen him for some time but were aware that he was intending to marry on his next leave. 'He will have his own family then, not just us,' Isabella said.

Anna, too, had moved to a new place. She and Isabella kept in touch, but she was not aware of how grave her sister's condition was. In her last letter she had written cheerfully, *I must visit soon – I haven't met Ann Eliza yet!*

Now, with Anna's letter clutched in her hand, Isabella called huskily to TF, 'Will you write to Anna for me? Dorrie got me a stamp.'

'What shall I say?' He dipped his pen in the ink bottle, took a sheet of paper, and waited. His mother's voice was hoarse as she dictated what she wanted him to say. When he had finished writing she asked him to catch the evening post.

Cook invited Anna into her kitchen for a chat and a mid-morning cup of tea. The 'lower orders', as Cook referred to them, had already been in and returned to work. She considered Anna to be 'a cut above' – parlour maids were often young ladies in reduced circumstances and so they were deferred to. Cook noticed that Anna was not her usual cheerful self. 'Anything wrong, my dear?' she asked, sipping her tea, into which she had put her 'secret ingredient' – a spoonful of brandy to keep her going.

Anna had a letter tucked in her pocket. On impulse, she took it out and smoothed the creases. 'My nephew sent me this. He tells me his mother is not well enough to write, but I am not to worry!'

'Of course you are,' Cook prompted.

'Yes – and more so because she doesn't want me to visit her either, as I had intended. I feel she must be really ill. I – I can guess what the trouble might be . . . so near the river.'

'Aah . . .' Cook nodded her head. 'She is thinking of *you*, my dear – the white plague shows no mercy.' This was just one of the names given to consumption by those who feared it. 'We'll put a box together for her: a bottle of beef tea, calves-foot jelly, nourishing things, and some of my cherry cake for her children. Oh, is that the doorbell? Must be the grocer with those quails' eggs for madam.' She bustled out, as Anna dabbed at her eyes.

White plague, Anna thought. Am I to lose my dear Isabella again – this time forever?

Sister Ursula had come prepared with an armful of towels and sheeting. She knelt by the stained mattress on the floor and waited for the next painful heave of the chest, as she covered the patient's open mouth with the last wad of clean cloth. Robbie had taken Mary to Dorrie but returned to keep vigil with TF. They wanted to help, but the nurse indicated for them to stay back. Irish Tom was there, too, head resting on his folded arms on the tabletop, an empty bottle on the floor beside him. His shoulders shook with sobs he was unable to suppress.

Sister Ursula, tired and pale, closed her eyes and murmured a prayer. 'Oh Lord, take this thy daughter and release her from her suffering.' The sister's apron bore the same ominous marks as the discarded linen. When she opened her eyes, she saw that Isabella had drawn her last breath. She rose with difficulty, for her knees were stiff, and said simply, 'Dear Isabella is at peace, at last.'

On her death certificate was written 'From Inflammation of the Lungs.' She was thirty-seven years old.

Charlie arrived home in Newcastle from his latest voyage a few days later to find Anna in his apartment. After giving him the sad news, she told him she had already arranged the funeral at the local church. 'It seemed the best thing, as she was not a Catholic.'

Charlie agreed. 'I will share all the expenses. Your employer was good to give you time off.'

'I would like to buy the children some new clothes and I hope you don't mind, but I looked in Pa's wardrobe and saw a suit which might fit Tom. But we will be the only ones from our side.'

'How is Tom? Is his brother in Malta?' Patrick was there to advise the military on armaments. His career had flourished at the Arsenal. Having lost his wife, he'd remarried and had a second family.

'Patrick cannot come. Tom is drowning his sorrows; you'll have to watch him at the church.'

On a bitterly cold day, TF and Robbie joined their father and uncle as pall-bearers. After the brief service, Mary, in her new woollen cape and bonnet, walked hand in hand between her brothers, following Irish Tom and Charlie to the graveside. In the church porch, Anna cradled Ann Eliza, swaddled like a baby, in her arms, to keep her out of the cruel wind. She wept as she said a quiet 'goodbye'. How could the children survive with Tom in that dreadful squalor, she wondered.

She was right to be worried, for within a few months little Ann Eliza was laid to rest beside her mother. She was two years old.

SEVEN

Emma

Wymondham, 1850

Martha was rising fourteen, and it was time for her to go to her first job. The ladies of the church had been looking out for a place for her, not too far from home, and Martha's chosen employer was a gentleman farmer who rode with the local hunt. She was very proud of her under-housemaid's uniform, and happy she had a small bedroom to herself under the eaves. There were many stairs to climb at bedtime, but she was up and down the main stairs all day long and used to hard work.

There was now a Sunday school at church, and Emma was chosen to help with the instruction – her class included her younger sisters. When she told them the parable of the prodigal son, Rebecca said innocently, 'Is Samuel our prodigal son?' Emma whispered, 'Shush!' for their father was in earshot, and she knew it upset him that her half-brother did not get in touch with him. Sophie too seemed to have cut herself off from the family, though when he heard that she was now training as a nurse at the new Norfolk and Norwich Hospital, William had promised Tobias he would try to contact her. However, Lizzie, raised as part of the second family, wrote home monthly and when she was earning more, generously contributed towards her siblings' school fees. This was much appreciated as Jerusha and Keturah had joined Emma at school and Rebecca would be starting soon.

In May, the children were given seeds in Sunday school to plant and nurture at home and told to present the biggest and best of their produce at the Harvest Festival in the autumn. Emma rushed home to show her mother the fat seeds wrapped in her handkerchief and asked Sophia if she could plant them in her vegetable patch.

'If you can wait until after I have dished up the dinner,' Sophia said, smiling, 'I will show you the perfect place for growing marrows.'

The younger children clustered round as Emma dug over a patch of earth which Sophia told them was sheltered from the north wind by the barn and soaked up the sun. Emma sowed the seeds one inch deep in the damp soil and then carefully placed a glass jar over them. 'Now, you must leave them to germinate for two weeks,' Sophia advised. 'Then you can thin the seedlings out and raise the stronger ones.'

Emma watched over the marrows diligently, and by September there were two huge striped ones and some smaller ones, which were picked off one by one and cooked in their vegetable pot. William dubbed the biggest marrow

'Goliath' and this one was selected for the Harvest Festival service. 'That will feed quite a family,' he observed.

When they sang all the harvest hymns, Emma glanced proudly at her contribution, which topped a pyramid of other colourful vegetables and fruit.

However, the vegetable they all preferred was the Swedish turnip, known as a swede. There was a plot of land set aside for growing these as this crop was vital for the cattle feed in winter. The cows did their bit by providing rich manure for the soil. Emma and her sisters loved to sit on the farm step and scrape the flesh from a juicy swede with a teaspoon, which Sophia had peeled and quartered for them. When Emma said it was much tastier than marrow, Sophia smiled. The other large marrow would be stuffed with forcemeat and onion, tied up with string and steamed in a pot. With new potatoes and carrots, that was a feast too, as they discovered.

In later years, Emma would say, 'Mother taught us everything we know, how lucky we were.'

Sophia's prayers had been answered, meanwhile, and the girls had two baby brothers: Jonathan and Joseph, born in 1848 and 1849 respectively. They were now active toddlers and Emma and Jerusha kept an eye on them before and after school.

One day, Tobias told Emma, 'Your mother is not too well, Emma. I'm sorry, but I'm afraid you will hev to leave school. Us need your support.'

Emma was shocked. She was ten years old and had hoped she would be able to continue her studies for another two years, when she might be considered as a future pupil teacher.

But Tobias was worried about Sophia. He had confided in William that she had a 'look about her' that reminded him of his first wife, who had succumbed to 'bronchitis' at around the same age. Most patients guessed it meant consumption.

William searched the bookshelf at home, trying to find more information. He told Sarah, 'This old book says this terrible disease spreads like the plague did long ago. You would think us would be free of it, due to the fresh air in the country, good food and plenty of milk. That is a puzzle which must be solved. But I hope to be an engineer one day, not a doctor, so it won't be me who finds the answer.'

Isabella and Sophia never knew of the other's existence, but Isabella, living in Tyne Street where the disease was rife, had no resistance to the illness. Sophia always had good food on her table, including dairy products and unlimited milk. It was indeed a puzzle.[1]

Life on the farm was not too hard for Emma at first. Her mother was still up and about, although not able to work

---

1. A French chemist and microbiologist, Louis Pasteur, was about to publish his findings about the latter, and this would lead to the pasteurisation of milk, to kill the tubercle bacteria passed from the dairy cows, in whom it was prevalent.

as she had done before. Emma's friends at church, keen for her to continue her education at home, lent her books and passed on what they considered to be suitable magazines, and William saved his weekly newspaper for her, so that she would be aware of what was going on in Norfolk and in the wider world. Sarah, with two small children in tow, helped in the dairy and on washing day. Emma cooked meals under Sophia's direction, while Jerusha kept an eye on her sisters before and after school. She was also a devoted part-time nursemaid to her small brothers.

Emma would, throughout her life, recall two 'magical moments' on the farm at this time. The first was before breakfast on a misty autumn morning when, jug in hand, Emma went to see William in the milking parlour to ask for milk. As she approached the door she saw smoke drifting from the direction of the small orchard where William had already picked the fruit. She set down the jug and went to investigate. It was only just past dawn, and as she drew near the trees, she heard a strange sound – a tinkling, as of bells – and then she saw that the smoke was curling from a small fire in a clearing. Beyond the fire was a high-wheeled cart, partly covered with horse blankets, which was an indication that the driver slept under cover. The shafts of the cart were empty, and Emma spotted an old horse standing under a tree with a nosebag of oats. She was startled by a loud braying from a small donkey tethered to the tailboard of the pedlar's cart. The tinkling intensified, and she realised it was indeed a bell, fastened to the donkey's head collar.

A figure emerged from the cart and a man lowered himself to the ground. He was holding a long-handled blackened pan in one hand, and Emma flinched involuntarily. Was she about to be bashed with this? Without appearing to notice he had a visitor, the pedlar, a stout fellow in a canvas smock which came past his knees, balanced the pan on the fire before he returned to the cart for the bacon to fry. The fatty slice soon began to spit and caused the fire to spark.

Emma felt rooted to the spot. Had he been given permission to stay here overnight? At last she spoke. 'Who are you? Does my father know you're here?'

He looked directly at her, his white hair and enormous beard illuminated by the flaring fire. He took a clay pipe from his pocket and lit it, before he answered. 'They call me the donkey man. I don't need a dawg, cos he warn me when someone is here.' One of his eyes was blue, the other white and blank. Emma felt a little shiver of nervousness. She looked down and saw the soles of his shoes were gaping, revealing his knobbly toes.

Then she felt a firm hand on her shoulder. 'I wondered where you were when I found the jug,' William said. 'If you'd come in, I would've told you Seth is an old friend. He hev been travellin' the country, us hev not seen him in years . . . He come after you were all abed last night.'

'I shall be off again after me breakfast,' the pedlar said. 'I want to git to Yarmouth. Hev a look at the sea. Wash me feet. 'Tis where I was born. Where I will end up, I reckon.'

'I like the donkey's bell,' Emma said. Seth felt in his pocket. 'Got a spare one, you hev it.'

'Let's take the milk back to the farmhouse now, eh?' William suggested.

'Goodbye, it was nice to meet you. Thank you for the bell,' she said to the pedlar. There was a muffled tinkling sound in her pocket as they walked away, which made her smile.

'Us should've have given him sixpence for the bell,' William said, 'He look on his uppers . . .'

'What did he mean about ending up in Yarmouth, Will?'

'Us all git drawn back to where us come from, however far we roam—'

'I'll never leave Wymondham!' she said firmly as they went into the farmhouse with the milk.

The following spring, Emma experienced her second 'magic moment'. She had been up since the early hours helping her father settle her mother after a feverish night. Jerusha came yawning into the kitchen as Emma was stirring up the coals in the fire. 'Wondered where you were, Emma,' Jerusha said. 'Can I help you get the breakfast?'

'What about the boys? You are usually chivvying them to get up and making sure they have clean socks when they need them,' Emma replied. They both had their own morning jobs.

'They are supposed to be washing themselves at this moment,' Jerusha said. 'They aren't babies any more, Emma. They have to be able to do things for themselves.' She stirred the porridge bubbling in the pan on the stove.

Just then, William appeared with an urgent request for Emma. 'I need some help with poor old Buttercup – she's about to calve and it seems the calf is acomin' hoof-first. Will you come, my dear? Buttercup do need a steady hand to hold her, while I help Father to git the calf born.'

Emma looked at Jerusha, who waved her away. 'Emma, you go – I can manage here, and will get the young ones off to school!'

'Put on your overalls,' William said, 'and your rubber boots. And a woolly hat, or you'll need to wash your hair, it's a mucky business – hev you ever seen a calf born, Emma?'

'No.' She shook her head. 'Father said it weren't a sight for little girls to see. And Mother didn't want us in the room when the boys were born, did she?'

'You were too young then, but Father told me to fetch you, he's worn out looking after Sophia all night.'

Emma felt weary too, but she swiftly changed and followed William out of the door.

The expectant mother was a Norfolk-and-Suffolk Red Poll cow. She was a lovely dark-rust colour with a touch of white on her switch, as the tail was called. This breed didn't have horns and were friendly creatures. Buttercup had been moved to a stall on her own, and plenty of fresh straw had been scattered on the ground to make her feel comfortable and secure. She was obviously feeling the strain of attempting to give birth and tossed her head impatiently when Emma attempted to give her head a stroke.

'Just hold the halter firmly and talk to her, she know you,' William advised. 'Stand firm, feet apart to keep your balance if she try to push you away. Poor old gal is in pain, she's usually so placid.'

Tobias handed a stout rope to William. 'We'll haul on it in turn, Will, and be at the back end,' he said, adding to his daughter, 'Do you hold tight, my dear girl, and keep talking to her, take her mind off what we're adoin' trying to turn the feet, and getting her calf born.'

'I'll try, Father,' Emma managed. She was thankful she didn't have to look at what was going on with the rope. 'Don't worry, Buttercup,' she said to the cow. 'Father and Will know what they're doing.' The cow blinked her eyes and emitted a pained 'Moo.' She couldn't swish her tail, for that was firmly tied too.

Emma found herself telling Buttercup a story, just as she did when she was sitting by a sick brother or sister to take their minds off pain from toothache or itchy chicken pox blisters; Buttercup's long eyelashes flickered, she relaxed a little and allowed Emma to caress her large domed forehead. 'Once upon a time,' Emma began, 'there was a beautiful cow called Buttercup, who was worried because her new calf hadn't come yet. Last year's calf, Daisy, was peeping into the pen where her mother was and wondering why she had been taken away from the rest of the herd.' She looked over into the big pen and saw the young heifer munching on a bundle of hay. 'Daisy is waiting, and so are the other cows, they know what is happening, I think.' She continued, 'Two strong men are doing all they can to help you, Buttercup.'

Just then, there was a shout from William. 'Pull on the rope, Father – turn the calf a bit more – watch out, here it come!' Buttercup gave a great heave, and the calf was born. Tobias fell back on the straw, then pulled himself up to remove the rope. The calf lay there, motionless. William began to rub its body with straw to clean it and stimulate its breathing. Emma was spellbound; it was the first birth she had witnessed.

'She needed help to give birth,' she told Jerusha later. 'Like our mother did from the midwife. Now I know what I am going to do when I grow up – I'll be a nurse and bring lots of babies safely into the world . . .'

'It won't surprise me if you do,' Jerusha said, making a new pot of tea for the men who were cleaning up in the scullery. She had bacon sizzling in the pan, and there were eggs to add, for this was a celebration. The new arrival was a heifer, not a bull calf, which, because this was a dairy farm, would have been sent to market, and Cowslip, as they had already named the calf, would join the herd with her mother.

The highlight of each week was the Friday market, where Emma now accompanied William in the cart loaded with farm produce to sell. From the dairy there were boxes of butter which she had 'knocked into shape' with wooden pats, a big round of yellow cheese, with a knife to cut the required pieces, a tray of brown and speckled eggs, cabbages and carrots, sacks of earthy potatoes, freshly dug, a churn of fresh milk with a measuring jug, and a smaller container of cream – folk brought their own jugs and bowls to be filled. Emma enjoyed all the hustle and bustle, even though she twitched her nose at the smell of the piglets and lambs in their pens, and a scruffy dog or two on the lookout for scraps to scavenge. It was a day which started at dawn and ended late afternoon, when she was despatched to look for bargains on neighbouring stalls, like Norfolk crab and shrimps, for teatime treats.

The big event of the year was the annual fair in September. When she was twelve years old Emma was trusted to take her three sisters, Jerusha, nine, Keturah, seven, and Rebecca, six, to marvel at what was going on. They were instantly recognisable as sisters in their matching cotton smocks, sewn by their mother, with their dark hair in ringlets restrained tightly by wide ribbons. Their bonnets were tied primly under the chin. Each one had a precious sixpence knotted into a corner of the handkerchief in their pocket. 'Hold Rebecca's hand,' Sophia cautioned. She didn't have to say why; all the girls knew there would be some shady folk at the fair not above dipping into others' pockets. There was a local lock-up for those caught in the act and Wymondham now had an organised police presence.

Swarthy men were there, with horses lined up for inspection while farmers in their best clothes and stove-pipe hats, contrasting with the colourful neckerchiefs and gold earrings worn by the Romanies, were examining the sturdier horses with a view to purchasing one to pull the plough, or a loaded wagon. Livestock was escorted through the crowds, causing them to scatter, especially when the young bullocks arrived. Whips were cracked, making the horses rear and neigh before moving back into line.

The children were more interested in the canopied stalls, particularly the penny toys, which were brightly coloured but made of tin, which could cause a nasty cut if handled carelessly, and the cries of the vendors, some of foreign appearance. They paused to watch a man stretch out his left arm and stack plates along it with his other hand. A duo with fiddle and drum approached the crowd hopefully, holding out their hats. As Emma and her sisters skirted the stalls, she spotted a few who were already too drunk to attempt to sell their wares. They stopped for a moment to stare curiously at a tent, which bore the sign *Curiosities of the World*!, but Emma soon shepherded them away, whispering, 'It's a *freak* show, they say.' There was also a boxing booth, where a huge man called out to passing lads, 'Anyone for fisticuffs?' But the sight of his ham-like fists put most of the boys off.

They bought small presents for their mother and father: sweetmeats for Sophia and a pocket handkerchief for Tobias. They had hoped to win a coconut from the shy, but had no luck. 'Will could have got one,' Emma sighed.

After a couple of hours, Emma led them back through the fair, past the waiting gigs and wagons, and they went home to tell their mother all about their exciting afternoon. Sophia was relieved to see they had come through unscathed, but she insisted they all have a good wash before their supper. 'You never know what you might catch at the September fair,' she told them, which made them scratch their heads.

When Emma was thirteen years old, Sophia had been bedridden for a year. Jerusha, now ten, left school to help Emma, but because she was not robust like her sister, she continued to look after the little boys and was concerned with the well-being of the younger girls. She also did much of the cooking. Emma had become her mother's carer, as well as tackling the more strenuous household tasks, with the back-up of her wonderful sister-in-law Sarah.

Tobias was noticeably frailer too, worn out with work and increasing worry over his wife. He, William and Emma were the only ones who came into close contact with Sophia.

She was painfully thin and sometimes semi-conscious. It was obvious to them that the end was near.

One evening, William and Tobias kept vigil by Sophia's bedside. They advised Emma to get some rest in bed, and they would call her if there was any change. Emma lay awake for some time, glad that Jerusha was asleep beside her and the small boys, too, in their small, shared bed by the window. There was no sound from Keturah and Rebecca in their room. Finally, Emma fell into an exhausted sleep herself.

Sometime after midnight, Tobias came for them. ''Tis time for you to bid your poor mother farewell, together . . . Stand in the doorway. She will know you are there, but don't come in the room.'

'Is Martha here? We promised to let her know,' Emma said anxiously.

'No – I could not leave Sophia,' Tobias said simply. Then he went back to the sick room.

The girls, in their nightgowns, hair plaited for the night, huddled together. Emma and Jerusha held the sleepy little boys whose faces they turned to their shoulders. 'They are too young to see this,' Emma whispered to Jerusha. Keturah put a comforting arm round Rebecca's waist.

William knelt by the bedside, reading a passage from Sophia's well-worn Bible in a soft voice. Tobias sat by his wife, holding her limp hand in his. Before the last words were said, William faltered, turned and addressed the children, 'She hev gone to heaven. Goo back to bed, pray for her. All is well.'

As Emma and Jerusha lay in bed, wiping away their tears, Emma realised she was now effectively mistress of the house. Her childhood really was over. She must discard recent dreams of becoming a nurse, like Sophie, the sister who left home before she was born.

The day after the funeral, at which a large congregation had supported her family in mourning Sophia, although the dissenters were not among them, Martha called her sisters to a meeting round the long pine table in the kitchen. She sat in her mother's chair, waiting for Sarah to join them. Jonathan and Joseph, now four and two years old, played on the rag rug before the range with the dog stretched out with them, allowing little Joe to rest his head on his flank. Now and again the dog flicked his long ears, for he was not normally allowed to be so near the fire because spaniels were prone to canker.

Emma sat next to Martha, who seemed so much more grown up than the girl who had left home three years ago. Martha's hair was swept up and secured with combs, which gave her the illusion of being taller than she actually was and she wore a black dress with a white lace jabot. Emma was still small and slight and her hair hung down her back because, after all, she was still a girl, not a young woman. Until this moment, when Martha had shown that she was in charge, it was she who had been responsible for house-keeping and childcare here, she thought.

'Sorry I'm late!' Sarah said breathlessly, putting down a basket on the table. 'Go and sit with the boys,' she added to her own children, who now numbered three, aged four, three and two: Jane, William and James.

'What's in the basket?' asked curious Rebecca, peering inside it.

'It's a meat pie – I used the big dish Sophia lent me a while ago – keep it after the pie's eaten.'

'You are very kind, Sarah,' Martha told her, indicating the empty chair on her other side. 'Do sit down. We have a lot to talk about before Father and William come in for their dinner, and the master is sending someone to drive me back to work later on.' She blushed, hoping it would be Elijah, the muscular young horseman on her employer's farm who had recently asked to take her out on her half-day off.

Sarah said tentatively, noting Emma's apprehension, 'I know you are wondering, Martha, if you ought to come home to look after the family, but Emma hev proved she can manage, and Jerusha, Keturah and Rebecca will help, too, I know. I can promise to continue doing what I can, and William, of course, will support his father as always. Emma knows she can share any worries with me. You hev been a tower of strength to your mother in the past, but us can manage now, my dear.'

Martha felt a surge of relief. She didn't want to give up her independence, and she knew she would feel resentful if she had to do so. The last thing she wanted was to have to go to church twice on Sundays, and ask permission to walk out with Elijah.

'If you're sure?' she asked.

They all nodded. 'Well, while we are sitting here, let's prepare the vegetables to go with this lovely pie!'

'Here come Father and William.' Emma looked out of the window. 'Children, come up to the table as there will be cooking on the stove. Who is peeling the potatoes? And wash your hands,' she added belatedly, 'after playing with the dog!'

Sarah smiled at Emma. She was taking charge again, she thought, and that was good.

Emma spread an old newspaper over the table where so many meals had been prepared, bread kneaded, pastry rolled and jars lined up to be filled with chutney or jam to be kept in the pantry – Sophia had never wanted a cloth to cover the scrubbed pine top, except on Christmas Day. The turned legs of the table were sturdy and there was a full width-end drawer which held the cutlery. The cups, a medley of different crockery, hung on their hooks on the dresser. Sophia liked to drink her tea from a delicate bone-china cup hand-painted with forget-me-not flowers. Emma had wrapped this cup and saucer in paper and put it away. A memory of her beloved mother. Tears welled in her eyes and she knuckled them fiercely away. She thought, I will never forget her. Why couldn't Mother have seen all her children grow up? Sophia was just forty-two when she passed away.

Tobias sat down heavily in his chair in the alcove by the stove. His face was grey and lined, his eyes puffy. Young Rebecca rushed to pull off his boots, and he gave her a hug. 'I can't do no more today,' he said gruffly. He wanted to go into the bedroom and grieve in private.

Sarah kissed his cheek and gathered up her little flock. 'We'll see you at the end of the day, Will, look after your father. I'll be back tomorrow morning, Emma. You'd best hot up the pie.'

Before they sat down to their dinner, there was a knock on the door for Martha. She gave them a quick embrace in leaving. 'I'll see you soon! God Bless you all! Take care, Father.' Then she was gone and being gallantly hoisted up into the front seat of the trap next to the handsome young driver.

EIGHT

TF

Newcastle, 1854

Having loyally supported Irish Tom and their sister Mary for the past three years, it was now time for Isabella's sons to leave Tyne Street. TF, who was seventeen, with the encouragement and backing of his Uncle Charlie and Aunt Anna, was about to join the Royal Navy as a boy sailor. Mary was now eight years old, she was a spirited child who stood no nonsense from Irish Tom, and since Granny had died and Dorrie had left, she had become very independent for her age.

'She is the sensible one of the two,' TF observed to Rob, as he now preferred to be known. Rob was a mature, steady lad of fourteen who was moving to Amble, Northumberland, on the Scottish border until he was old enough to join the merchant marine. Again, this was at the suggestion of Charlie, who arranged lodgings for him with a local family. Charlie had been at sea with the widow's late husband.

On their last evening in Tyne Street, Tom, gaunt and unshaven but trying to stay sober until after they had gone, opened Isabella's trunk. 'I want each of you to have something to remind you of your mother,' he said. 'Then I will give the trunk to Anna to keep for Mary.'

The contents were as the boys remembered them. The cloak, wrapped in brittle, yellowing paper, the opera glasses, the drooping feathers of the ostrich fan, the water colour picture of Isabella's family, her parents unsmiling; the sewing basket she had been given as a child, and the box of paints. They each took a book. No jewellery remained, except for the little brooch intended for Mary. Tom passed it to the child. 'Have it now, it was left to you by Aunt Nesbit.' She pinned it to her dress. 'Isn't it pretty! Did I know Aunt Nesbit?'

TF chose the sewing basket. All sailors were expected to be adept with needle and thread. Uniforms issued were 'standard size', but with generous seams and most needed adapting to fit – in TF's case, as he was unusually tall and well-built, he would have to unpick hems and cuffs on trousers and jackets to lengthen them. Rob decided on the paints as he was artistic like his mother, and drawing and painting was a favourite past-time of sailors, he knew.

'I suppose you will soon forget Newcastle, and who can blame you,' Tom said heavily.

'Dada, we will always be Geordies,' TF said. 'And we promise to keep in touch. When I've finished my training, I'll be serving queen and country, most likely in the Crimea.'

TF was on *Monarch* during his four-month training and passed out as a 'Boy, First Class'. He was given money from navy funds to purchase his uniform: a blue cloth jacket (17s. 8d.), and trousers (11s. 7d.), blue serge frock (smock) for winter wear (8s. 6d.) and a white duck frock for summer (2s.7d.), black silk kerchief (2s.10d.) and black shoes (6s.7d.). He was indeed kept busy taking the tighter garments to pieces and resewing. TF, along with a few boys released from workhouses into the navy, taught this skill to those from more affluent homes.

On board the ships they were supplied with all they would need: a hammock, one blanket and a bedcover, plus mug, plate, knife, fork and spoon, which they were told wouldn't be replaced and must be guarded zealously.

There was no grog ration for those under eighteen years of age, but a pound of tobacco was available for a shilling, and soap was 4d. a bar. The boys might grumble at that, but they were expected to keep themselves clean and tidy at all times.

TF tackled all tasks with enthusiasm. He was the first to climb to the top rigging, as he had a good head for heights after nipping up and down ladders when helping his father. He learned to swim in the safer waters of the harbour where he observed sea-going vessels coming and going and gangs of men repairing and refitting ships, which could take months, and finally loading craft in the docks. Later, he would realise the significance of the altercations between the idle crew members and officials, because the men were not paid until just before sailing. Families were getting deeper into debt meanwhile, and whenever ships departed, desperate women rowed out to them pleading for their share of the men's wages. Sailors could allot half their pay to support them, unless in debt, which invariably they were.

When he left the *Monarch* TF joined the *Curlew*, a small warship known as a Screw Steam Sloop, which had recently been launched and was intended to serve mainly in the Mediterranean. The smaller boys often became 'powder monkeys', charging the ship's eight guns.

Unlike some of the lads, TF soon conquered his sea-sickness, thriving on the discipline and orderliness of naval life. There were 500 sailors on board, including commissioned officers and naval tradesmen with special skills. Their assistants were called petty officers. Quartermasters, experienced seamen, could steer the ship, keep watch and send and receive signals. Able seamen were dedicated sailors who were a good example to the boys.

Off-duty, there was some lively entertainment below decks – banjo and harmonica playing, the lads sang songs like 'A Sailors Life for Me' and TF discovered he had a talent for whistling. Boys often whittled driftwood as they sang, some knitted or sewed, others listened to the music while they painted pictures to send home, preferring to do this rather than write letters.

The diet on board ship was rather monotonous, but most of the younger members thrived on it.

Food had to be nutritious and easy to store, easy to carry and long-lasting. Fresh vegetables and fruit were soon exhausted and needed replenishing whenever in port. Dairy products soon became mouldy. As TF wrote home: *Even the rats can't nibble the hard cheese* . . . Game, caged on board, was limited but fish could be caught in deep waters with a line slung overboard. The latest vessels now had cooking and baking facilities on board, and cereals became an important part of navy rations. Fresh loaves were seized upon with relish, but sea biscuits kept better than bread. The recipe was simple: 1lb of flour and 4oz salt were mixed with water to a stiff dough. This was left to stand for half an hour then rolled out thickly into six long biscuits. These were baked in a hot oven, then put in a warm place to harden and dry. There were occasional variations with added caraway seeds or currants, which were counted gleefully by the boys to see who had the most. The biscuits were enjoyed by those with good teeth, but some had to soak them in tea.

Canned food had been introduced in the early part of the century and beef was preserved in tins from 1842. Having discovered that citrus fruit prevented scurvy on long voyages, limes and lemons were purchased en route, and lemon juice was also added to the rum ration. Exotic fruit like pineapples and bananas were a real treat.

As for Rob, he immediately took to life in the coastal town of Amble, which was situated on land jutting out from the mouth of the River Coquet, with panoramic views out to sea. It was possible to row out to Coquet Island where there was a colony of seals and many sea birds. The countryside was lush and green, with rich seams of coal now being mined, bringing prosperity and work to what had been mainly a fishing community grouped around the harbour, but was now a busy port. Rob lodged there in a fisherman's cottage and had his first experience of going to sea as a deck hand on a trawler along with his landlady's two eldest sons.

Amble would be home to Rob for the rest of his life, the place he always returned to after long periods away once he had joined the merchant marine a year later. When he learned something of the history of the place, he discovered the name Amble was derived from Annebelle. He wrote to Anna, *I must have been meant to come here . . .*

Like his brother he grew to six feet tall, his hair was bleached even fairer by the sun and sea air, and his pale skin was bronzed. Isabella would have rejoiced to see her boys so fit and happy.

Rob became firm friends with Jane and Margaret, the local innkeeper's daughters in Amble, and it was Margaret whom later he would marry, although Jane was also a constant presence in his life.

Sebastopol, 1854/5

The *Curlew* was in action in the Crimea, a peninsula situated on the northern coast of the Black Sea. In mid-1855 the British prime minister, Lord Palmerston, bowed to public opinion for Britain to join with France and Turkey in the assault on the Russian naval arsenal at Sebastopol in the Black Sea. In 1853 the Russian Black Sea fleet had annihilated a Turkish squadron at Sinope. Britain, anxiously regarding her trade with Turkey and access to India, wished to maintain the Ottoman regime, and regarded the action by the Russians as an insult. The Allies decided that a vigorous response was necessary. The Royal Navy was sent to destroy the Russian fleet and the docks and ordered to secure Sebastopol. It was ironic that in 1851, despite the rapidly deteriorating relations between Russia and Great Britain, the Russians had placed an order with British shipyards, which were ahead of them in nautical engineering, for powerful propeller-driven engines. These were commandeered at the outbreak of the Crimean War by the British government and used by our navy, having been paid for by Russia.

TF, still classed as a boy sailor, had another year to serve before he became an able seaman, but he was involved in the fierce, bloody hand-to-hand fighting in the streets of Sebastopol and witnessed the death of several close friends. The musket was the new weapon of choice for the British and French, but the blades of their opponents flashed and inflicted mortal wounds. The booming of the guns from the waiting ships was deafening, and he suffered from ringing in his ears for the rest of his life. The nightmare of Sebastopol, the memory of maimed men who cried out in foreign tongues, would never be erased, although he was fortunate not to have been badly wounded.

The independence of the Ottoman Empire was guaranteed by the Treaty of Paris in April 1856 and by order of the Admiralty, the Crimea Medal was awarded to sailors and marines present during this campaign between September 1854 and September 1855. TF received this medal, along with four clasps awarded to those present not only in Sebastopol, but in Inkerman, Balaclava and the Sea of Azoff, an arm of the Black Sea.

After four years, TF changed course, and went to the *Impregnable* in Devonport for signalman training. Following this, he joined the *St Jean d'Acre* as a yeoman of signals, the equivalent of a petty officer. This large wooden battleship, a two-decker, was the navy's first 101-gun screw, with a crew of 950. She had also served in the Crimean War and later took dignitaries to the coronation of Czar Alexander II at St Petersburg in 1856.

Despite his promotion and further prospects, during the following two years, TF had doubts about completing his promised ten years' service with the Navy.

While her brothers pursued their maritime careers, TF and Rob's sister Mary, with a sick father unable to work, left school in 1856 when she was ten years old and became a fur puller. It was a common industry in London and in other city areas, like Newcastle. It was thoroughly unpleasant work, usually performed by young girls and older women in small barns or outhouses, which were freezing in the winter months. Mary learned to pull the skins of rabbits by removing the loose down off them with a blunt knife. The reward for this was around a shilling for the down from five dozen skins. The down was returned to the furrier, who supplied the rabbits, for stuffing mattresses, sofas and pillows. During the Crimean War output considerably increased and many more employees were needed as soldiers' jackets were lined with down to keep them warm in the bitter cold; it was also popular as a lining for women's and children's cloaks.

Mary sat on a low stool with a trough at her feet into which she deposited the fluff as she pulled it. Now and again, she paused to rub the knife with whiting to remove the grease. She coughed continually as she breathed in fine, floating fibres through her nose or open mouth. There was very little communication between the workers, for lungs soon became affected and breathlessness was the result. Her red hair looked as if it was powdered with white snow, and the awful smell clung to her clothes and person.

Sometimes she would have to assist with cutting open the rabbits' tails to extract the bones, which were sold for manure. The fur obtained in this way was used in the manufacture of cheap blankets and hats. Mary could make 8d. per pound for this work.

The highlight of Mary's long day was the arrival of the carter to take away the results of all that hard graft. She helped him carry bags out to the cart and count them. Alexander, who was the son of a Jewish docker, became a friend. He liked to tease her, calling her Irish Mary, and boldly told her, 'If you was to wash off all that dust, you'd be the prettiest gal in the whole wide world.'

'You want to watch out, I ain't got red hair for nothing!' she replied.

'Fancy comin' round to my place for a plate of rabbit stew?'

'What d'you think! Poor creatures, I could never put one in a pot.'

She went back to Tyne Street, cleaned herself up, and made a meal for herself and her dada. She was too tired to cook anything, but smiled to herself as she served the usual bread and cheese, thinking, Rabbit stew indeed! I have seen enough of 'em to last me a lifetime . . .

'You'll make someone a good wife,' her father said unexpectedly as she passed him a cup of cocoa made with the milk Sister Ursula had brought them that day.

'Who would ever want to marry me, smelling like I do?' she lamented.

When Mary was sixteen, in 1862, she and Alexander were married and she gave up the fur-pulling to ride on the cart with him, and before long, they had a little daughter Margaret.

Alexander loved his wife dearly, despite her quick temper, and he bought her fancy clothes to wear. She looked quite the lady sitting up top on the cart, wearing a fur-lined cloak. But the years of fur-pulling damaged her health and Mary died before she was thirty. TF and Robbie were affected all their lives by what happened to their sister, the feisty little girl with the mop of glorious red hair and blue eyes that matched the brooch left to her by Aunt Nesbit. TF hoped her daughter would have a better life, and that she would wear the lapis lazuli brooch.

As for Irish Tom, he was lonely and depressed when Mary left home to marry Alexander. She stopped calling on her father when it became inevitable that he would end up in the workhouse, drunk and in debt. He must have been there a while unknown to his sons, both away at sea, before he passed away in the infirmary, some time before his daughter.

NINE

Emma

Wymondham, 1858

In July 1858, Tobias Wright suffered a disabling stroke and was admitted to the infirmary some distance from Wymondham. It was a bitter blow that he was no longer able to communicate with his family and they came to realise that he was very unlikely to return home.

Sarah said quietly, 'He be all wore out, poor old Father, bringing up two families, and losing two good wives.'

'How long will us be able to carry on?' William wondered. Sarah was unable to be involved with the family at the farm as before because she had just given birth to their fourth son, Jeremiah, and with the help of their only daughter Jane, now almost ten years old, Sarah was also caring for four-year-old John, born a year after Sophia died. John was gravely ill following complications with measles, which he had contracted from his older brothers after there had been an epidemic at the school. The family were still in the farm cottage from which they had hoped to move on long ago, for as Sarah sighed, 'Us be a real houseful now.'

William's firm reply to this was, 'Us must see things through to the finish.'

Sarah knew he was talking about the farm, and the responsibility he felt for the youngsters there. Neither of them wanted to believe they might lose their son.

'Are things really bad?' Emma asked when William came in for his morning break.

'Father hadn't paid the rent for the past six months. Sophia used to deal with that. He should hev told me—'

'He thought you had enough to worry about,' Emma told him. 'But I can help! I like being outside, especially now it's summer. We can work well together; just tell me what is needed. The children are growing up. Ru will continue as she is, and the other girls will help.'

'Us can try – but I can't promise 'twill all turn out as us would hope. Us hev other bills too.'

The following morning Emma joined William in the milking parlour. She'd spent the previous evening shortening the legs of Tobias's ancient corduroy breeks, and making another notch in his leather belt to hold them up round her narrow waist. She wrinkled her nose a bit at his jacket, which had never seen a washing tub, but she needed it first thing before sun-up. Her long hair was bundled up under his hat, a shapeless affair like an up-ended bucket with a feather stuck in the brim. She drew the line at Tobias's boots, which were in their usual place beside his chair. William had cleaned the mud from them and polished them up, even though he knew they wouldn't be worn again. William greeted her with a smile. He wouldn't mention that he had sat up most of the night with his sick child.

In September came the news that he and Sarah were expecting again and Tobias died of 'Natural Decay'. He was sixty-six years old. He was brought home to Wymondham and buried in the Abbey graveyard. The farming community turned out in full force to mourn a good man.

'He be at peace now,' William told the young ones as he tried to comfort them.

'Will we be able to stay on here?' Emma asked him fearfully, after the funeral when the rest of the family were not in earshot.

'Father wanted me to carry on, I know that, but us hev no money behind us, Emma. The farm is not what 'twas. The landlord will, I believe, say he must find a new tenant at Michaelmas. The stock and the contents of the house will hev to be sold to settle our debts. I hope to be allowed to take the pine table and chairs that Father promised me, so the family can sit around that table when us can all be together. The rector hev said the church will support us while us are in need. I won't be able to take on the children, as I would wish to do, and the law say *you* are too young to be their guardian, even though you hev been that for so long.'

'What will happen to us all?' Emma exclaimed. Then, seeing his face: 'Oh no – not the *workhouse*!'

'I don't know yet,' he said. But the spectre of that loomed large.

Emma clung to her brother's arm as they walked resolutely away from the farmhouse, not looking back. All was silent now, after the noise of the auction, which she and William had attended. Before the sale William was allowed to take the table and chairs as he requested, and at the end the landlord waived his right to some of the chattels that were left and he was told quietly, to 'help yourself'. He chose the old washstand and the cornflower-patterned bowl and jug which still stood on it, his father's boots, Sophia's precious forget-me-not cup and saucer, which he would give to Emma later, and his own mother's chest, filled with good linen for Sarah.

'Here you are at last,' Sarah cried thankfully as she opened the door of the cottage.

William enveloped her in a fierce hug, whispered: 'Is he . . .?

'He is waiting for you,' she sobbed. 'Goo straight up.'

At dawn, their long vigil was ended. In Jane's adjacent small room, the baby woke and began to cry. They heard creaking, as Jane rocked the cradle. William gently helped Sarah to her feet; they had both been on their knees by John's bed, which had been drawn up close beside their own.

'The little 'un do need you now, Sarah. I will do what must be done. All is well.' But, of course, they knew it was not.

Wicklewood Workhouse had been built in 1777 as 'a House of Correction'. It was all arranged: Keturah, Rebecca, Jonathan and little Joe would be taken there by the rector. The only consolation for Emma was that the children would be able to continue with their schooling and this would stand them in good stead when they were able to leave the workhouse and go to work.

There was no alternative – they were destitute.

The ladies of the church rallied round as always, and Emma and Jerusha were soon in employment, due to the efforts of their friends from the church. The rector's wife said stoutly, 'You will not be *skivvies*.' Emma, now eighteen, became an assistant cook to the squire and his lady in the 'big house'. Fifteen-year-old Jerusha was now a nursery maid in another village; Martha was settled, and engaged to Elijah, the groom. As for William, he had yet to find employment on another farm as an agricultural labourer, not a farmer, as he had been at Browick Bottom.

Emma, in the big house at Wymondham was highly regarded by Milady, as she was known.

She was still hungry for knowledge and she was allowed to take away and read avidly all her employer's magazines, which Milady had only given a cursory glance through. These were not as earnest as the religious papers she had read in the past, apart from *The Christian Lady's Magazine*, but she particularly enjoyed Mrs Isabella Beeton's *The Englishwoman's Domestic Magazine*, which had just started in 1856, and was written in a lively fashion. She was permitted to try some of the recipes on the family, and so widened her expertise. However, she was still an assistant cook, as the old cook often tartly reminded her. Cook did not approve of favouritism. 'I hev been here thirty year, do they think o' that? Emma hev big ideas, but she is wet behind the ears,' she muttered to the butler, who feigned deafness.

Emma wrote to Jerusha, *The family like my cooking, but Cook says it is too fancy!*

Jerusha was in her element looking after the small children of a master builder and his wife near Norwich. However, a great deal was expected of her and she was told 'not to make a fuss' when she suffered an attack of asthma, as servants were not expected to take time off for illness. The children had their meals in the nursery with Jerusha, as their mother was often entertaining guests at dinner in the evenings, and out and about social calling during the day, unencumbered by her progeny. This gave Jerusha a free rein to deal with the children in the only way she knew: following the example of her mother, Sophia.

Jerusha wrote to Emma, *I am fortunate to live in this lovely house, and am mistress in the schoolroom!*

At the workhouse, Keturah, aged twelve, and Rebecca, eleven, clutching the bundles which contained their few possessions, were taken to the superintendent's office and told to wait for his wife to come to interview them. They had already been parted from their small brothers, who were escorted to another room to await their turn. Men and women were segregated, which was very hard on married couples, likewise the older children, although the latter met up at mealtimes. Mothers with babies cared for them in a communal nursery but all inmates who were fit enough were expected to work for their keep. Single women scrubbed floors and did other chores, mothers with older children were often involved with cooking and serving the meals and did the piles of washing up with those not at school. The laundry was another busy place. Older women and girls would sew and mend, or knit baby clothes. 'Idle hands' were not permitted.

The able-bodied men tackled the gardening, cleaned and mended boots and shoes and cut wood for the fires and stoves. There was a sick room, presided over by Matron, with an elderly nurse, but very old patients were transferred to the infirmary and rarely returned.

'The old people all look very sad,' Rebecca observed.

'That's because they have been parted from their husbands and wives,' Keturah said.

Matron was a tall, angular woman dressed in black, with an assortment of keys fastened to her chatelaine belt. She was not intimidating but she didn't smile much as she went through the rules of the establishment. The girls were not expected to speak until she had finished. Keturah was told, 'You will be known by your second name here, Hannah, we prefer good plain names. Rebecca is acceptable.' Matron indicated the bundles. 'In the girls' room you will find a cupboard. Your personal effects will be kept there. You will be given a name tag to mark them. When you leave here, these will be returned to you.' She looked them up and down. 'You will wear the good clothes we provide here, we find it best for the girls to be dressed alike. Have you any questions?'

Rebecca, the bolder of the two girls, spoke up. 'When will we see our brothers again?'

'At dinner time. However, the boys sit on the benches on one side of the table and the girls on the other. Now, have you had a bath as we requested?'

'Yes, Matron,' they said in unison. They had enjoyed their session in the bathroom at the rectory in a proper bath with plenty of hot water and scented soap. Emma had helped to wash their hair and rubbed it dry with the fluffiest of towels afterwards.

'Your hair – did your sister go through it strand by strand?'

'What for?' Rebecca asked, rather too innocently. They had never suffered from head lice, due to Sophia and later, Emma's diligence.

'You know very well what for. But we are aware that you come from a good home. No curls, please; braids are much more practical. We do not have a fixed bath here. We find portable baths quite sufficient, but you will be expected to immerse yourself fully each month.'

As they followed an older girl up the stairs to see the sleeping quarters, Rebecca whispered to Keturah, 'I thought you were only immersed fully if you were baptised in the River Jordan.'

'Shush!' Keturah cautioned her nervously.

They entered a long room with a row of narrow beds a few inches apart. The girl showing them around said brusquely, 'That one's yours, and that one's yours,' She went to the cupboard opposite. 'Bring your bundles. Your new clothes are here. Get changed and put your old clothes in the same place.'

'They're not old,' Rebecca muttered, but they complied with instructions.

'When you are ready, come down to the dining hall. It's the door to the left of the stairs. I have to go to help get the table laid.' And she was gone.

Keturah sank down on her bed. 'Ouch! It's a *straw* mattress!' she exclaimed in dismay.

Rebecca thumped the one pillow. 'This is filled with straw, too! But, see, there's a chamber pot under each bed!'

'I can guess who has to empty those, Becca. Look at this dress. Thick, horrible material; I expect it's scratchy to wear! Starched petticoats and pinafores—'

'These stockings aren't new, Ket, they're darned at the heels – I shall still call you that, because I always have!'

'The drawers are stiff and starchy too,' Keturah said dolefully. 'Sit down carefully in them.'

'At least we can wear our own boots. Only one washstand for all – d'you think we'll have to use the same water?'

'Yes. So we'd better try to be the first in line in the mornings, eh?'

'The only thing to look forward to is the day we leave here – William is hoping to get a bigger house when he gets a job. He would take us in if he could.' Rebecca was optimistic.

Keturah said, 'Even if that doesn't happen, we won't have to stay here when we are old enough to go into service – but the poor boys will be here much longer.'

When they went down to the dining hall, they were shown where to sit at the long table. The knives and forks were laid out on the bare wood with a mug in each place. They spotted their brothers a little further along across the table and managed a few words before the superintendent arrived to say grace.

There was only a year between the boys, Jonathan was nine and Joseph, eight, but Jonathan was a big, sturdy boy whereas Joseph was small and puny for his age. Jonathan told them that he was now known as Ebenezer (his second name) as there were other boys with his first name.

Keturah sympathised. 'And I am now Hannah! I like the name, but I still feel like Keturah.'

'Well, I will never like being *Ebenezer*!'

'Cheer up,' Rebecca said; she was never down for long. 'The dinner smells good!'

There was a sudden hush as the superintendent stood at the head of the table, hands folded together, his keen gaze on every face in turn. He waited until the children were all standing, before in ringing tones came the familiar words: *For what we are about to receive . . .*

'*Moses!*' Rebecca whispered to Keturah, as they bowed their heads. He was very tall with long, white hair and an even longer beard, like pictures in the Sunday school texts.

Plates were passed from one to the other to the end of the table. There was a generous slice of salt beef, a plump Norfolk dumpling, two large potatoes, diced carrots and dark greens. The gravy was in a jug and the children poured it carefully on the food. There was a thick slice of bread for each of them. Water was limited to half a mug per child. The drinking water was pumped up in the yard once a day. They ate in silence. It was good food, well cooked and there were no complaints.

'Oh, we're in luck – rice pudding!' Becca whispered, hoping for some of the brown skin on top. But there was no home-made raspberry jam and cream as they had with this pudding at home.

Wicklewood really was as 'cold as charity' with only one fireplace in the big day room. The floor was always clean, but very chilly to the feet as all floors were either brick or tiled, and there were no mats. The day room was below the level of the adjoining yard which meant the floor was also damp in winter. In fact, all the rooms were bare and cheerless with no comfortable furniture, just hard chairs and a square table in the centre of the workroom.

That night the two girls slept fitfully, for the straw prickled their faces as they lay on the hard pillows, the blankets were adequate but of harsh wool, and the mattress rustled as they tossed and turned. They thought of their brothers and hoped they were together, as they were. They wouldn't allow themselves to cry.

They didn't know that Emma and Jerusha shed tears for them all.

Emma wrote regularly to her siblings and, being in Wymondham, was able to visit Wicklewood at times specified by the matron, but she wept in private after she left. It was such a grim place, but she was consoled by the thought that Keturah and Rebecca supported each other. It seemed much harder for her brothers. Joseph, who was often ill, could barely read and write, but Jonathan was doing well at lessons, although the Wicklewood children, conspicuous in their workhouse clothes, were picked on by some of the other schoolchildren. It was Jonathan who fought back on his brother's behalf, and suffered a bloody nose on occasion.

William had secured a new job on a bigger farm, with a tied cottage. At Christmas, the first since they left home, the children at Wicklewood were allowed to join them for two weeks. No doubt they hoped they would be able to stay longer, but the house was not much bigger than the cottage where William and Sarah had lived since their marriage, and they had four children of their own. Reluctantly, the boys and girls returned to Wicklewood, with the promise of a summer holiday to help with the harvest.

Rebecca clung to her sister when Keturah emerged from Matron's office, clutching a letter in her hand. 'What happened?' she asked fearfully. Such summons invariably meant censure of some sort for often a minor demeanour.

'I will be fourteen next week and I suppose I should have known this was coming,' Keturah replied. 'I will leave Wicklewood and' – she flourished the letter – 'this is from the – place – they have found me.'

'Oh, but that's good news, isn't it?' Rebecca glanced around, but they were not observed, so she gave Keturah a hug.

'You'll miss me though, won't you?' Keturah wiped away tears with her sleeve.

'Course I will, but I'm going to work hard at my lessons and you'll write to me, won't you, and I'll still be here to keep an eye on the boys. And Ket, you'll be able to wear nice clothes again.'

She brightened at this, remembering how earlier Matron had said, 'You're a young woman now,' in a disapproving tone. Keturah was conscious of her changing shape and was aware that the one-size-fits-all, from skinny to well-built, of the Wicklewood clothing did nothing to enhance it. She was good at sewing, she thought, so that could be an advantage. She would take her bundle, but only for sentimental reasons.

Rebecca, at twelve, was still straight up and down, which met with Matron's approval. 'Young women' were sent out into the world, but a few of them inevitably returned, usually with a baby in arms. The facts of life were never discussed with girls in care, though morality was heavily emphasised in the superintendent's daily homilies. But the euphemisms went over the girls' heads.

So Keturah left Wicklewood for good in 1857 and worked as a mother's help in Great Yarmouth for a family of modest means, who treated her well.

Rebecca, resilient as always, enjoyed her school days and although she was unaware of this, she was actually Matron's favourite, and consequently was found a good place a year later as house servant to a solicitor's clerk in Wymondham. Later she also worked in Great Yarmouth where her elderly employers became fond of the cheerful, articulate girl who brightened their rather mundane lives. Like Keturah, Rebecca loved living near the sea and, best of all, she could meet up now and then with her sister.

Then it was Jonathan's turn to leave Wicklewood, at an earlier age than his sisters; he was twelve and apprenticed to a shoemaker. Sadly, his ailing young brother Joseph did not live long after they were parted, but Joseph spent his last days with William and Sarah, who loved and cared for him as one of their own family.

Emma had been with Milady for two years when she began to peruse advertisements for cooks in London. Emma's well-written letter stood her in good stead when she applied for the post of cook-housekeeper. She was now twenty years old, although she thought she had more chance of the job by saying she was twenty-three! She was accepted by return of post and soon she was off to London, to Kensington, to work in an even grander house!

TEN

Emma

London, January, 1861

When Emma awoke, she wondered for a moment where she was, for she had arrived quite late at the house in South Kensington after travelling for the first time by train. This had been a somewhat unnerving experience, with all the steam and smoke from the great engine and the sight of folk scurrying along the platforms, worried that the whistle might blow and the train would depart before they could find an empty carriage and climb thankfully inside. The rector had escorted her to Norwich to catch the afternoon train to London and made sure she was safely settled with her trunk, her hand luggage and a book to read. She was in a Ladies Only compartment, but her companions were engrossed in their magazines and did not speak to her or to each other. When she reached her destination, she obeyed instructions to wait for a hansom cab sent by her new employer. The driver, identifying himself, reassured her that Mr Summers had paid for the journey in advance. 'I know the gentleman well, I often calls there.'

This was another new experience for Emma. The hansom bowled along on two huge wheels, and she had to be assisted up into the cab. The driver sat on high behind the cab, controlling the horse out front with reins that stretched across the roof. It was fortunate that Emma didn't realise the only part of the horse visible to the driver was its expressive ears. The front of the cab was open so she was provided with a rug over her knees and was thankful it wasn't raining or snowing. Communication with the cabbie was only possible through a trap door in the roof, but fortunately it was not necessary for her to contact him as the journey was uneventful.

Even at dusk, the three-storey, white-stuccoed building in the exclusive crescent, with its balconied upper windows, decorative cast-iron railed steps leading to the basement and wider steps to the impressive double front door, appeared to Emma to be like a fairy-tale palace in a children's picture book. It was the end house, next to the railed and gated communal gardens to which all residents possessed a key. An elderly retainer opened the door, ushered her in, and her belongings were carried into her quarters on the ground floor, a bedroom which led to a private sanctum where she could relax when she finished work. Beyond was the servants' hall. She was relieved she wouldn't have to climb the many stairs to the top floor where the other staff had their bedrooms.

'Mr Summers and his sisters are at dinner. He suggests you have supper in your room, the maid will bring it to you and tell you where everything is. Mr Summers will see you tomorrow after you have recovered from your journey. The family wish you a restful night.'

After the poached eggs on toast and a pot of tea, brought to her by a pleasant girl who introduced herself as Nan, the under housemaid, Emma slept well in a comfortable brass-railed bed with gleaming knobs – she was cosy because a warming pan had been placed in the bed earlier and the blankets were soft woollen ones beneath a pretty hand-sewn patchwork quilt.

'Mr Summers' sisters made that,' the young maid said when Emma admired it. Emma was aware there were three of them, unmarried ladies, and that Mr Summers was a widower, a solicitor, with a daughter, Frances, who went to an Academy for Young Ladies. There were also two sons, but as Mr Summers wrote in his introductory letter, they were boarders at Westminster School and only at home in the holidays. He also mentioned, 'It is a busy kitchen, for my sisters often entertain friends from the church.'

She sat up in bed, plumped the pillow behind her and turned up the wick on the nightlight on the bedside cabinet. She gazed around the room. There was a framed text on the wall, embroidered in coloured wool. *His mercy is everlasting*. She wondered which sister had done that. She reached for her Bible, which she always read for ten minutes each morning before rising.

There was a tap on the door, and another young maid brought in a can of steaming water. She placed it on the washstand, with its tiles patterned with yellow tulips. 'Good morning, Cook. I hope you slept well?' she asked politely, adding, 'Slops will be collected later.' She indicated the cupboard below the washstand in which the chamber pot was concealed. This matched the yellow bowl and jug, soap dish and hair-pin holder. A flannel and hand towel were provided. What luxury! Emma thought.

'Thank you, I slept very well indeed.' She smiled at the girl, who suppressed a yawn as she opened the door. It was only just past six o'clock. She paused in the doorway for a moment or two.

'Cook – Mrs Love – made sure you would have everything in place before she went yesterday. She's gone to look after her old parents. I was told to wish you all the best.'

'It was kind of her to take so much trouble,' Emma said. 'I've never stepped out of bed on to a sheepskin rug before!'

After she had washed and dressed, she made her bed, and unpacked some of her things into the tall chest of drawers. She felt confident and smart in her new black dress and capacious snow-white apron and cap. The keys on her belt, which she had been given yesterday, jingled pleasantly. She gazed at her reflection in the mirror, thinking, I look just like Mother with my hair parted in the middle and in a knot in the nape of my neck. What would dear father say? *'Bootiful!'* Then she went along the hall, down a short flight of steps to the big basement kitchen and through the double, baize-covered swing doors where she explored her new domain.

There was a sturdy, well-scrubbed table with two drawers where she would do most of her preparations for meals. One of the drawers contained lists of tradesmen who called regularly, a ledger of household accounts, which she was expected to record meticulously, and a locked black cash box. In the other drawer were recipes written by several hands, a ball of string and a set of Apostle teaspoons. She admired the rows of gleaming copper pans, the huge dresser with its display of blue-and-white plates, mixing bowls, jugs in various sizes, large tureens, and the locked canister of tea to which only she kept the key. In the cupboards were sacks of flour and dried fruit. She looked in the larder at the goods, which had to be replenished regularly, everything in its place on slabs of marble. Most impressive of all was the coal-fired range with the oven to one side and a tank on the other, which provided hot water through a tap, but required much topping up with cold water each day. The cast-iron kettle on the hob was steaming gently. It would soon be time for the staff to gather for their breakfast, which Emma was about to make, and after that there were the jugged kippers for the family breakfast to be delivered to the ground-floor dining room by dumb waiter. The maids, she guessed, were now laying the table there.

Emma went through into the scullery, hearing a clatter within. Nan, the youngest maid, kept it spotlessly clean. They had met briefly last night and Emma guessed Nan was the first to begin work in the mornings and the last to leave at night. She didn't live in but had a long walk from a less salubrious part of the city where she lived with her aunt, whom Emma had yet to meet. She was the washerwoman employed here on Mondays to deal with the household linen. The maids hand-washed the ladies' delicate garments and pressed them with flat-irons.

Nan looked up from washing up the family's early morning cups and saucers in the sink. She was small and thin with a sallow complexion and an anxious expression. She dried her hands, sore from the soda in the hot water, hastily on her over-apron which was made of sacking. 'Good mornin', Cook. Is everythin' orlright?'

Emma smiled reassuringly. 'Yes, Nan, it is.' She made a mental note to mix up a solution of glycerine and rose water into a salve for Nan to rub into her hands. She added, 'You do a good job black-leading the stove. It really shines.'

'It'll be greasy agin by tomorrer,' Nan said with a rueful grin, which reminded Emma of her youngest sister Rebecca, whose cheerfulness in adversity helped her sister and brothers to cope with life in the workhouse.

'Can you find me a large pan to fry the bacon, please? Then I'll be grateful if you would crack a dozen eggs and whisk them in a bowl, so I can scramble those. Add a little top of the milk and salt and pepper—'

'*Bacon!*' Nan said in awe. 'We on'y had it on Sundays before, and scrambling eggs is me fav'rite!'

The young maids were back from delivering the cans of hot water to the Summers family in their bedrooms on the second floor and ready for breakfast before they tackled the rest of the morning chores. Like Nan, they sniffed appreciatively: '*Bacon*! Thanks, Cook.'

'Emma,' she said, 'call me Emma, everyone does. I know you are Lily and Rose.'

'And I am Anna, the parlourmaid,' a newcomer introduced herself, smiling.

This was Anna Lister, Isabella's sister and TF and Rob's aunt. The two of them would become lifelong friends, but of course they weren't aware of that then.

The post of cook-housekeeper was an important one. Emma would discuss the day's menu with Miss Maria, the eldest Miss Summers, each morning after breakfast was over, until it was time for them all to assemble for morning prayers in the drawing room. She was already aware that she would be responsible for the purchase of meat, poultry, fish, and vegetables in season, eggs and dairy products, as well as keeping the store cupboard well-stocked, all within a designated budget. She was expected to enquire about bargain buys from the tradesmen who called at the house. After that she must keep account of every item to add to the lists in the table drawer. These would be inspected periodically by her employer, who would also replenish the petty cash.

On her first morning, she was excused the menu appraisal and prayers as Mr Summers had asked to see her in the library before he left for his office.

Mr Summers was a kindly man in his early forties, with a good head of hair fashionably parted in the centre and Dundreary whiskers: sideburns with a full, bushy beard and an impressive moustache. He invariably wore dark, single-breasted jackets with narrow legged, checked trousers and a silk cravat rather than a necktie tucked under his high white collar. Mr Summers seemed a trifle overwhelmed at times, being the sole male in a house full of females apart from his manservant, whose duties were few now he was old, although he had the key to the cellar and kept an eye on the wine, especially when the two lively boys, aged sixteen and seventeen, were at home. 'Boys will be boys,' Mr Summers, a modest drinker himself, observed tolerantly. When the chatter in the drawing room in the evenings became rather too animated, particularly if his sisters were joined by other ladies, he would make his apologies and retreat to the library, with its shelves full of legal books, and study the sheaf of papers brought home from his office.

He had been a widower for some years, his wife having died when their daughter, Frances, was less than a year old. Actually, Frances had known her mother hardly at all, for the older Frances had been an invalid and was sent with a nurse to Brighton for the sea air. In the last resort, she was sent to a sanatorium in Capri, where sadly she passed away. The baby was cared for by a nanny until she went to school.

Emma knocked on the door and was instantly told, 'Do come in, Miss Wright.' They shook hands, and then Mr Summers pulled out a chair and waited for her to settle down opposite him.

'Now, how do you find us?' he asked diffidently.

Emma could hardly say that the glimpse she had had of the Misses Summers was not as she expected. They were dressed much more extravagantly than Milady and her friends in Wymondham. She had yet to meet young Frances, although the staff seemed very fond of her.

'She was Mrs Love's pet. After school, she is usually downstairs in the kitchen, with the cat on her lap – her aunts don't seem to know how to get on with an eleven-year-old girl – it's an awkward age, especially as she has no mother,' Anna had said earlier.

Emma said now, 'I am happy to be here, Mr Summers – and, oh, I am only ever called Emma – do you mind that?'

For a brief moment he looked nonplussed, then he cleared his throat and said, 'Emma . . . well, you look nothing like most cooks I have known, although they have always been good at their job, but you, I have a feeling, may surpass them all.'

'Thank you, Mr Summers,' said Emma, not knowing what else to say.

'I shall look forward to my dinner tonight. I must leave now. My sisters would like to make your acquaintance in the drawing room. Don't worry, I'm sure they only wish to compliment you on the excellent breakfast. I hope you have a good day, Emma.' He ushered her out.

The Misses Maria, Rosalie and Adelaide were preparing to go out too. At thirty-eight, thirty-six and thirty-four, there were only four years between the eldest and the youngest. They were in the process of having their hair arranged by Anna, who doubled up as a ladies' maid. Her duties were much less arduous than the housemaids'. She supervised the meals in the dining room, made tea in the drawing room and looked after the ladies' clothes.

Miss Adelaide was the most talkative. 'We are joining our friends for a sewing morning to raise money for the poor of the parish, which is why we will only require a light lunch at one thirty. Our hostess today will no doubt provide an abundance of sweet cakes mid-morning as usual. Do you like to sew, Miss Wright – or may we call you Emma, as Anna suggests?' She sounded very girlish despite her age, and the ringlets Anna was coaxing with a comb round her face added to the illusion. The latest hair-styles were very time consuming.

Emma replied, 'Yes of course.' Adding shyly, 'I made my frock!' She had actually used Milady's new sewing machine for this, but she enjoyed hand-sewing and embroidery.

'We have a good supply of remnants,' Miss Rosalie put in. 'The ladies of the church are very generous. Would you like a bag or two of those?'

'That is very kind of you, thank you.' Emma thought, Perhaps I can make a nice dress for Nan!

Miss Maria was pulling aside the heavy curtains at the window to look down on the street below. 'The cab is here! Girls, hurry! Might I suggest the smoked salmon, Emma, on our return?'

Emma and Anna were left in the drawing room. 'We'll go down together,' Anna said, tidying up. 'There are some things I think you haven't been told – I propose to enlighten you!'

Emma looked round the room appreciatively. There was an impressive fireplace, with a mantel and mirror over it, but the fire had not yet been lit. Paintings in ornate frames were arranged on the walls, including the portrait of a lady with a pale face and sad expression. 'Mr Summers' late wife,' Anna informed her. There was a polished piano, open, with the morning's hymn music on the stand and silver candlesticks on the piano top. Elegant chairs were grouped round small tables, one laid ready with crockery and a spirit kettle. Glancing up, Emma saw that gasolines had supplanted candelabra. In one corner was a ladies' davenport, where the sisters wrote their letters.

'This is a lovely room,' she said, 'but I feel sorry for the maids having to carry heavy buckets of coal for the fire up all those stairs. The new lights are brighter, but I don't care for the smell of gas.'

'You mentioned smells,' Anna said, when they were in the kitchen. 'and that you don't like the smell of gas, but I promise you there are far worse smells in London, if you venture away from here. Especially in the slums, which are so overcrowded and absolutely stink of sewage, as does the Thames. Anyway, speaking of water, it is only available between certain hours, so we all have to use it sparingly. So, baths only once a month for everyone, even the family. And not too may pulls on the lavatory chain. Of course, *we* have the earth closet in the backyard and that is emptied when necessary by the night soil man.'

'On the farm where I was brought up, my brother William had that task. There are smells in the countryside, too, and not all of them pleasant, what with privies and cesspits, as well as manure which is spread on the fields, but there is plenty of fresh air to compensate,' Emma told her. 'However, I haven't got time to be homesick; I must see if the washing up is all done!'

Later that afternoon, Frances, a shy girl with a rather anxious expression, appeared in the kitchen after finishing school, and at around the same time the maids mysteriously disappeared for ten minutes. Anna enlightened Emma, 'They both have followers, young men who come along about this time most days and lurk round the side of the house. Maids rarely stay more than a year or two – they dream of being married and having a family, I suppose.'

Emma detected a note of wistfulness. 'Weren't you like that at their age?'

Anna shook her head. 'My parents weren't happy together. I was glad to leave home. Anyway, I have my nephews and niece – they are grown up now – I think the world of them.'

'And you have *me*,' Frances put in, sitting by the stove, stroking the large tabby cat on her lap.

'Of course, I do! And I shouldn't be surprised if Emma has made a hot, buttered muffin for you!'

'Here you are.' Emma passed the muffin to Frances. 'Would you prefer cocoa to tea?'

'Please! This muffin is much nicer than usual.' She brushed a crumb or two from the cat's fur.

'That's because I baked it myself! I'll teach you how to make them, if you like, Frances.'

'Mrs Love never offered to do that. *She* always said, "Eat your greens! Or you'll get worms!"'

ELEVEN

TF

London, 1861

In March 1861 TF was in Cadiz on the *St Jean d'Acre*. He had served as man and boy with the Royal Navy for an eventful period, but he was only half-way through the ten years to which he had committed himself. He had spent his last shore leave with his Uncle Patrick, his father's brother, in Woolwich, and it was then he realised that despite the camaraderie aboard ship, he was lacking a home and family of his own.

Uncle Pat offered to advise him if an opportunity arose for a new career and in July he wrote that the committee of the London Fire Engine Establishment, the LFEE (which would eventually become the London Fire Brigade) was recruiting experienced mariners as firemen. This followed a catastrophic fire in Cottons Wharf, Tooley Street, which started in a warehouse storing hemp and jute on Saturday afternoon, 22 June. Fire doors were left open as workers fled and the blaze spread quickly as a result. The loss of property was estimated at two million pounds. James Braidwood, the long-time Superintendent of the LFEE, was with his men offering support and brandy when the wall at the west front of the warehouse collapsed on to him and a colleague. Both were killed instantly. Queen Victoria wrote an emotional tribute to James Braidwood when his body was found on the following Monday. She ended with: *It made me very sad.* Church bells tolled all day on the funeral route from the brigade headquarters in Watling Street to the cemetery at Stoke Newington.

TF found the history of the fire brigade fascinating. He learned that steam power had been employed on the Thames fireboat for the past ten years, but now the latest steam engine, pulled by horses, was used by the LFEE. They had moved on from buckets of water passed along a human chain to a manual pump invented by Richard Newsham in 1721, which could pump 110 gallons per minute continuously.[1] Wheeled escape ladders were kept in churchyards during the day and at street corners at night in the city, a temptation, of course to mischievous lads and petty criminals intent on stealing lead from roofs. When there was a fire, a barrel of beer would be rolled out from the nearest pub to fortify the weary firefighters, as well as eager volunteers from the crowds who gathered to watch the conflagration. When the barrel was empty,

1. One of these early pumps was in use for 200 years.

pumping would grind to a halt. But another barrel would be at the ready!

Before this new era, after the devastation of the Great Fire of London, insurance companies were formed to reduce losses from fire. These companies each had their own fire brigades and a fire mark or 'plate' marked insured buildings to show which insurance company was responsible for that building. The fire brigades only dealt with fires covered by their particular insurance company, which meant that often those crying, 'Fire, fire!' and pointing frantically, would be disappointed as the fire engine would not stop if the building wasn't covered by their insurance company. By the early 1830s, the insurance brigades realised they would have to amalgamate and so the LFEE was formed in 1833.

TF left the Royal Navy and joined the LFEE as a second-class officer following a successful interview with Captain Eyre Massey Shaw, Braidwood's successor at Watling Street. 'Ah, a fellow Irishman,' Captain Shaw observed as they shook hands, adding prophetically, 'I expect you to go far in the firefighting world.'

Captain Shaw shared his predecessor's belief that ex-naval personnel were the best choice, being well disciplined, healthy and strong, used to hauling heavy equipment and ladders, nimble, fearless climbers and calm in adversity. The LFEE also employed successful, skilled tradesmen, including surveyors, to great advantage. Recruits were between eighteen and twenty-five years old.

TF was twenty-four and his starting wage was twenty-one shillings a week. He was proud to wear his new uniform, a grey tunic with brass buttons, matching grey trousers and a buckled belt, together with a black leather helmet with chinstrap, and knee-high boots.

He found lodgings near the fire station in Northumberland Street, where the bell often rang out in the middle of the night.

During his training period TF met Charles (Chas) Holmes, who matched him for height and physique, but was dark-haired contrasting with TF's striking blond looks. Chas was a year younger than TF and the two were inseparable thereafter and from the start worked as a team. This was approved by Captain Shaw, but TF, the more extrovert, was the leader of the two.

Chas, like TF, had had an unsettled childhood, although he never experienced poverty. He was the youngest son of a wealthy currier, an expert in the leather industry, in Chichester. But his parents had died when he was young, and his eldest brother had sent him to boarding school when he was six. He was not invited to return home in the holidays. Chas was a diligent scholar, and although he accepted his lot, like TF he had missed out on a normal family life. And also like TF he had joined the Royal Navy as a boy sailor.

TWELVE

Emma

London, 1861

It was coming up to Christmas and Emma was busy in the kitchen preparing for the feast to come, when they heard the shocking news that Prince Albert had died of typhus at Windsor Castle on 14 December, aged only forty-two. Queen Victoria and the royal household were in mourning.

The Summers showed their respect for the queen's loss and spent the Christmas quietly at home. Everything was draped in black and there were no bright decorations. Like the queen at Osborne House, where she had retreated, they dined alone on Christmas Day, and in South Kensington there were no jolly gatherings of the sisters' friends.

Emma packed the excess food into baskets and this was distributed to the poor of the parish by the local church. It was a sombre time, and young Frances spent most days down in the kitchen with Emma, Anna and Nan. She sat by the range with her Christmas books, and a purring cat on her lap while they bustled about.

The following spring, Emma could hardly believe that she had been in London for over a year, but she was well aware that she was very fortunate to be where she was, with employers who appreciated all her efforts. She was glad to know that her own family were now all doing well, and though she was sad about losing her little brother, that had been expected. She corresponded regularly with her sisters and was excited about the prospect of becoming an aunt, as Martha, married to Elijah, was expecting her first baby. They had moved up country where Elijah was now a mill carter and lived in a tied cottage. William and Sarah kept her up to date with Wymondham affairs. Sarah was helping in the village shop, and they were saving hard to fulfil their dreams. They vowed that one day there would be a Wright again at Browick Bottom Farm.

Emma had become fond of Frances and Nan, who was only a couple of years older than Frances; she thought they both needed her love, just like her own sisters had in the past. She encouraged Frances to be more involved with her aunts. 'Ask them to teach you some of their card games, and how to make a scrapbook, and perhaps Miss Rosalie might agree to teach you to play the piano? Oh, they are so clever with their needlework! Did you see those pretty net purses they made for the church bazaar? Perhaps you could write poetry like Miss Adelaide . . .' She paused for breath and inspiration.

'But I prefer being in the kitchen with you, Emma, learning to cook, with Dizzy the cat – did you know I called him after Mr Disraeli? That's how the queen refers to him! Papa says he is sure to be prime minister one day soon. I do like his curly hair and twinkly eyes,' she added dreamily. 'He writes books, but Aunt Maria says I am too young to read them.'

Emma smiled. 'Your Dizzy doesn't earn his keep as kitchen cat – we had to set a trap for a mouse Nan saw in the pantry.' The cat's ears twitched on hearing his name, but he feigned sleep.

'He's my best friend – after you, of course!' Frances said. 'Can I stir that jelly and pour it in the mould? I do like to see it wobbling on the dish when you turn it out.'

'Which flavour would you prefer?'

'Raspberry, please.'

Anna came in with some exciting news. The communal gardens, which had been closed over the winter, had reopened to residents who possessed keys and enjoyed their walks. It was a Saturday morning and a sunny day, just right for a stroll. Mr Summers was lunching at his club and the ladies were off to Kensington High Street for the day, visiting the couturier and the milliner, and would be eating out with friends after shopping. They would all be back for dinner, though.

'I asked if we might take a picnic in the gardens,' Anna said. 'We are all to have the day off. Miss Maria said Frances could accompany us.'

'I must get changed, I can't promenade like this!' Frances was excited at the prospect.

Nan was busy with dustpan and brush getting rid of the breakfast crumbs under the table.

Emma saw her wistful look. 'You can come too!' she cried. 'I've finished the frock I am making you – well, almost – and I only have two buttons to sew on the cuffs. I was too weary last night; I didn't get to bed until after ten. I'll pack the basket and maybe Anna will be kind enough to dress our hair?'

Anna nodded. 'Of course I will. Hurry up, and we can be out of here by eleven.'

'My hands are all sooty – Miss Maria called me upstairs to dust round the gasolines, as the maids on'y flicked their feather dusters round, bein' eager to git out, I reckon,' Nan sighed.

'I'll find you a pair of gloves,' Frances offered.

The communal gardens were part of the housing estate and had been planned before the crescents, some of which were still being constructed. Following the death of his wife, Mr Summers had joined forces with his sisters to buy their house when it was new. The Misses Summers were of independent means and had also invested in the house in Brighton where their sister-in-law had stayed before her premature death.

Anna had the key safely in her bag, while Emma and the girls took turns in carrying the picnic basket. The gate swung open and they were in the gardens, which were a sight to see. Gravelled paths were set in a triangular pattern around sweeping green lawns with colourful shrubs and beds of early spring flowers. There were wooden benches under the shade of leafy trees where walkers could rest and admire the vista.

Anna observed, 'Who would think we are in London still? D'you know, when our crescent was being built, for a time the land here was leased by a racecourse – it was called the Hippodrome. Now they say *our* gardens are the most beautiful of all.'

'I would like to have seen the horses galloping round,' Frances said wistfully. Coming towards them along the path was a lady with a lively cocker spaniel on a lead. 'Oh, I wish the aunts would allow me to have a dog, but they say animals have fleas and shed their hair on the carpets.' She bent to pat the dog, which rewarded her with an enthusiastic lick on her hand. 'What lovely floppy ears! Such a cold, wet nose!'

'You have Dizzy,' Emma reminded her as Frances straightened up.

The two young girls plumped down on the grass, under a spreading horse chestnut tree. 'When are we going to eat our lunch?' Frances wanted to know.

'It's not midday yet,' Emma said mildly, but she sat down on a convenient bench and motioned Anna to join her. They smiled to see the girls making daisy chains and Emma thought how different Nan looked in her rose-pink frock with lace collar and cuffs. The skirt was not as full as Emma would have liked, but she'd had to cut the material carefully as it was a remnant given to her by Miss Rosalie. Nan had borrowed a bonnet as well as gloves from Frances. Even her scuffed boots had polished up quite well. The bonnet concealed her wispy hair, because as Anna confided quietly to Emma, 'Poor girl can't wash it very often.' Frances was at rather an unattractive stage, being somewhat chubby and pasty-faced, but Anna had tied her thick mass of hair back with ribbon to match her blue serge frock, which was more practical than becoming.

'Thirsty?' Emma called, uncorking a bottle of lemonade, coloured bright yellow from lemon peel steeped in boiling water. They munched left-over rolls from breakfast, slit and buttered, with a fat sausage slotted in. Anna peeled the hard-boiled eggs and passed them round in a napkin, and there were flat cakes cooked on the griddle and dusted with sugar. They finished the meal with rosy apples. Emma closed the basket. 'Let's do some more exploring and see where this path leads us.

At four o'clock she and Nan were back in the kitchen, preparing the evening meal. Nan's face was flushed from the fresh air and sunshine. Her new dress hung in Emma's closet. Unexpectedly she hugged Emma round the waist as she was rolling pastry on the table. 'Emma – I had a luverly day! Will we go agin?'

'Of course, we will,' Emma said softly. 'No one deserves a treat more than *you*, Nan . . .'

Upstairs, the aunts were opening their hat boxes to show Frances the fancy confections. 'In a year or two, you'll be old enough to come shopping with us. I hope your day was not too dull?'

'We went to the gardens and had a picnic,' Frances said. She couldn't tell them how magical it had been, how much she had enjoyed her outing with friends. 'I saw a nice black spaniel.'

'Time for your piano practice,' Aunt Rosalie said firmly.

'It's my nephew's birthday soon,' Anna said one morning at breakfast. 'If I provide the ingredients, could you make him one of your wonderful fruit cakes, Emma, please? He is a firefighter, you know, and because he is always on call, he eats his meals when he can. I know he is fond of fruit cake.'

'Of course, I will make him a birthday cake! He's the one who left the navy, isn't he – I know the other one is still serving – doesn't he have a wife to cook for him?'

'No, he isn't married. He'll only be twenty-five next week. About your age, Emma.'

Emma hoped she wasn't blushing; she hadn't got around to revealing her real age to any of them yet. She had actually come here a few days after her twenty-first birthday in January the previous year, but had told her employers she was twenty-three in her letter. What had her mother told her children? *Always be truthful for it will come out anyway.*

The cake was duly baked and delivered by Anna to TF's lodgings. 'My friend Emma – she's our cook – made it at my request!' She saw how fatigued he was, his blue eyes dark-circled from too many nights fighting fires, especially at the dockside warehouses. There was always the fear of another Tooley Street disaster, but the brigade was well-prepared with the new steam engines.

'Dear Anna, let me fetch a knife and we'll have a slice with a cup of tea! My good friend Chas will probably join us! Nothing like home-made cake, is there, especially one bursting with fruit and nuts!'

When Chas turned up and was introduced to Anna, she took to him immediately. She knew TF must miss his brother, as the two had been so close, but Chas and he had that same easy rapport together. Like Emma and me, she thought.

She said, 'When we can manage an afternoon off at the same time, you must come and meet Emma, TF. We can walk in the communal gardens. Then you can compliment her on the cake!'

The meeting came about on a day when the entire family went to watch the Summers boys in a cricket match at their school playing fields.

'TF has the afternoon off, but he is back on duty this evening,' Anna said. 'We should wear our best summer frocks, and you might let me brush your hair in a chignon, so much prettier and looser than that tight knot you think suitable for your profession! Let's hope the sun shines all day.'

'Nan reported a cloudless sky. She's going home after she's finished in the scullery. Do I really look as severe as all that?'

'Emma, you're always smiling! But it's a day for relaxing the rules. I hope you've made something filling for a young man to eat?'

'A raised pork pie. The smaller of two. The other is for the family tonight.'

'What about a fruit cake?'

'I decided on a cherry cake this time.'

TF was waiting at the gate for them and waved as they approached. He saw that his aunt's companion was a diminutive young woman in a white voile dress, patterned with tiny blue dots, a light shawl round her shoulders and a round straw hat. He noted her bright, dark eyes, and the tendrils of hair that framed her face, having escaped the soft loops of hair in the chignon. This was no large stout cook as he'd imagined, but she shook his hand firmly and looked up at him, with a mischievous smile. 'I didn't think you would be so tall.'

'And I didn't think you would be so small! Or so pretty!' Then he turned to kiss Anna. 'Are you matchmaking?' he murmured in her ear.

'D'you mind?' she returned demurely.

'Not at all,' he said, well aware that Emma was blushing.

'I thought you would be in uniform,' Emma ventured, as they walked along in a threesome, arms linked, with herself in the middle. TF held the basket, and Anna carried a parasol, as well as her bag. Emma almost felt as if she was being carried along by the two of them. It disturbed her, being so close to someone she'd never met before. She thought he was the most handsome man she had ever seen. Such blue eyes, cropped, golden hair under his straw hat, and the soft Geordie–Irish voice, as Anna had described it.

'I don't get much chance to wear anything else. It was the same when I was in the navy, but my friend Chas lent me his frock coat and I bought a new pair of trousers,' he said disarmingly. 'Chas said I must look smart if I was escorting two ladies. However, the cravat is mine, fortunately silk doesn't crumple.'

'I expect you thought I would be in my black dress with white cap and apron.'

'I don't believe I would notice if you were.'

Emma didn't quite know how to take that.

'Here we are.' Anna detached herself from them and walked over to their favourite bench under the chestnut tree. 'Bring the basket over and I'll unpack the picnic.' She brandished a kitchen knife. 'I'm about to slice up the pork pie.'

'Lemonade?' Emma offered TF a glass. She had packed this carefully in paper in case of breakage. 'We've some washed watercress to go with the pie. Take a plate and help yourself.'

TF certainly had a healthy appetite. 'Cherry cake. The fruit cake you baked was much appreciated by two hungry firemen, and this is – almost – as good.'

Anna was waving at a mother with a baby in a perambulator coming towards them on the path. 'Oh, there's our neighbour – this must be her first outing with her baby. D'you mind if I go and admire her new daughter and cross her palm with silver – I've got a sixpence in my purse.' She hurried across the grass to look into the perambulator and to chat to the young mother.

TF didn't move away from Emma, in fact he shifted nearer. 'You and I have a lot in common I believe. We are the same age—'

Emma felt so comfortable in his presence she allowed the words to spill out. 'I have a confession which is overdue. I am twenty-two, three years younger than you – I added to my age when I applied for my job. I thought they would think I wasn't old enough for such a responsible post. I know you have had your troubles and lost your mother. I was about the same age when my dear mother passed away. You lost a little sister too . . . and I, a young brother. When my father died and we were forced to leave our home, my younger sisters and brothers went to the workhouse. That was a very sad time for all of us.'

'My father is still alive, but he doesn't know us. He has been in the infirmary for several years. My brother and I are miles apart, he is mostly on the high seas, and my sister

Mary, I hear, intends to marry when she reaches sixteen in a few months time. However, I have some family, Anna and my Uncle Charlie, though he is at sea too, and my father's brother, Patrick, at Woolwich.'

'My family are still in Norfolk, but I keep in touch with them all. Anna is a good friend to me. I – I have a feeling . . .' She looked up into those bright blue eyes. 'I can't explain it, but . . .'

He said softly, 'I can, I think . . . I never believed it could be like this, Emma. For me, this is love at first sight. I have never felt so happy in all my life before . . . May I dare to hope, you feel the same?'

Emma took a deep breath, 'Yes – *yes*, I do!' She felt exultant. It's all so sudden, she thought, but I'm going to marry him one day!

'I wish I could kiss you, Emma, but look, Anna is about to return, I think, she just waved!'

Emma squeezed his hand. As Anna bid goodbye to her friend, he said urgently, 'Emma, we were meant to meet, I'm sure.'

'So am I,' she said, suddenly aware that they were holding hands. They sprang self-consciously apart as Anna arrived and cried brightly, 'Oh, I can't resist a baby!' Then she saw their faces. 'Oh, you two like each other, I knew you would!'

THIRTEEN

Emma, London, 1862

Mr Summers would like to see you, Emma, in the drawing room,' Anna said, as she came into the kitchen. 'Oh, and may I have the bicarbonate of soda, please. Miss Adelaide has indigestion.'

'I hope it wasn't caused by the smoked haddock she had for breakfast! D'you know what Mr Summers wants to speak to me about?'

'Well, I can guess, but it's not my place to tell you! I'll just say it could be a nice surprise.'

Despite the reassurance, Emma felt flustered as she went up the stairs to the first floor. She knocked politely on the door, then entered the drawing room. Mr Summers was standing by the window and turned at her approach. He smoothed his moustache with finger and thumb, as if thinking what to say.

'Ah, Emma. You know, of course, that we are going for our annual visit to Brighton shortly? We always invite one or two of the staff to accompany us to carry out, ah, less onerous duties, for the ladies in particular, and Anna has suggested that you might like to take care of the catering. A simple breakfast and an evening snack. No need, ah, for you to slave over a hot stove. In fine weather we may require a picnic or will visit a restaurant.' He hesitated. 'You could regard it as a holiday, though I suppose the seaside is not a novelty to you, coming from Norfolk?'

'Oh, sir, I've never even been to Yarmouth! My father was always too busy with the farm to take us, and we were a large family, you know. I would be very pleased to go to Brighton.'

'That's good. We always buy our provisions after we arrive there, by the way. Mrs Love will step into the breach here.' As she still stood there, he asked, 'Is there anything else you wish to say?'

'Please, can young Nan come too? She and Frances have become friends, and I would be responsible for her, but she's a good girl, and she, well, she deserves a holiday more than anyone!'

Mr Summers cleared his throat, as he always did when he was wondering what to say. 'You may give her the good news. It is a modest dwelling, so she will have to share a room with you and Anna. Is that all right?'

'Yes, thank you, Mr Summers!' She couldn't wait to tell Nan and Anna.

Mr Summers regarded his wife's portrait. 'I think you would approve, Frances – didn't you always remind us "Charity begins at home?" Though I'm not sure what the girls will say!'

Brighton had certainly changed from the tiny village known originally as Brighthelmston. As Daniel Defoe wrote over a century before, it was 'on the edge of the sea'. At that time the fishing industry was in decline, and many had sought work elsewhere while those left lived in abject poverty.

The town's fortunes turned when the Prince Regent, later King George IV, began to visit on the advice of his father, George III, who had developed an enthusiasm for sea-bathing. He believed the eminent physicians who claimed this practice promoted good health. Drinking sea water was considered a cure for such varied complaints as asthma, rheumatism, cancer and consumption and, inexplicably, deafness. Holidays by the sea became fashionable among the gentry.

Brighton still had its bleak side, with areas that were inadvisable for visitors to explore. There were the same problems as in the slums of London – overcrowded lodging houses, pickpockets, beggars and ragged children, and overall the putrid odour of poor sanitation, for many cess pits were dug in shifting shingle, resulting in contamination of local springs. Disease was endemic.

However, the trains that first linked London to Brighton in 1841 conveyed the prosperous middle classes to holiday by the sea. Most of these, like the Summers, had bought or built properties along the front. Some of the latter were rented out in the season. When the railway started to offer third-class tickets, they were joined by a much larger group of visitors who worked hard to afford this experience. Queen Victoria, who until that time had enjoyed private family holidays in Brighton, decided to change the royal holiday destination to Osborne in the Isle of Wight.

The Summers boys were spending the final days of their summer vacation in Gloucestershire. 'Their hosts have a new tennis court!' Frances told her friends in the kitchen. 'They are both keen on sports, unlike me – but I am the swot in the family! Then I overheard Aunt Rosalie say I was unlikely to marry because I had opinions of my own, as they have, and *wives* aren't expected to be like that.'

'One should only marry for love,' Anna said unexpectedly with a sigh, then they all looked at Emma, who blushed in embarrassment. Is it so obvious I have a beau? she wondered. Despite their closeness, she had not even shared her secret love for TF with Anna.

September, after the influx of visitors at the height of summer, was a good time to visit Brighton. The house had bay windows overlooking the sea, where boats of all kinds bobbed on the breakers, and a bracing wind blew the hair and clothes of walkers crunching along the shingle into disarray. Emma took deep breaths of the salt-laden air and delighted in venturing along the beach, clinging to Anna's arm, while Frances and Nan dipped their toes in the briny water with shrieks of, 'Oh my, it's cold!' Their hastily discarded boots and stockings were in danger of being washed over by the incoming tide, which had already obscured the strip of muddy sand where children made wobbly sandcastles. Screeching gulls hovered hopefully over a fishing boat on the horizon.

'It was so kind of the ladies,' Emma said to Anna, as they moved these articles further up the shingle, 'to buy Nan some new clothes – she looks so bonny in that navy skirt and jacket with the sailor collar, don't you think?'

'I think what she is wearing underneath is more important, especially as they have bundled their skirts round their waists – she is very lacking in that respect!'

They came upon a line of beached rowing boats where a man and a dog sat together waiting for customers next to a sign that read: *Boat trips*. 'Not today, but later in the week,' Anna called out. 'It looks too rough out at sea,' she added to Emma.

'Aunt Adelaide said they are going to the Theatre Royal with Papa this evening, I wish they would ask *us*!' Frances said, when the girls caught up with them.

'Oh, Anna and I have planned to light the fire, make toast and—'

'Scrambling eggs!' Nan chimed in.

'Why not? And then we'll play games and make as much noise as we like!'

Emma received a letter during their first week in Brighton. She tucked it in her pocket, for she was boiling the breakfast eggs when Nan brought the post in to sort on the kitchen table. She would have to contain her impatience to open it. She knew the letter must be from TF, for he was the only one she had given their holiday address.

Life was very informal here. Family ate with the staff in the dining room, sitting at a round table with a vase of flowers in the centre. Frances and Nan passed the plates round, Miss Maria poured coffee, while Emma was in charge of the teapot. Anna made sure the table was properly laid and it was she who had fetched the hot rolls from the bakery earlier, along with Mr Summers' newspaper. He waited his turn to be served and glanced at his paper meanwhile. Emma was hoping to catch him on his own after the meal, for she had something to ask him.

When the ladies had departed to make ready for the day's excursion, and Nan, Frances and Anna were washing up, Emma seized her chance, after quickly perusing her letter. 'Mr Summers, I have heard from a friend who would like to visit me here on Saturday, if that is permissible,' she began.

Mr Summers folded his newspaper, looked up and smiled at her. 'Your young man, I take it, Emma? The handsome fireman who sometimes walks with you, Anna and Frances in the gardens?'

'Yes, sir. Thomas Meehan, Anna's nephew. I hope you don't mind him accompanying us?'

'Not at all, but Emma, *you* have no need of a chaperone in a public place, you know!' He cleared his throat, fingered his collar. 'Of course, your friend is welcome here. However, you shouldn't, ah, feel you must take the young ones wherever you go. We had planned a picnic on the Downs, I don't think they are too old for a donkey ride, do you? You may have the day to yourselves.'

'Thank you, Mr Summers – you are so kind!' Emma said gratefully.

She was there to meet him from the excursion train. He was waving his hat through the open window to attract her attention, but of course she had already spotted his blond head and hurried along the platform to greet him. He saw that she had let her hair down and it tumbled to her shoulders beyond the confines of her bonnet. She was wearing a full-skirted, floral-patterned frock – it had taken her hours to sew all the ruffles in place in the latest fashion – and her mother's wedding shawl, fastened with a shell brooch she'd bought from a stall in the market.

'Here, you can pin this on with your brooch,' he told her, as he took from his lapel a single rosebud. 'I thought it was the safest place for it on the journey,' he said.

Emma's face was as pink as the rose as she bent to secure it. 'Thank you, it's very fragrant.'

'Now, where do you propose we go?' They linked arms. She carried only her purse while he had a valise in his free hand. She had not packed a picnic as he had written that he would treat her to lunch.

'I don't mind. Why don't we walk and talk but, later, could we go on a boat trip? It only takes half an hour to the marker and back again, apparently. You wouldn't even have to row!'

'Well, I'd rather sit alongside you, holding on to you while the boat rocks, and whisper sweet nothings in your ear. But let's find a tea shop first – I'm dry as a bone!'

They strolled along a parade of small shops, including a photographic studio, where they studied the amazing portraits of local worthies in the window. 'Would you like to have your photograph taken?' TF asked Emma.

'Oh, I'm too windblown today – and they all look so poker-faced! Maybe back in London, eh?' Much later she would regret that she had refused.

He was interested in the map shop. 'Think of the hours and patience it takes to make a map!'

Emma spotted a tea shop and bakery. 'I'm dying for a cup of tea, too!' They went down stone steps to a low-beamed room beyond the counters piled with loaves and cakes under glass domes. The basement room was rather dark, but they found a vacant table by the window, so that they could look out and see the world go by, or at least their feet at that level.

They were the only customers apart from an elderly man who put up his newspaper as a barrier so he didn't have to speak to them, though they only had eyes for each other.

'Anna says I am to bring you back to the house for supper. You can't come and go without seeing her! It's my day off, so she will be cooking something tasty, assisted by Nan.'

'Does that mean I will meet Mr Summers and his family?'

'Would you mind that? They have been more than kind to me – and Anna.'

'I imagine they would not like to lose you—'

'I haven't thought of leaving!' she said, as the waitress arrived with their tea and scones.

They buttered the split scones and took a spoonful of raspberry jam in turn from a little pot. When they had eaten and sipped some of the hot tea, TF said, 'Emma – I know it hasn't been long since we met, but I expect you can guess how I feel about you?'

She looked into those blue eyes. 'Of course I know how you feel, because, well, I feel the same way about you. I used to think it couldn't be true, stories about love at first sight.'

'I don't want to wait; I intend to marry you, Emma.'

'It won't be two years until January, since I came to London. I've been so happy in my work.'

'I know. I also know we need to be together. Let's go and enjoy the rest of the day, eh?'

TF spread his jacket on the stones, and they sat on the beach during the afternoon. Emma looked for unusual pebbles and shells, filling her bag with a selection. TF watched the fishing boats come in to shore and recalled his days at sea. The man and dog were tidying up the hire boats. A new sign was up: *Last trip of the day.*

'We mustn't miss that,' TF observed. He helped Emma to her feet. 'It'll be sunset soon, and we still have supper to come at the house, and then I have to catch the last train home.'

The blue-painted boat of their choice was launched, the oars were plied, and Emma sat close to TF on the wooden seat, with his arm supporting her back and her face pressed against his shoulder as the spray flew up at them. The dog lounged in the well of the boat, while his master puffed on his clay pipe and pulled on the oars. As they approached the marker, they became aware that the water around them shimmered with reflected light from the sky above, which was streaked with glorious crimson. By the time they arrived back on the shore, it was dusk.

As they walked back across the stony beach, deserted now, they paused at the wrought-iron bench at the top.

'Let's rest here for a bit,' TF suggested. He hugged Emma to him and for the first time, they kissed. She trembled, as his hands strayed under her shawl. She stretched her arms up and tentatively stroked his hair. He released her suddenly. 'I'm sorry, Emma, I couldn't help myself.'

'Nor could I,' she whispered. 'I must find my comb; we both need to tidy our hair before I introduce you to the family.' They didn't realise that their bemused expressions gave them away, not only to Anna, but to Mr Summers, recalling when he'd fallen in love himself, twenty years ago.

Back in London on a pleasant October afternoon, Emma and TF met for the first time since Brighton. In Hyde Park, the trees were turning and flowerbeds reflected the seasonal change too, with clumps of purple chrysanthemums and Michaelmas daisies.

'Such a lovely earthy smell to autumn,' TF observed. 'Leaves on the paths and grass, the smell of bonfires and mist. Time to roast chestnuts by the fire . . .'

They smiled at each other: it was a nostalgic memory for both of them, though TF could only remember one such occasion when he was living with his family in Harbottle. He gave a little sigh, we were happy then, as a family, he thought.

'Let's listen to the band,' he suggested. They made their way to the bandstand and joined the audience who were tapping their feet to the infectious beat of the brass band. The bandsmen in their scarlet jackets played with verve. Later, they had planned a special treat – fish and chips, the latest food sensation, which was now available all over London.

The smell was irresistible, the queue long, but they waited patiently by the flaring gas light attached to the side wall of the shop. 'It makes a nice change,' Emma said, 'not cooking my own supper!'

TF agreed. 'It's bread and cheese usually for me, that's if I'm not called out.'

They were walking home, for it delayed the time when they would have to part. They paused now and then to extract chips from the newspaper parcel, having decided against the fish. 'You need to sit down at a table to eat that,' TF said.

The chips were hot and greasy, and Emma remarked, 'I am enjoying them, but I could do with a nice cup of tea!'

When they had eaten their fill, they walked on, past the noisy beer houses on every corner and now and then, when no one was about, TF would steal a kiss. 'Your lips are all salty, Emma. I wish we were going to our own little home together. I wish . . .'

'I know what you wish, Tom.'

'You haven't called me that before.'

'D'you mind?'

'Not at all. Our own little home, Emma – I will be entitled to that when I get married – we won't have to struggle like most newlyweds. Will you marry me?'

'Yes, Tom – yes!' Like TF, Emma was finding it difficult to hold back, but she was her mother's daughter and believed in waiting until she was wed.

Christmas had come around again but Emma waited until Boxing Day to tell the family that she and TF hoped to be married in January. She wished that TF was with her to offer his support, but he was on duty as this was always a busy time for firefighters. She had opened his presents early on Christmas morning and was delighted with the polished wooden writing box filled with cream, water-marked paper and envelopes but, even better, was *Mrs Beeton's Book of Household Management*. He had written inside: *To dear Emma, from her loving husband-to-be, Tom. Christmas 1862.*

The staff was invited to join the family in the drawing room for hot mince pies and Christmas cake, handed round on dainty blue-and-white plates by Frances. Mr Summers poured small glasses of sherry and walked round with these on a silver tray. The ladies wore their new crinoline gowns and chatted pleasantly of this and that. The Christmas log fire gave out a good heat, and after the sherry, eyelids were seen to droop. Miss Adelaide rustled to the piano and began to play favourite carols, urging the company to 'Sing up and be merry!' They drowned out the snoring from the old retainer, who was guarding the decanters, while the boys admitted defeat, sloping off to their room. Emma was sitting by herself at the back of the group, rehearsing silently what she must say when her eyes suddenly brimmed with tears. She fumbled for her handkerchief, hoping no one would notice.

Mr Summers was sitting nearby, apart from all the female singers.

'Here, take mine,' he said. He beckoned to her. 'Come and tell me why you're upset, Emma, we can't have that at Christmas.' She took the large handkerchief and dabbed her eyes.

'I was remembering Christmas at home. We went to church in the morning and had our Christmas dinner in the evening. My mother was a wonderful cook, and we would all sit up at the table, while Father carved the goose and I watched that my little sisters didn't spill gravy on the best tablecloth.'

'You must miss them all,' he said quietly.

'I do! But I have been so happy here, Mr Summers—'

'You put that in the past tense, Emma. Is there something else you wish to tell me?'

'Oh, sir – Tom has asked me to marry him, next month, if we can find a church where we are welcome, as he is a Catholic and I am an Anglican, but I shall be sad to leave you all.'

'My dear Emma, we guessed this would be the case, when we saw you and your young man together at Brighton. As for a church, I will have a word with our rector at St Stephen's.

Also, Emma, ah, I must speak with my sisters first, naturally, but I am sure that they will be excited and wish to be involved.'

'Mr Summers, could Frances be my bridesmaid – and – would you consider giving me away? I know my brother William would want to do so, but I can't expect him to travel all this way.'

'I should be honoured,' Mr Summers said. 'Make your announcement after the singing.'

FOURTEEN

London, 1863

On 26 January Emma awoke at 6 a.m. and her first thought was, today is my wedding day! She had celebrated her twenty-third birthday three days before by making three large sponge cakes, slicing them and sandwiching the halves together with home-made lemon curd. Then she dusted the tops of each cake with fine sugar. The birthday cakes were much appreciated by those upstairs and downstairs and by TF when he arrived for a brief visit during the evening.

She rinsed her face and hands in cold water, for it was her decision to be up so early and the maids would not yet be at work. She snuggled into her flannel wrapper – oh, it was chilly this morning, but not snowing, she hoped. She didn't pull the curtains to find out. Then she tiptoed quietly along the corridor to the kitchen where she lit the lamp and went into the pantry to fetch the wedding cake. Now that the royal icing had hardened she could place the final decorations, including the tiny china figurines of bride and groom, which Mr Summers had presented her with. 'These were on our wedding cake – they can be your "something borrowed", eh?' Then she would garland her masterpiece with a silver ribbon.

Emma was so absorbed in what she was doing that she didn't notice she was no longer alone in the kitchen. Nan had arrived, face red from the cold and out of breath, for she had run some of the way to get her circulation going. 'My, it's freezing outside, Emma, and whatever are *you* doin' in 'ere on your weddin' mornin'?'

'I'll leave you to guard the cake – it's going back in its box in the pantry – then I'll return to my room and pack up the rest of my things. Anna is fetching me to have a bath upstairs later on. What time do you expect Mrs Love to arrive? Will you manage the breakfast on your own?'

'Cook will be 'ere 'fore ten and will foller your menu for the weddin' breakfast,' Nan said. Then she added proudly, 'I'm to be assistant cook from today, Miss Maria said it was your idea. And course, I can do scrambling eggs for one an' all! Anyway, Lily and Rose are givin' me an 'and.'

'Don't forget the grapefruit for the ladies.'

'I won't, Emma – good luck! I'll see you in the church!'

'Oh, one last thing, remember you are a witness, and have to write your proper name.'

'I've never been called it, but I'll be *Ann* Butterworth, jest for today,' Nan promised.

I shall miss the yellow tulips on the washstand, Emma thought later, as she looked around her room. I was the luckiest girl in the world to come to this house; everyone who lives here is a true friend, upstairs and down. I will miss them all. How kind of Mr Summers and the ladies to allow us to have our celebration meal here. I am grateful to the ladies for helping me choose my wedding dress and paying for it too, and to dear Anna who insisted on buying the flowers.

At that moment came a knock on the door. It was Anna with two cups of tea and some shortbread biscuits. 'Lily and Rose are filling the bath tub, but we are tiptoeing about as it is so early. Old Joseph is seeing to the fires.'

It was the first time Emma had been inside the family bathroom upstairs. The steam was rising from the hot water in the white bath with its mahogany surround. Anna closed the door. Everything was ready. Towels folded neatly, soap in a dish, a new flannel. Emma slipped out of her robe and nightgown. She leaned over the bath and felt the water. It was not too hot, so she was able to climb in the tub. Anna had fastened her hair up in a topknot, for Emma had washed it the day before.

Anna sat on a chair, towel on her lap, waiting to wrap her friend in it when she emerged from the water. She averted her gaze from Emma's naked body for this was a sight reserved for her new husband. There was a bag with Emma's new underwear, but she would need to cover up again with her robe before she went downstairs, where her wedding gown, along with the bridesmaid's outfit, hung in the closet. But first they would eat breakfast together in Emma's room. Then Anna must leave her while she attended the ladies. Frances should have joined Emma by then.

'The scrambled eggs are perfect.' Emma tucked into her breakfast.

'Thanks to you teaching young Nan how to cook.' Anna took a curl of butter from the dish and spread it on her toast, then helped herself to more soft, golden egg. 'Well, Miss Wright, you'll be answering to Mrs Meehan before the wedding breakfast!'

'While you, dear Anna, will be my aunt by marriage – but still my best friend!'

'The flowers have arrived,' Frances told Emma, when she appeared just as Anna left the room. 'I'm to help you dress, then Anna will come back and arrange your hair – and mine, I hope.'

Emma thought wistfully, I should have had my younger sisters as bridesmaids too. She had received gifts from them all: a lucky silver horseshoe from Rebecca, a pressed flower picture from Keturah and a leather-bound book from Jerusha for her wedding and family photographs. Martha had sent a picture of her two small children and Lizzie had embroidered a pair of pillowcases. William and Sarah sent the young couple a tea service with a pattern of forget-me-nots like her mother's cup and saucer. She still treasured that, and always would. That special cup and saucer were bone china, but the new set could be used every day because it was more serviceable. It was lovely, she thought, they had remembered the original cup and saucer and what it meant to her . . . Her family were doing well, it seemed. She blinked back sudden tears as she put the new tea set carefully back in its box. If only my mother and father could be here with me today, she thought.

It was time for Emma to don her wedding finery. The crinoline was gradually being superseded by a different shape, straight-cut at the front with all the fullness at the back of the dress, the forerunner of the bustle. Not that Emma had worn one of those cumbersome contraptions – like a cage which held out enormous skirts. They were for formal occasions, not for working women. However, she had been persuaded by Miss Maria that she should wear a laced corset over her chemise, to accentuate her bosom and flatten her stomach. 'Help!' she appealed now to Frances. 'If I hold on to the back of the chair, will you pull the laces tight?' It was quite a struggle, and they emerged from it thankfully. 'My mother was right,' Emma said ruefully, 'a corset is an instrument of torture.' She'd never had the need for one before because she had a trim figure, with high, firm breasts.

The sleeves of the beautiful red velvet gown were cleverly fashioned from two pieces of material, sloping at the shoulder, then wide to the elbow, tapering to the wrist and fastened with tiny mother-of-pearl buttons. More of these were on the tight bodice, from the lace-trimmed high collar to the waist. It was just the right material for a wintry day, warm and glowing with colour. Emma had chosen it because it reminded her of the sunset over the water in Brighton, but only TF would know that.

Frances stroked the white fur cape which Miss Adelaide had lent Emma to keep her warm. 'I hope she leaves me this in her will!'

Emma exclaimed reprovingly, 'Frances! What a thing to say – don't repeat it to your aunt!' she added with feeling, 'I shall be glad to take this wretched corset off by the end of the day.'

'Are you going to use the muff Aunt Rosalie gave you?' This was also made of white fur.

'In the carriage, but not down the aisle. I have my prayer book and flowers to carry.'

Anna returned to dress their hair. While she attended to Emma, covering her shoulders with a cotton cape, Frances changed into her bridesmaid's frock. Gold velvet, in a more grown-up style than the calf-length skirts she usually wore, as this skirt skimmed her ankles.

It was not considered seemly for a bride to wear her hair loose, but ringlets or loops of hair could cover the ears, while back hair was parted and coiled in the nape of the neck. It was actually a good style on which to perch her hat, which was in the new, small style and was white felt, decorated with a red silk rose and skewered with a hat pin. Emma was not too sure about the hat, but Anna assured her it would stay in place. Once she had finished with Emma, she turned to Frances. 'Now, let's see what I can do for you!'

The staff stood in the doorway, waving and calling, 'Good luck!' to the bride and her bridesmaid who were escorted by Mr Summers, elegant in a new single-breasted suit, which revealed a glimpse of the high, starched collar, gold cravat and matching brocade waistcoat. He doffed his top hat to those watching, as he joined Emma and Frances in the carriage. A second carriage awaited the Misses Summers, Anna and Nan, for Anna had requested that the girl should not make her way there on foot in the drizzle.

St Stephen's Church was of the era, but with traditional features. It served the thriving new estates in the area, which had spread out to South Kensington where the Summers lived. The church already had a well-deserved reputation for community work among the less fortunate in the slum areas of London, and its support of missionaries overseas.

Although the wedding was on a Friday, there was a good congregation and a warm welcome for the wedding party. The bridegroom and his best man were already in place at the steps to the altar, awaiting the bride. TF and Chas were dressed in their best uniforms but had placed their helmets on a side table. Their colleagues from the fire brigade had taken the back pews in order to make a quiet exit, for they would form a guard of honour when the newlywed couple emerged from the church.

Emma endeavoured to compose herself as she waited with Mr Summers and Frances in the porch for the bells to cease ringing, and the music announcing their arrival to begin. Frances held the modest posy of flowers with a lace handkerchief round the damp stems to protect Emma's prayer book. 'Keep your hands in the muff until the last minute and then lend it to me,' she whispered.

Holding tight to Mr Summers' arm, Emma proceeded down the aisle to the stirring 'Wedding March' by Felix Mendelssohn, to join the bridegroom, who turned his head to watch her progress. He caught his breath at the sight of her in her jewel-bright gown. There were gasps of appreciation from those gathered to witness Emma's marriage to the handsome young fireman.

They made their vows, knelt for the prayers, the gold band was slipped on her finger, they sang 'Love Divine All Loves Excelling', and the vicar delivered his homily. Then suddenly it was over and time to sign the register with their witnesses: a fellow fireman and friend to TF and Chas, and young Nan, who duly signed herself as *Ann Butterworth* in her best handwriting. It was thoughtful Anna who had suggested her for this important task.

The newlyweds emerged into a flurry of snow, and hurried, laughing under the arch of fire hoses, fortunately not connected to water on this happy occasion.

Back at the reception, there was another surprise, a photographer with his bulky camera, and there were several flashes before they took their seats at the dining table for the wedding breakfast.

Although Emma missed the presence of her family, and TF missed his brother Rob, she thought how very fortunate she was that her employers were also friends. She would be leaving them later today but she hoped they would always be in touch.

The bride and groom took pride of place at the top of the table. Mr Summers was on Emma's left with Frances, while TF had Chas, for moral support, on his right. Miss Maria was at the far end with her younger sisters. Anna helped them arrange their voluminous skirts, then sat alongside. Nan, of course, had gone straight to the kitchen to help Mrs Love, who grumbled a bit that, 'Things is not where they used to be.' Old Joseph poured the drinks and the maids hovered by the serving hatch, waiting for the first course to be delivered after the wedding party had partaken of the sliced fresh pineapple with half a glacé cherry on top.

Tender fillets of beef with hot, onion gravy, tureens of roast potatoes, buttered parsnips and diced carrots; a basket of fresh bread rolls and a pot of horseradish sauce – a meal to warm them up on a winter day, one which Emma's mother had often cooked for her large family back on the farm.

For dessert there was apple pie: Mrs Love had not lost her light touch with the pastry, and the side with the cloves was marked with a 'C'. Nan had made the custard and it poured, lump-free, from a tall jug. Those in the kitchen then sat down to enjoy their own meal after a job well done.

It was decided that the wedding cake should be cut later, before the departure of the bride and groom, but champagne fizzed in the crystal goblets and Mr Summers led the toasts, followed by a few words from the best man and the bridegroom. Emma was glad she was not called upon to speak, for she suddenly felt overwhelmed and tearful. TF passed her his handkerchief to dab her eyes.

When it was time to leave, Emma exchanged the fur cape for her mother's wedding shawl, and she and TF were at last alone in a cab, with a blanket tucked round their knees while the cabbie overhead flicked the reins and urged the horse to 'gee-up!' as they moved away from the big white house into the dusk.

'We'll soon be home,' TF assured her. Emma had not yet seen their rooms in Marylebone Passage, a narrow, cobbled street between Margaret Street and Wells Street – the latter ran between Oxford Street and Mortimer Street. Tall, gloomy old buildings were crowded along the passage, some multi-tenanted, but their new abode had been built more recently and housed two fire service families. TF had been fortunate to secure the ground floor apartment, with a shared cellar area for the delivery of coal, an outside privy and a yard with separate washing lines for the tenants.

They left the comforting gas lights of the main road and turned by the Gothic church at the corner. The notorious Golden Lion Alehouse at the head of the Passage had been demolished in the 1790s to make way for the Marylebone workhouse, which became too crowded and ill-equipped and was condemned in turn. A modern, purpose-built workhouse replaced this in Northumberland Street and became the largest workhouse in the country. The old site was taken over for residential building. Although TF had mentioned the Golden Lion to Emma, he thought it wise not to say that they would be living where the original workhouse had stood.

Once inside the living room, where the stove was already lit, the shiny new kettle singing on the hob thanks to TF's friend upstairs, Emma sank down thankfully on the nearest chair. The furniture was second-hand but adequate, and the table would soon look more inviting, she thought, with a tablecloth and crockery set out from the boxes which waited to be unpacked. Off this good-sized square room was a scullery with a deep sink and copper for boiling the linen. A cupboard housed the new brooms, mops and slop buckets. There was even a shelf for books, and a mantelpiece for the clock and ornaments. TF lit the oil lamp. At least there was no smell of gas here, Emma thought, and there was a small pantry for food storage.

'The bedroom is across the hall,' TF said, 'and there is a further room which can be used as a parlour or second bedroom if . . .' He paused as he saw Emma blush. They hadn't discussed it, but they were both hoping for a family of their own. He busied himself with the teapot. 'Cup of tea?'

'Oh, yes please,' she agreed. 'Shall we have it with our share of the cake?'

Later, when a modest blaze in the small bedroom grate had taken the chill off the room, they prepared for bed. It had been a long day, a happy one, of course, but it was a moment for reflection. Emma sat on a chair by the washstand in the flickering candlelight and followed her usual ritual. She undressed to her chemise but was unable to remove the corset without his help. TF soon loosened the lacing and she gave a sigh of relief. He was already in his nightshirt and ready for bed. 'Thank you! I shan't wear that instrument of torture again for a while,' she said with feeling, as he padded over the bare floorboards and dived under the covers. She brushed her hair, washed her face and hands in the warm water TF had poured into the basin and then turned her back to the bed while she slipped her new nightgown over her head.

'Are you coming?' his voice was muffled by the purple eiderdown, a wedding present from the Summers, under his chin.

'I must hang my dress in the closet,' she replied. She glanced at the old trunk in passing. 'Oh, where did that come from?'

'It was my mother's. Anna was looking after it for my sister Mary, but she said she had her mementoes, as we all have, and Anna should give it to you.'

'That was kind of her. Is it empty?'

'No. There are a few things which Mama considered precious – reminders of her old life, I suppose. You can look at them tomorrow.'

'I must just read a passage from my bible and say my prayers, and then I'll join you,' she promised.

'Nip the candle out, when you are ready,' he said.

He moved over, so that she could slide into the warm hollow where he had lain in the bed.

'A feather mattress – you are spoiling me, Tom,' she whispered appreciatively when she joined him.

'Mama always longed for a new soft mattress, like the one Aunt Nesbit provided all those years ago. She would have loved you, Emma, she had lots of spirit too before we ended up in that awful place in Newcastle.'

'I feel I know her, from what you and Anna have told me.' She hugged him to her breast. One of us has to make the first move, she thought, it might as well be me. I wish I could tell Isabella how much I adore her precious son – but I am about to prove that to him.

FIFTEEN

London, 1864

January 1864 had come and gone, with another birthday for Emma, followed by their first wedding anniversary, which they celebrated at home with TF's favourite steak and kidney pudding. Emma had been unable to wear her lovely red dress for she was heavily pregnant. The baby was due in six weeks. The local midwife was booked and the family crib had already arrived by carrier from William and Sarah. Emma had been busy hemming two dozen squares of terry-towelling for the baby's napkins. Her sisters knitted tiny vests and jackets while Anna contributed four warm flannel gowns, which would be worn for the first months, whether boy or girl.

Emma sighed. She had a pile of washing to do, but it would freeze if hung outside, she thought. All summer she had taken a daily walk, although she found the surroundings depressing, for the grim buildings and narrow road occluded sunshine and light. But at least she got to talk to the shopkeepers and meet up with other fire service wives. Bess, who lived upstairs, told her these acquaintances had dubbed Emma 'the duchess'. 'They say you look and sound like a lady!'

TF had been called out in the night and returned to work after a brief visit just after dawn to eat a hastily prepared breakfast. Emma hadn't gone back to bed and had been restless all day.

'Don't wait up for me,' TF had advised earlier. So Emma wrote a note telling him what there was for his supper. *Chicken soup in saucepan and plate of ham sandwiches and pickle in pantry . . .*

She glanced at the clock on the mantelpiece. Ten minutes past nine. As she folded her work and put it in the sewing basket, she felt a twinge in her back. Best get into bed and rest, she thought.

Just after midnight she threw back the bedclothes and, gasping with pain, managed to swing her legs out of bed. She gripped the bed rail, thinking she must be mistaken – it couldn't possibly be the baby on its way – could it? Despite the chill, for TF hadn't returned to light the fire in the bedroom so she guessed he was still tackling that big blaze at the docks, she felt sweat trickling from her forehead and running down her face. When the contraction subsided, she made her way on wobbly legs to the door. She went into the hall and reached for the walking stick in the stand. 'Bang on the ceiling with it, and I'll come,'

Bess had said the morning before when she called in to see Emma. She must have observed I was restless and put two and two together, Emma thought.

It took a few knocks to rouse Bess, but she came down as promised, to find the door on the latch. She took one look at Emma and decided to run around for the midwife. 'I'll borrow your shawl!'

She turned at the door, 'Get back into bed, I should. I'll be as quick as I can.'

It seemed an eternity to Emma as she struggled to cover the mattress with the newspapers they had saved for weeks, and heaved the precious purple eiderdown on to Isabella's trunk, as she was determined it should not be spoiled. Then she subsided onto the bed and pulled the sheet over her and prayed help would come shortly. Surely TF would be home soon?

The midwife was a local woman who had followed her grandmother and mother into this age-old profession. Her qualifications were experience, patience and strength. She was a large woman with a reassuring manner. She gave brisk instructions to Bess, whose own two small children were being looked after by their grandmother, who lived with the family. Her husband was out firefighting with TF. Bess soon had the bedroom fire crackling and fetched hot water and towels. She made the crib ready, though she interpreted the midwife's warning glance that the baby might be too small to survive.

It was mercifully a short labour and within three hours, still before dawn, a tiny baby girl gave her first feeble cry. She was swiftly wrapped in a soft flannel sheet and given immediately to her mother. 'Is she . . .?' Emma managed. The midwife nodded.

'She is best in your arms, my dear. Keep her warm and secure. We cannot expect too much – but you must give her a name. Have you one in mind?'

Emma had been sure the baby would be a boy, she couldn't say why. 'The baby was to be called Thomas if it was a boy . . . Emma, I suppose, after me – and Augusta, which was my husband's mother's second name – we both like that.' She looked at the baby, 'Oh, she has her Irish grandfather's red hair! Augusta is too regal a name for one so small, we'll call her Gussie!'

TF, with his face blackened by smoke, knelt by the bed some two hours later. He gently stroked the tuft of red hair, which was all that was visible of the baby and asked, 'Has she blue eyes?'

'I haven't seen them open yet . . .' Emma said. 'She hasn't even been washed or dressed, but – she's here, and breathing, thank God, and her name is Gussie. I hope you approve?'

'Dearest Emma, I do,' he said tenderly.

Anna was the first to hear the news. She arrived with presents from the Summers family, including some rather comical oversized bootees knitted by Frances. The new cook made up bottles of beef tea and Nan sent two big oranges with a home-made card of congratulations, *From your friend* (sic) *Miss Ann Butterworth*. The postman made daily deliveries from Emma's family, too. Jerusha wrote, *I hope to see you soon!*

Emma sighed. She wasn't experiencing the euphoria expected of a new mother. In fact, she was anxious and tearful. She carried the tiny baby about with her all day, tucked inside her bodice, to keep her warm. At night, the crib was drawn up to the bed and Emma remained vigilant, turning her back on her husband. She wasn't aware that he was longing to comfort her and was worried about her as well as Gussie. When he tentatively stroked her shoulder, she stiffened, and he moved away.

Gussie at three months old weighed only as much as a normal full-term baby; she was like a doll, with her big blue eyes and curly bright hair. But her development was spasmodic due to recurrent chest infections and she had a chronic cough. Each month was a milestone. Feeding times were a nightmare for poor Emma, for the baby would only suckle feebly for a few minutes at a time. There was no time to cook substantial meals for TF as Emma had done in the first year of their marriage, and he returned, uncomplaining, to the Newcastle routine of bread and cheese.

As summer gave way to autumn, Gussie's health seemed to improve a little. Enough to give them hope that she might grow stronger. Emma was still very protective of her precious firstborn, and Gussie was sitting up and attempting to crawl by the time they celebrated her first birthday. She could say a few words, including *Dada* and *Mama*, and she smiled a lot. Emma still carried her about, now on her hip, but she dare not take her out in the perambulator, for fear she would suffer another bout of bronchitis in the cold weather.

TF had been very patient, but he missed the intimacy of the marriage bed. Finally Emma turned back to him, finding comfort in his arms, and the following March she realised she was pregnant again.

In June, Jerusha was leaving Norfolk for a post in Sydenham. She wrote to Emma, 'My new employers expect their first baby in September, so I will be needed to prepare the nursery a few weeks before this. May I spend the time between with you, Emma? It is so long since we were together! I can't wait to meet TF and young Gussie as well!'

Chas Holmes offered to meet Jerusha from the station and to escort her to Marylebone Passage. He had thought that no other young woman could equal Emma in beauty and intelligence, but he kept these feelings to himself, because her husband was his best friend. When the carriage door opened and Jerusha stepped out onto the platform, he caught his breath. She was small like her sister, with dark hair and eyes, but slighter in build. A porter followed with her luggage on a trolley.

'Charles Holmes?' her voice was husky, her smile dazzling. She was wearing a navy-blue jacket and skirt, hardly the outfit for a warm day, which her grateful employer had presented her with as a reward for her faithful service, saying, 'You *must* look the part in London! I can't get into these since I had the children . . .' Jerusha expressed gratitude, despite the candid admission.

'Oh, call me Chas – everyone does! You, of course, are Jerusha!' They shook hands. 'This way, I have a cab waiting,' he said. He looked at the loaded trolley.

'I'll foller you up,' the porter said, hoping for a tip. He was not disappointed.

Jerusha's reaction to Marylebone Passage, being a country girl, was quickly disguised dismay. The door opened immediately they arrived, and Emma stood there, with little Gussie in her arms. 'Ru – here you are at last! Come in. You too, Chas – the tea is brewing and I have made some muffins!'

As Jerusha kissed her sister and then the top of Gussie's head, she whispered, 'You kept your secret well! It seems I have come at the right time to help you. You mustn't overdo things.'

'I can't stay long, I am due back on duty at five,' Chas said, adding shyly, 'I hope we will meet again soon!' to Jerusha.

'I hope so, too,' she replied, and she meant it.

'This is your room.' Emma ushered her sister inside. 'I'm sure you will find the bed comfortable – it's the one I slept in at Kensington! My successor, so my friend Anna tells me, is a stout person, and needed a larger bed! Anna suggested to Miss Maria that we might be glad of this one, and it was delivered to us only last week, together with the washstand, as Anna also mentioned that I missed the tulips – just in time for your visit!'

'Your employers must have been fond of you, to be so kind – look at me!' Jerusha said ruefully. 'I was given my mistress's cast-offs! I felt I had to wear this outfit today to please her – but now I am going to change into something more comfortable!' She noticed the cot-bed in the corner. 'Oh, does Gussie sleep in this – it will be nice to have her company!'

Emma said, 'She may start the night off here, but she always ends up in bed with us!'

'You need your sleep – you must try not to worry so much about her – your poor husband will feel neglected. I have come to help, in any way I can, Emma.'

Emma shifted the baby to her other hip, and thought, Everything will be better now Jerusha is here!

Later, as she prepared a special supper, which would be shared with TF when he came home, Emma glanced at her baby crawling on the blanket Jerusha had spread on the floor and smiled to hear her sister talking to Gussie as she knelt beside her, encouraging her to play with a multi-coloured woolly ball that she had made for her. It was so good, she thought, to have both hands free for a change, so she could concentrate on her cooking. Tom would be pleased.

'You always had a wonderful way with babies – wouldn't you like to be married and have one of your own?', she said to Jerusha, then bit her lip, realising that that was a little tactless.

Jerusha smiled at her. 'Oh, I don't think that will ever happen somehow. Gussie is very special, Em. Mother and Father said *I* was a poor doer, d'you remember? I don't suppose I'll make old bones, but I've held down my job since I was fifteen, despite the asthma, and have a warm reference to take to Sydenham.'

'I'm glad you don't intend to stay in London, the air is not good here – though you won't be far away from me any more, but on the edge of the countryside.'

'Tomorrow,' Jerusha said, 'we'll wheel Gussie out in the perambulator to the nearest park. Now she's sitting up, she can see all the flowers, green grass and ducks on the pond.'

The summer months rolled by and suddenly it was the end of August and Jerusha was leaving for Sydenham. Emma was more relaxed, her old sunny self, despite being, as she said ruefully, 'As big as a barge!' The baby was due in early October.

Chas had offered to escort Jerusha to her new place and it was obvious to Emma and TF that he was smitten with her, but it seemed that Jerusha was determined to think of him as just a good friend.

'As you are not expected until the late afternoon, we could leave your luggage to be collected at the station as your employer instructed, and spend the day at the Crystal Palace – would you like that?' Chas asked her diffidently.

'Well, I don't suppose I'll get much time for jaunts after the nursery is occupied,' she replied. 'I'd like that very much.' She'd wondered why he was all dressed up for a train journey and was glad she was wearing her best dress and not the stuffy costume she'd arrived in!

The sun beat down on their heads through the dome above and showed up the dusty streaks on the glass panels. They were moving with the crowd through the tropical greenhouses. Glancing up Jerusha exclaimed, 'Oh look, Chas, a beautiful blue butterfly!' They paused for a moment to watch it fluttering among the exotic plants, though Chas had his eyes on his companion, like a butterfly herself, he fancied, in her cream voile dress, the skirt of which seemed to float around her neat ankles.

He dabbed his forehead with his pocket handkerchief. He was sweating and wished he could remove his jacket, but it would not do to be in a public place in shirtsleeves. He couldn't help noticing that although most of the visitors were smartly dressed, there was an unpleasant odour emanating from some of them. Maybe it was the clothing, for best clothes were worn on special occasions only, and were often not of washable material. No wonder the ladies carried small vials of perfume or vinaigrettes in their bags and strong-smelling salts which, when sniffed, brought tears to the eyes.

They were now passing through the display areas. Some of the exhibits had been in the original Crystal Palace before its move to its present location, and there were marvellous examples of craftwork from all over the globe. Jerusha was particularly impressed by a huge plaster reproduction of an Egyptian sphinx. Although scratched and dented by past visitors, it remained aloof, she thought.

The sideshows were becoming seedier as they walked through, with traders' intent on persuading folk to buy their goods by outdoing one another with their strident shouting. 'Look, my luv, fancy some crown jools?'

'Tell yer fortune for sixpence, lidy?' 'Granny's toffee – have some stick jaw!' Chas steered Jerusha skilfully through the crowds surrounding each booth.

With sighs of relief they ventured through an exit into the gardens, discovered a shady spot and a table and Chas went to buy refreshments from the outside traders.

Jerusha sat there dreaming – her new boots were feeling tight, and it was good to be out in the fresh air. Wouldn't it be lovely, she thought, to attend a concert in the great hall here and listen to the music? However, there were still the gardens to explore and the dinosaurs to marvel at.

After sandwiches and a pot of tea, they walked to the tidal lake, which, their guide informed them, sometimes flooded and eclipsed some of the vast stone sculptures. 'Cleans them off, I suppose,' Chas said. Some of the towering strange creatures looked a trifle weatherworn; they had been very popular in the original Crystal Palace in Hyde Park when they were displayed in groups on raised platforms. Now, it seemed to Jerusha and Chas, they had been scattered here and there and did not have the same effect on visitors. Small children were inclined to try to climb on them and were not overawed by their strangeness. Not so long ago, their authenticity had been questioned, especially after Darwin published his findings on evolution.

They were walking slowly, hand in hand, when Chas turned to Jerusha and asked, 'May I continue to see you sometimes, Jerusha? I know you will be busy when the new baby arrives in the nursery, but I do so enjoy your company, and hope you feel the same about me?'

'You know I do! Emma and TF obviously consider you to be one of the family, and so do I.'

'I would,' he began, 'hope for something more . . .'

'Shush. Don't spoil what we have now, Chas. I have my reasons for holding back.' She hesitated, then said, 'My health for one. The doctor says I have chronic asthma, no cure for that.'

'You know I would care for you. If you change your mind.'

'You will be the first to know,' she assured him. Then she smiled and squeezed his hand. 'There is no one else,

I promise you. We had better think about leaving now, I think.'

After bidding her goodbye on the doorstep of her new abode, a handshake because they had spotted the front curtains twitching, he walked to the station and waited some time for the London train, thinking how much he would miss her.

Emma missed her sister too. Little Gussie was deteriorating, a spell of wet, cold weather had resulted in what the doctor diagnosed, as usual, as bronchitis, and she seemed to lose her ability to crawl and play. Emma tucked her up in the perambulator and wheeled her about indoors. The rattling of the baby's small chest alarmed her, but she obeyed instructions to keep the little girl warm both day and night, when they would also have a steaming kettle on the trivet of the bedroom fire.

Emma had not had time to worry about what might happen in labour this time. She was thankful when it was obvious this would not be a premature birth. The midwife suggested that the monthly nurse, who would attend Emma and the baby, might be able to help with the sick child until she was needed for maternity duties.

Gussie was moved back to her own room and the other bedroom was cleaned thoroughly in readiness for the new arrival. TF decided that he would sleep in the single bed next to Gussie's cot when he was home at nights. Their coal allowance from the brigade was increased and his deputy, Chas, was ready to take over his duties in an emergency. The brigade looked after its own.

The baby did not arrive until 17 October, almost two weeks after the expected date. The midwife eventually advised Emma to drink a wineglass of castor oil. It was a real struggle for her to swallow this foul liquid, but it worked. Even as she lay in her bed in the early afternoon, with the midwife in attendance, she could hear the comings and goings in the other bedroom. 'Your husband asked the doctor to call,' the nurse said. 'You mustn't worry my dear, concentrate on getting this baby born.'

'He said nothing before he went to work this morning, before the pains started,' Emma said faintly. She offered up a silent but fervent prayer that all would be well.

As the baby gave its first indignant cry, she thought she heard the front door slam. Had TF come home?

He had actually been back for some time and received grave news from the doctor, 'I'm afraid we are going to lose your little girl. There is a slight chance, if I can take her to hospital.'

TF gently lifted Gussie and wrapped her in a blanket. 'Dada,' she murmured feebly. They were the last words she would utter. She was so frail, so vulnerable, and so precious. He had to make the decision alone, because Emma was not in a fit state at this moment to do so. He passed the little bundle to the kindly old doctor.

Shortly afterwards he was summoned to his wife's bedside. 'A fine, healthy girl,' the midwife announced proudly. 'The image of her mother!'

He knelt by the bed, and with tears in his eyes, he agreed. 'She's beautiful, like you, Emma.'

Emma was smiling, stroking the small dark head. 'My dear father would have said *bootiful*.'

'What shall we call her?' he asked.

'Isabella Mary, after your mother and sister. Would you like that?'

'I would!' He swallowed hard. 'I have to tell you that Gussie has been taken to the hospital—'

'All is not lost?' she cried.

'She is in the right place, Emma.'

'She hasn't yet been baptised, Tom – we said we'd have the two babies baptised together—'

'The padre at the hospital will attend to that. The doctor asked me about it.'

'Your wife should rest, try to sleep,' the midwife advised quietly. She took Isabella Mary from her mother and placed her in the crib.

On 14 November Gussie passed peacefully away. Isabella Mary (Immi) was baptised two days before this in All Souls Church, Langham Place, together with Marianne, the infant daughter of the wharf inspector at the London Salvage Corps, Edwin Goodchild and his wife Fanny. Immi would always be extra special to her parents after the loss of the sister she never knew. 'She gave us strength to carry on,' Emma said.

SIXTEEN

Southwark, 1866

Emma and TF decided to move from a place with too many sad memories. The LFEE had become the Metropolitan Fire Brigade, responsible for 'all life and fire' in a 120-mile radius. TF, together with Chas, applied to the London Salvage Corps, a new brigade in London. After receiving a glowing testimonial from Captain Shaw, which he treasured all his life, TF was offered a post as a full foreman, a well-paid position which provided the family with excellent housing in Southwark Bridge Road, and other good benefits. Chas was to be his deputy, as before.

Emma, TF and little Immi shared their new accommodation in Southwark Bridge Road with the Goodchild family. Fanny was always willing to listen to Emma when she felt low, and Edwin similarly supported TF through the grieving period. Their two small girls, who were baptised together, would grow up to be firm friends.

The houses were large and well-designed with three storeys. Emma appreciated the extra space and airiness of the rooms – there were no damp patches on the walls here. Chas found lodgings with other single colleagues opposite the fire station. This had originally been a slum area, which had been cleared and regenerated as a decent place to live.

Later, Chas would tell Emma about the Evelina Hospital for Sick Children built in 1869 on the site of the demolished South Sea Court, also once a slum. The hospital was endowed by Baron Ferdinand de Rothschild as a memorial to his wife, who had been involved in a train accident and gone into premature labour, when both she and her baby died.

The hospital was a cheerful place with its light, airy rooms, cosy cots and special nurses, there was a playroom for convalescent children, and although there was heartbreak because of the nature of some of the illnesses, all were handled with compassion and kindness. The staff was willing to listen to parents who called in for advice. After losing Gussie, this hospital would be where Emma would turn for reassurance.

Emma also attended St George's Church in the Old Mint area of Southwark Bridge Road. Old Mint was a place of narrow courts, winding alleys, and large, lofty dwellings, often roofless, but some of the lower floors were inhabited.

It was not, TF counselled Emma, a place to venture to after dark. Historically, St George's had a close connection with Charles Dickens and his novel, *Little Dorrit.* A relic of the Marshalsea prison was part of the church boundary. Although Emma still read the worthy magazines of her youth, including Mrs Beeton, and of course, her bible, she had been introduced to the novels of Dickens by her friend Fanny, and these were given to her by TF at her request on her birthday and at Christmas. She found *Little Dorrit* a sad and disturbing tale, but a compelling read none the less.

Emma had been at Southwark Bridge Road for some two years when she received an unexpected invitation. She had heard from Anna that the Summers family had moved from South Kensington into the suburbs, to Bromley, where Mr Summers now had his practice. Anna had gone with them, as companion and ladies' maid, with Nan, who had been promoted to cook. The only other member of staff was a local maid of all work, it being a smaller establishment now that the Summers' sons and daughter were no longer much at home. Frances was boarding at a College for Young Ladies, William junior, having qualified as a solicitor like his father, was spending a few months travelling abroad before joining the family firm and Henry had recently become a student of theology in Shropshire.

Bromley Kent.

Dear Mrs Meehan (Emma),

The Misses Rosalind and Adelaide Summers invite you to an informal luncheon in honour of our dear sister Maria, who is leaving for the mission field. We have planned a surprise reunion for her with friends and former staff who have provided valuable assistance in the past.

Please say you will come! It is an easy journey by train, and you would be met and escorted from the local station. Luncheon will be at 1 p.m.

We do look forward to seeing you again after all this time.

Sincerely, etc.

'Of course you must go, I'm sure Fanny would look after Immi for you,' TF said immediately, when she read this communication to him over breakfast.

'What could I wear?' Emma wondered.

'I don't suppose it is a dress parade! Just go as yourself!'

She sighed. 'I wish you had been invited too.'

'I'd be a fish out of water among all the ladies, and anyway I can't take time off.'

Fanny was more helpful. 'Of course Immi can come to me! What about the new frock you are making for the warmer weather?'

'I haven't nearly finished that.'

'I'll help you; we'll have a sewing session here this afternoon!'

'You are a friend indeed!' Emma said fervently. They were not alike in looks, for Fanny was tall and well-built, with a rosy complexion and fair hair, but they were very compatible. Fanny was of Scottish descent and had enjoyed a private education. Fanny knew about Emma's family struggles and she was the only one, apart from her husband and Anna, to whom Emma had revealed the painful facts about the workhouse.

A week later, Emma boarded the train for Bromley South wearing her new mauve silk frock with frilled overskirt, fitted bodice with pearly buttons, a small matching hat and a cobweb-fine wool shawl lent by Fanny, round her shoulders. She carried a parasol, for she had learned from Anna that if it was a fine day, lunch would be served in the garden.

At first, she didn't recognise the young woman who had been sent to meet her. Then, 'Frances!' she exclaimed, beaming. Frances had been a schoolgirl last time they met – shy and awkward – but now she had *blossomed*, Emma thought. That was the only word for it. She had grown taller and her mass of brown hair was attractively styled – Anna must have had a hand in that, she guessed. Frances wore small, round, gold-rimmed spectacles and no hat, but looked cool in a cream frock in fine tussore material with a jaunty blue-spotted bow at the neck. There was just a glimpse above her ankles of blue stockings, which had long been worn by those who could not afford the silk variety but were now adopted by women who were at last receiving higher education.

'I am home for the summer,' Frances said, as they linked arms, 'I hope you feel like a walk. It's not far.'

Emma confided, as they walked along towards the Common, 'I felt nostalgic when I knew you had moved from Kensington. It was such a lovely house, and surely you must all miss being there?'

'The family decided to move out of London after Aunt Rosalie suffered from bronchitis most of last winter. Papa was afraid we would lose her, like my mama. The doctor told us it would be an excellent idea to come here. Did you know that Anna looks after my aunt and is her companion now?'

Emma nodded. 'You will note other changes too. Aunt Maria said she thought the three of them had led a privileged life – that they ought to leave all that behind and work to help others in a more positive fashion.'

'But Frances, they were so good – think of all the sewing parties and the bazaars . . .'

'It was not enough, Aunt Maria said. That's when she decided to become a missionary. Prepare yourself to see a new woman! I may decide not to return to college – I was studying classics, but I could continue my course by correspondence. My aunts tell me I am old enough now to run a smaller household and I know it would make Papa happy to have me at home.'

They turned into a side road and Emma saw a row of identical villas facing the common. These were new houses, no basements, but useful attic rooms and were specially designed for families with one or two servants. They opened the gate and walked up the path to the front door, with its small round window of stained glass, and a plaque proclaiming *The Summers House.*

'We have a lovely garden at the back,' Frances said, opening the door with a key taken from her purse. 'Aunt Adelaide has taken up gardening and has great plans for planting – and if I stay, Papa has agreed I can have a little dog – he suggests a King Charles spaniel. We had to leave Dizzy behind at Kensington, you know. He was too old to disturb from his routine. The new owners took him on.'

Maria came hurrying along the hall to greet Emma. She wore a plain grey frock and her hair was drawn back in a bun. Gone were the extravagant trappings, the expensive clothes and ringlets. '*Emma* – I am all in a whirl! I knew nothing of all these arrangements, you know – and you are the first guest to arrive. Nan has made a big pot of tea, and when you are ready we must go into the garden and have a long overdue chat! Mr Summers has taken the afternoon off from his office in town and is looking forward to meeting you again, too.'

Mr Summers was pushing a wheelbarrow full of grass cuttings along the side of the kitchen garden, where he tipped the contents into a compost bin. He dusted his hands on a green apron, which he untied before shaking Emma's hand warmly. 'Ah, Emma, you see I was put to work directly I arrived home! It is very good to see you again. How are the family?'

'Both my husband and our little daughter are well, thank you, Mr Summers.'

Nan arrived then with the pot of tea and a tray of cups and saucers. She placed these on a garden table, one of several with matching cast iron chairs. She looked just the same, Emma thought fondly, a wisp of a girl, but one confident in her role. The cockney inflection was still there, but she had mastered the aitches in her speech. 'The ladies will join you in a minute, Emma, they are greeting some guests.' She indicated the long trestle table on the lawn with its contents concealed by a snowy linen cloth. 'I will see you later, I have something ready to come out of the oven,' she added.

Mr Summers had joined them for the welcome tea. He mopped his brow with his handkerchief, then replaced his straw boater 'A real summer's day – please forgive the pun.'

'It is lovely here,' Emma said. 'It reminds me somehow of when we were at Brighton.'

'Except there is not a pebble in sight and no sea breeze, eh?' He smiled.

'Yes, but a wonderful scent from the roses.'

'You must take a selection of those home with you,' Maria said. 'I intend to press one of the dark red blooms in my bible, to remember this happy occasion.'

Then the French doors to the garden opened wide and others came across the grass to join them. Emma recognised Mrs Love, who had come out of retirement, and looked overheated in her best black satin, followed by Rosalie, pale, but pretty in pink, accompanied by Adelaide and Anna, then Frances with the curate and his wife from their old parish and the vicar from their present church, with two ladies from the overseas mission committee. Last came a young man who was introduced as a newly qualified barrister who was lodging with the family at present. 'He is working with Mr Summers for a few months,' Maria informed the company.

Rosalie told Emma, 'I'm afraid old Joseph is no more, and other good friends were unable to come from London, but all have sent their good wishes to dear Maria.'

Anna greeted Emma with a kiss. 'We don't see enough of each other these days!' she whispered. Close to, Emma was startled to notice the little wrinkles around her eyes. Anna, she realised, was now over forty, like the Misses Summers. I am twenty-seven, and Mr Summers must be fifty, she thought. How time goes by.

Mr Summers had risen to escort the visitors to sit at the table. Frances removed the covering and there were murmurs of appreciation at the spread. Plates of several kinds of sandwiches, with the crusts removed, including cucumber, ham and smoked salmon; bowls of salad; fresh mayonnaise; cheese tartlets; small pork pies; and dishes of pickle. There were also freshly baked hot rolls, curls of butter and a selection of cheese. However, it was a modest repast compared with the old days in Kensington, Emma thought. No wine, for she soon gathered that this was now a temperate household, when Nan reappeared with jugs of iced lemonade.

Later, after they had finished off the meal with fresh fruit, including sliced pineapple, Frances and Nan brought out the coffee pots and cups and saucers, and a tray of home-made fudge. It was time for the farewell and good luck speeches.

Mr Summers rose from the table. He caught Emma's eye as she was sitting opposite, and smiled. 'Thank you, all of you, for coming along today to wish Maria all the best in the future. We are extremely proud of her, but we shall, of course, miss her. When I lost my wife, ah, and was left with three young children, I wondered how I could carry on. Maria and her sisters rescued me from my depression and have been supportive ever since. Maria, wherever she is in the world in the future, will be in our thoughts, and still an important part of this family.'

Others expressed their appreciation of her community work and pledged support, before Maria spoke. 'I'll keep it simple, because, well, if I say too much I will cry. Thank you, every single one of you, for the splendid send-off.'

At 3 p.m. all the visitors departed, except for Emma who was to spend the hour until she had to catch the train home with Anna and Nan in the latter's comfortable bed-sitting room off the hall, which was convenient for the kitchen. She would talk again with Frances when she walked with her to the station.

There were a couple of comfortable chairs for Emma and Anna to sit on while Nan went off to brew tea for the family, and for the three of them. Meantime the young maid tackled the washing up with a friend she had recruited to help that afternoon.

'I saw Mr Summers' face light up when he saw you, Emma,' Anna observed.

'I was pleased to see him – and all the family – too,' Emma returned.

'I think, you know, he thought you were *irreplaceable* . . .'

'I never . . .' Emma paused. 'But, as you know, Tom is my first – and last – love.'

'Of course I know, and I'm glad! I could guess what Mr Summers was thinking, but I also knew he was too much of a gentleman to do anything about it.' She sighed. 'I'm glad he didn't know how much *I* admired him – in the past.'

'Oh, Anna, I never realised!' Emma said softly.

'Now, don't be sorry for me, because the whole family has been so kind to me over the years. However, when

I heard about Miss Maria's new venture – she has given up her worldly assets, you know, to fund her work, hence the changes here, for she has been most generous over the years, helping Mr Summers pay for everything, the children's education included. When I learned that, I began to think I needed to change my comfortable life too and do good for others.'

'Then I hope you will find what you are seeking and Tom, for I know I can speak for him, and I will support and encourage you as much as we can.'

'You two look very serious,' Nan said, coming in with a teapot covered in a knitted cosy. 'Here's some news! That young law man has asked Frances to go with him to a performance by Charles Dickens. She is all of a flutter!'

'I'm not surprised,' Emma sounded wistful. 'I'd love to go to one of those readings, but Tom is unlikely to be able to take me, as evenings are always busy for the fire brigade.'

Later, as she said goodbye to the family, Mr Summers shook her hand and then raised it briefly to his lips. 'Don't leave it so long before you visit us again, Emma,' he said.

TF was working late that evening when Emma collected Immi and thanked Fanny for having her.

'She was no trouble at all,' Fanny said. 'How did your day go?'

Emma had divided the big bunch of roses, and now presented Fanny with her share. 'We had lunch in a lovely garden, and I watched a bumble bee on these same roses. It was just like being back in the country, only Bromley is a thriving town with lots of shops. The Summers live by the Common.'

'The roses smell beautiful, thank you, Emma. Do you still miss Wymondham?'

'Oh, I do! I will return there one day, I know it.' For a fleeting moment Emma recalled the old traveller they called the Donkey Man who had stayed the night in the orchard on the farm back home. William had said that everyone was drawn back to where they came from.

'That's how I feel about Scotland, too,' Fanny said nostalgically.

SEVENTEEN

1868

Emma's nickname 'the duchess' carried on from Marylebone Terrace. Later, her children would refer to her affectionately in the same terms. For three years there was just Immi, who grew into a delightful child, loving and kind who, having heard stories from her mother about the animals on the farm, especially Emma's dog, Fly, asked, 'Please can I have a little dog of mine own?'

While Emma hesitated, thinking of the havoc a boisterous pup might cause in her nice new home, TF came home with a kitten, one of a litter from a stray cat that had been adopted by the firemen at the station. The kitten was black, with blue eyes, which would turn gold within a few weeks. 'His name is Tip,' Immi pronounced, noting the white tip on his tail. 'And I like him cos he's got black hair like me.'

Emma's worries about having another unhealthy child were fading and she felt ready to grant another of Immi's wishes for 'a little brother to play with me'. To the delight of parents and sister, Thomas Frederick the second arrived in 1868. He too favoured Emma in colouring, and he was a strong, healthy baby. By the time he was toddling, Tommy and Immi were inseparable.

Emma now had help in the home, at TF's insistence. She enjoyed the company of a young woman not unlike Nan, who was just as willing to learn how to cook and clean. When the children took their nap after lunch, and Tillie was cheerfully washing up in the kitchen, Emma followed TF's suggestion that she should also rest while she had the chance. Some days she read, and once a week she wrote letters to her family, and to a newer correspondent, Rob's wife Margaret in Amble. Rob, who gained his Masters and Mates Certificate in 1871, was often away from home as he trawled coal up and down the coast and to London, but Margaret had the support of her unmarried sister Jane, who was seven years her senior and lived with the family. Jane was a dressmaker. Margaret wrote, *My dear sister brought me up when our mother died, I could not leave her behind when I married.* As Margaret had a small daughter, Lizzie, the same age as Tommy, and was expecting a second child, she and Emma had a lot in common. They hoped to 'meet one of these days.' Amble sounded a good place for a family holiday, and TF mentioned that he and Rob had not seen each other since they left home, when both boys felt guilty at leaving their young sister Mary with their father. However, it was proving difficult for the brothers to take leave from work at the same time.

Perhaps Emma was too busy with her growing family at first to notice that Immi had begun to have short 'absences' when she would sit staring into space and seemed not to hear what was going on around her. The first couple of times this happened Emma thought Immi had been daydreaming. She was due to start school after Christmas, and TF said reassuringly, 'Don't worry, Emma, she'll soon be told by her teacher to pay attention!' After an episode she would suddenly come to and behave as if nothing had happened. Then it could be weeks before the problem reoccurred. Otherwise Immi was bright and happy, and had already learned to read.

Emma decided to consult the Evelina Hospital before enrolling Immi at school. The sister listened patiently to Emma's concerns about her daughter's health and asked a few questions.

'Isabella is generally in good health?'

'Oh, yes! She doesn't seem any different after this happens.'

'The name for this condition is *petit mal*, a milder form of epilepsy, often seen in childhood. Isabella has not suffered any rigours?'

'Fits? No, nothing like that.'

'Please don't upset yourself, Mrs Meehan. She may well grow out of it. Do you know of any other instances of this malady in your family or your husband's?'

'I haven't heard of anything on either side,' Emma said, which was true.

'You must return here if you have any further concerns, but carry on as you are. Isabella should not be treated as an invalid, however be watchful for her welfare. Goodbye, Isabella, I am very pleased to have met you.'

'I would like to be a nurse like you when I grow up,' the child said shyly.

'Thank you for your reassurance, sister,' Emma said.

That evening, she talked about what she had learned at the hospital to TF. 'I can't help thinking of what the future holds, Tom. Our lovely daughter. I would like to teach her myself at home at present – maybe she can attend school when Tommy is ready to go, too. I hope you agree?'

TF hugged her to him. 'Dear Emma, of course I do.'

By this time, they were leading a comfortable life in Southwark Bridge Road and TF, as senior foreman with the LSC, had seen his salary increase the previous year from £130 p.a. to £155, plus clothing, rent and coal allowance. Chas, as deputy foreman, had an increase from £98 p.a. to £114, plus clothing and rent allowance, which was good for an unmarried man.

Keturah visited at this time, hoping to find employment in London, having left the household where she had been in service since the age of fourteen when she left Wicklewood. 'They were kind folk but there was no prospect of a better position – I was the only servant,' she confided to Emma. Even in humbler abodes, if the husband was in work, there might be a general maid, usually known as 'the girl'. Keturah had grown into an attractive young woman, but she had never been as confident as her soul mate, Rebecca. Shortly, as she and Keturah grew closer again, Emma learned the reason behind Keturah's sudden decision to come to London.

Emma enjoyed her company and, after discussing it with TF, asked Keturah if she would like to stay on help her with the children. However, Keturah confided that she was hoping to be married shortly to Harry Barnes, a ships' carpenter whom she had met in Yarmouth. 'He was born and brought up there and is from a large family like ours. Harry doesn't want us to be apart, and I miss him too,' she said. 'He works hard and says he can support a wife! I'm not sure I am suited to work in London; I only wanted to earn and save more for our wedding. Emma, d'you think I could be married here in Southwark? TF could give me away, and you could be my matron of honour!'

Emma smiled. 'Oh, Keturah – why don't you ask Rebecca if she will be your attendant? You two have always been so close. But there is one thing I could do. I am willing to lend you my own wedding gown. It is perfect for a winter wedding, which I presume you are about to decide on?'

'Yes! I don't think Rebecca will be able to come; her present employer is about to have another baby. She is not one for travelling on the train either because she says the motion makes her feel sick. She will have to get over that,

I imagine, for her future husband works as a porter on the railway! Wymondham is as far as Becca will go to see the family.'

'That's a shame, but I'm sure Jerusha will be here on your big day!' Perhaps, Emma thought, Jerusha would think again about marriage herself – Chas had been so patient, and never lost hope she would change her mind.

'Martha and Elijah have moved yet again, he really has a roving spirit!' Keturah said. 'She would have come, I know, if she could. D'you know, after you left for London to work, Martha wrote to Rebecca and me every week, as you did?'

'I didn't know.' Emma felt a pang of regret. She and Martha had never been close and she felt now that she could have made more of an effort to please her elder sister when Martha was in charge of the family. She hoped she was happy in her marriage.

When Keturah tried on the red velvet gown, it only needed a small alteration, to let down the generous hem on the skirt, as Keturah was an inch or two taller than her sister. 'Are you sure you want me to borrow it?' she asked Emma.

'I'm sure,' Emma said ruefully. 'I don't think I will be as slender as that again.'

The banns were called in Southwark during the first three weeks of December 1869, when Keturah was described as 'Spinster of this Parish'.

Harry Barnes arrived in London with his friend, who would stand as best man. Emma and TF were impressed by their future brother-in-law. He was a few years older than Keturah, who was twenty-three, and he reminded Emma of her beloved brother William, with his broad Norfolk accent. He loved his woodcraft and was ambitious for the future. He had already rented a cottage in Royal Road, Yarmouth, which Keturah would run as a lodging house. 'In a year or so we hope to move to Jarrow, where there is plenty of work for skilled carpenters in the shipping industry – they have been recruiting already in Great Yarmouth,' Harry said in his thoughtful way.' I promise to take great care of Keturah for I know how hard her life has been at times.'

The wedding was on Boxing Day and despite the inclement weather, the bride, looking very like Emma on her special day, walked proudly, holding TF's arm, to meet Harry at the altar. She wore her mother Sophia's wedding shawl round her shoulders, 'in memory of our dear parents'. In the front pew, little Immi gave an excited clap of her hands, while Tommy, a wriggling one year old, wiped his pudgy hand which clasped a soggy rusk, on Chas's trouser leg, and Emma and Jerusha wiped away a sentimental tear or two.

After a special meal cooked by Emma, the young couple departed for Great Yarmouth where shortly they would have their union blessed in their local church so that those who could not come to London might share in their joy. They then spent a brief honeymoon settling into their new home.

After this happy event, there was sad news of one who had earlier played a big part in TF's younger days. His Uncle Charlie, who had inspired both his nephews to go to sea with his lively stories and songs of his life as a jolly Jack tar and had been so generous with support after Isabella had died, had passed away. He'd married during the 1850s and afterwards contact had ceased.

Anna had received a black-bordered card from his widow, without a personal message or a postal address, which stated that Charles Henry Lister of Birkenhead, born 1822, son of Abraham Lister, of Newcastle, had died in Birkenhead, aged forty-seven.

The notification arrived some time after the event as it had been forwarded to Anna at the Bromley address, from Kensington. However, Anna had moved on again. She was now the matron of a church school in Birkenhead, and she was devastated to think she had been so near her brother at the end, but not known it.

There were nine boarders at the school, which was supervised by the local curate from the church. They were young men aged between thirteen and nineteen who were studying to be ministers. The majority were sponsored by missions overseas. Two of the scholars were from Mexico, one from Paris, one from Spain, one from Valparaiso in Chile and two from London and Kent. Anna was a mother figure to these boys. She wrote, *I am happy and the job is very rewarding, I hope to stay here a long time . . .*

She had heard of the position from Maria, who visited there before she left for the mission in China where she worked alongside women from America and Canada. Anna wrote to Emma, *Can you imagine Miss Maria in a rickshaw? She finds the Chinese very courteous and cultured, but is unsure many will be converted . . .*

The following June, 1870, Margaret and Rob in Amble had their second daughter, another Isabella, named for his mother and sister. In December, Keturah and Harry wrote to say that they had been blessed with a baby son, Harry jnr. and that they were hoping to move to Jarrow sometime in the New Year. Emma and TF had some news of their own: they were expecting their fourth child and this time Immi was hoping for a sister.

Immi was thrilled when Emma Alexandra, soon to be known as Alice, was born after a quick, easy birth, with a qualified midwife in attendance. Alice was blonde like her father and fair-skinned with blue eyes. She was not a placid baby like Immi and demanded attention. TF said fondly, 'She is spirited, like her mother!' For which remark Emma gave him a mock cuff round the ears and cried, 'Oh, you!'

But two years after these happy events, there was worrying news when Margaret's sister Jane wrote from Amble to say that Rob's wife was suffering from consumption, complicated by the fact that she was expecting another baby in September. Sadly, the baby inherited the condition and did not survive long. Margaret's condition became worse and she passed away two years later, aged thirty-three. From then on, the two girls, Lizzie and Izzy, were cared for by Jane. Rob, despite being grief-stricken, had to carry on as captain of his ship, in order to support them. He was fond of Jane but although he might have been expected to marry her eventually, no one could ever replace his gentle, sweet-tempered Margaret. Jane was made of sterner stuff and was not so indulgent with the children. She determined they would grow up to be independent and strong-minded, like her.

'I'm sad we never met,' Emma wept, her face pressed against TF's shoulder in bed, the night after they received the news, because she didn't want to upset the children. 'I thought of her as a true friend. I tried to comfort her as best I could when they lost baby Margaret. She knew I understood because of Gussie.'

It would come as a shock to them to learn later that Izzy, a precocious child who was obviously very bright, displayed the first signs of epilepsy after losing her mother; there was obviously a family connection. 'Perhaps it came from my mother's family; I never knew of this on the Irish side,' Tom said reflectively when he heard the news.

Emma comforted herself with the thought that she'd never heard of it in her family, either, although they had other afflictions to bear.

EIGHTEEN

Keturah, 1871

Keturah looked back just once at Buckenham Cottage, the place she and Harry had moved to immediately after their marriage and where their baby had been born the past December. She didn't want to think of the empty rooms inside. Their furniture had been removed to the saleroom earlier in the week, after the lodgers left. On impulse, Keturah wrapped the pair of Staffordshire china dogs from the mantelpiece in newspaper and tucked them among the tiny clothes in the baby's bundle. These would remind her of home and Rebecca, whose wedding gift they had been – of Fly, Emma's spaniel at Wymondham, and of the cottage here in Yarmouth. It had been an eventful year since she married Harry. Her only regret at leaving was that she would miss Rebecca's wedding in the summer.

It was now spring, 1871, and they were about to embark on their great adventure, which would begin that day when they stepped aboard the steamship *East Anglian* for the overnight trip to Newcastle. However, they would disembark before this at South Shields, where accommodation had been arranged. South Shields was situated at the mouth of the River Tyne, which flowed inland to Jarrow, then to Newcastle upon Tyne. Workers at the Jarrow shipyard were transported there by wagon, as it was only a few miles away.

The carter heaved their luggage aboard, and then assisted Keturah up, while Harry held the baby until she was settled on her seat. He had a sack slung across his shoulder, with provisions for the journey, for they had been warned that food for passengers was rationed. Regarding the jostling crowds, waiting to board, Harry observed, 'It'll be like feeding the five thousand, I reckon.'

They had joined other families on the South Quay who had been recruited mainly by Palmers, the big shipyard in Jarrow. Keturah recognised a familiar face. It was Liza, who like herself had been in service in Great Yarmouth. They had been great friends and on their afternoons off the two girls had walked along the sandy beach and dipped their stockinged feet into the waves as they lapped and receded. They popped the seaweed bladders and allowed the sea breeze to loosen their long hair, even though it was quite a task to remove the tangles later, especially for Keturah, with her curly locks. They chattered and giggled like the children they still were at fourteen and fifteen years of age. Liza had married Francis when she was twenty and the young couple had moved out of town to live with his parents on their farm. Francis was a tailor by profession and rented a small shop in Yarmouth along a side street, but there was not much call for his services among the fishing community, who needed more rugged wear and were not interested in fashion. Keturah wondered what had prompted them to travel into the unknown. The delicate-looking Francis, with his elegant hands and tapering fingers, so sure with needle and thread, seemed unlikely to be heading for the shipyards at Jarrow or the mines in Newbottle, a village further inland. She waved at her old friend and hoped to get a chance to chat before they retired for the night. Liza, too, had a babe in arms, fastened within her shawl, however, there was no sign of Maybelle, her first child, who must be three years old. Francis was carrying his precious violin and Keturah recalled that Liza had said he was musical and had never wanted to follow his father into farming.

They made their way with difficulty, trying to get to one another. Francis had disappeared by then to find a cabin, as had Harry. Keturah managed to get to her old friend first. It was not possible to embrace while holding on to their babies, and they had to shout so that they could hear each other.

The milling crowds on the quay reminded Keturah of a story Liza had told her years ago. 'It must have been a crowd like this when your grandfather was at that beef and beer celebration to mark the end of the Napoleonic Wars,' she said to her.

'Fancy you remembering that ... All that beef, and seventy barrels of beer! And they made a mistake by celebrating a year before Napoleon was defeated at Waterloo in June 1815! It must have been a sight to see, Grandpa said his father took off his belt and *striped* his bottom for being drunk at fourteen years old.'

They gazed out to sea where the fishing fleet were already out – Yarmouth was famous for its herring industry; a staple food which could be preserved in salt – and Keturah felt a sudden constriction in her throat. She was leaving her loved ones, especially her beloved sister Rebecca, and going far from home. Would she ever see them again, or the old familiar places?

'Why are you going to Bottle?' she asked her friend. 'It's a mining village, isn't it?' She couldn't imagine Francis digging coal deep down a mine.

'We needed to get away – to be by ourselves, masters of our own destiny for once, is how Francis put it. He's prepared to work hard and we'll save up so he can return to his tailoring,' Liza said. 'How about you?'

'Well, Harry is a ship's carpenter and he seized the chance to earn more and have a more responsible job; it does sound much more interesting than his old job in Yarmouth. He wants me to be a lady of leisure, he says, and enjoy bringing up our future family – little Harry is the first!'

'We should find our cabin,' Harry suddenly appeared. 'I had a job to find you. Our boy is sucking his fist, he hev need of his mother,' he reproved her mildly.

'Shush!' Keturah whispered, thinking he sounded like her brother William. She looked to see if anyone was listening. There were folk everywhere, some leaning over the rails to call a last goodbye to friends and family while children ran around exploring and being rebuked by grizzled old sailors with leathery skin from constant exposure to the elements. Language was ripe, and Keturah was thankful that their baby boy was too young to take it in. Mother would have been horrified, she thought. The gulls screeched overhead, circling the boats and there was the overriding smell of fish from the crates on the quayside. The deck rocked beneath their feet. Full steam ahead!

'I'll see you later,' Liza said quickly, 'I expect my husband is searching for me, too.'

Their cabin was tiny and claustrophobic, with two narrow, hard bunks, one above the other. There was a slop pail, a wash bowl and a jug of water. Keturah sat on the bottom bunk, which was covered with a rough blanket, to nurse the hungry baby. She thought, I won't be getting undressed tonight!

Those without sleeping quarters would sleep on deck, resting their heads on their bundles. Some were already feeling queasy and were hanging over the rails as they gazed down into the darkening, heaving sea below. Others, fortified by swigs from bottles they'd brought along, and encouraged by a couple of the crew with banjo accompaniment, obviously intended to dance and sing the night away.

There was a tap on the cabin door, and Liza and Francis were revealed with their baby. 'May I come and be with you, Keturah, for a while? We are two cabins along from here – only Francis has been roped in to play his fiddle for the dancing.'

'I couldn't say no,' Francis said apologetically. 'Perhaps Harry would like to join me? Then the gals can have a good old chinwag.'

Liza was wearing similar clothes to Keturah: long skirt, high-necked blouse, a hand-crocheted shawl and boots. In cold weather the shawl would be worn over the head and shoulders and then they appeared much like the fisher girls. But the similarity ended there, as she was taller than Keturah, fair-haired with freckles. When they were younger, she had always been protective of Keturah, who had been small, shy and nervous after her long stay in the workhouse. Liza's baby was also a boy, almost the same age as little Harry. He too was dressed in a long flannel garment suitable for both day and nightwear. He was named Albert, a name still popular despite the demise of the prince consort.

'Our Maybelle is staying with her grandparents but I hope she will join us later in Newbottle. 'Did you know there are three pits in Harbottle. Francis will be employed at *Dorothea,*' Liza explained, answering Keturah's unspoken questions. She added: 'I'm glad your Harry is with Francis – some of those men on deck look as if they enjoy a fight. Francis is a gentle soul . . .'

'Harry may be large, but he's not one for drinking or fisticuffs, he's a real family man,' Keturah said defensively. 'I hope little Harry will grow up to be the same.' She cuddled her baby close and kissed the top of his dark head, just visible over the folds of the shawl.

'I didn't mean . . . oh dear, Keturah, I didn't mean to put your back up! I've missed your company since I married – my ma-in-law is a bit of a tartar and believes young mothers should stay at home! I had to pull my weight on the farm, too. She's one reason, though I would never repeat that to Francis, I'm looking forward to our new life in Newbottle.'

Keturah thought, I couldn't leave a child of mine behind, but she didn't say this to Liza. 'We won't be so far apart, Liza; we'll be living in South Shields, in a company house. We won't be going as far as Newcastle on the boat, thank goodness.'

Liza gulped. 'Oh dear, I think my supper's coming up.' She laid Albert down at the other end of the bunk and dashed for the bucket.

Up on deck, those who weren't similarly afflicted, were suddenly spellbound, as Francis drew his bow over quivering violin strings, under the stars.

They parted from their friends at dawn, waving and shivering in the early morning chill on the dock at South Shields after promising to keep in touch and exchanging addresses. Then they were herded on to the waiting wagons and trundled along the road towards their new home. Keturah was glad to be on dry land at least.

As it was a coastal town, Keturah had imagined South Shields to be like Yarmouth. It came as a shock to be told that it was the second largest town on the Tyne after Newcastle, with a growing population due to the shipping yards in the locality and the coal mines. It would be some time before she discovered the miles of sandy beaches, the coves, the dunes, and the river frontage with the massive North and South Piers, which she explored with Harry. On Lowe Top there were two cannons, which had been captured from the Russians during the Crimean War. They would walk along the Leas above the limestone cliffs and learn the history of the Grotto pub, cut into the cliffs. Seabirds cried raucously overhead, reminding them of the place they had left. The wild side of South Shields was quite breathtaking, but despite this, Keturah didn't feel happy living in the town. It had an unpleasant stench of the river in the summer months and she wished she was in a village like Liza, for it was taking time to make friends.

Letters winged back and forth between South Shields and Newbottle. Liza wrote: *Dear Francis comes home as black as the coal he has worked with his pick and shovel. I get the tin bath ready and scrub him all over – the sight makes Bertie laugh! His poor hands, rough and red, he is too tired to play his fiddle in the evenings, but sometimes he sews, and has made Bertie a sailor suit.*

Harry, too, was working in a different environment. The great iron-clad ships were awesome to see, towering above the workers who toiled like so many ants far below. He worked long hours on cargo boats and on ships with revolving twin gun turrets, which cost in excess of a thousand pounds to build. Harry, like his fellow workers, sometimes dreamed of going to Australia on one of these vessels and was proud of being involved with the construction of these aristocrats of the high seas, including *C.M. Palmer, Dilston Castle* and *Hebburn Hall*, and he was devastated at the news in 1873 that the latter had sunk in Northern Spain.

When he arrived home, he sometimes found his young wife in tears, with a fretful baby and no hearty meal waiting for him on the table. Young Harry was not thriving, it seemed. Keturah was alarmed when she found that just a couple of years ago, there had been an epidemic of smallpox in the town. The house they lived in was pleasant enough and they were not short of money, because Harry's skills as a carpenter were rewarded well by his employers, but she constantly worried about her little boy.

Harry thought privately that if she had another baby, she wouldn't have time to worry so much, but he kept silent, for he didn't wish to upset Keturah who had already said, 'How could I cope if I had other children to care for?'

Then in April the following year, tragedy struck. Young Harry had a high fever one day, and the next morning Keturah discovered him lifeless in his cot. Nothing could be done to revive him. He was eighteen months old. For days after the funeral Keturah was unable to speak and, grief-stricken himself, Harry comforted her as best he could, making all the arrangements and passing on the news to the extended family. When he came home from work to find his wife had been unable to make the bed, let alone cook an evening meal, he quietly set about the household tasks.

'They were so happy, with Harry in a good job, and Keturah hoping to increase her family,' Emma said tearfully to TF when they received their letter. 'The only consolation for me is that after all those years apart, I got to know my sister again when she stayed with us before her wedding.'

NINETEEN

1873

TF received not altogether unexpected news from the LFC that he had been appointed as the Inspector of Wharves and Warehouses, 'in consequence of Mr Goodchild's resignation'.

Simultaneously, Chas, who was now the senior deputy foreman, was promoted to the rank of full foreman and directed to take charge of the Central Division in place of TF.

Emma gave her husband a hug. 'Oh, you both deserve it – we're going up in the world, Tom!'

'We will miss our good friends,' TF said. 'I had hopes, you know, after Edwin told me he was leaving to be superintendent of the Glasgow Fire Brigade but didn't say, in case it didn't happen.'

'We must keep in touch,' Emma said firmly.

The towering warehouses under TF's supervision were linked by many gangways. The Thames lightermen in their large, flat-bottomed boats unloaded goods from ships at the dockside and then rowed to the warehouses where the cargo was hoisted up by stout ropes attached to metal pegs jutting out near the top of the building into the designated storage area. It was dangerous work and accidents were not uncommon. The lightermen were cheerful chaps who sang traditional songs as they rowed, as well as more ribald offerings from the music hall.

Inspecting the warehouses was a vital, but exacting occupation: TF needed to be vigilant at all times. Internal combustion of goods was a hazard still, despite the safety rules put in place after the Tooley Street fire. There were many stairs to climb, narrow, dark passages to walk along with a lantern, and TF, who had been so fit after his years in the navy, began to suffer from claustrophobia and breathlessness due to poor ventilation. Added to this, he was still called out for fires when greater manpower was needed. He didn't confide his anxieties to Emma because she was pregnant again.

Emma and TF had thought their family was complete before they had a second son, Ernest Robert (Ernie). Ernie, TF thought, took after Irish Tom, with red hair and bright blue eyes. He was to grow up to be handsome, lively and charming, but also possess a strong character, and he was very close to his mother in particular.

Soon after Ernie's birth, when TF was carrying out his inspections in a particularly grim old warehouse, Chas ventured along the endless corridors in order to locate him to tell him that he was needed back at headquarters.

He came across his friend slumped unconscious, lips tinged blue, and had to revive him with a nip of brandy from the flask all firemen carried for emergencies.

'Has this happened before?' Chas asked anxiously, as TF sat up, still breathing torturously. TF could only nod in reply. Chas helped him to his feet, and steadied him with an arm around his shoulders.

'Take it easy. I was sent to fetch you to a meeting in the office.'

'You won't – say anything?' TF managed.

'No – but I think *you* should.'

'I can't – I could lose my job.'

'Does Emma know?'

TF shook his head. 'Emma has had so much to bear in the past, I couldn't bring myself to say, and now she is so happy with her babies . . .'

'These duties are too much for you on your own. You should request an assistant.'

'I promise you, I will . . .'

However, when it became apparent that TF was very unwell, he was asked to attend a medical examination arranged by the Committee of the LSC.

April 1874

TF's health was deteriorating fast and after further tests, they discovered he had valvular heart disease. Emma again sought the advice of the Evelina nurses. When the symptoms were described to her, of fatigue, shortness of breath, swollen feet and ankles, she realised that TF suffered all these. The erratic heartbeat was the only thing she had missed. She was advised to conceal her worries from her husband and to support him as best she could. 'You must be strong for him, and your family, Emma.' She vowed to herself that she would follow this advice, whatever the future held.

The LFEE committee expressed their sympathy and suggested he take a break from work for a month, which they would help to fund.

On hearing the news William wrote back by return of post: *Come here! Us have plenty of room for you all now.* The letter ended with his usual words, *All will be well, may God bless you, love from Will and Sarah.*

Chas made the travelling arrangements and accompanied them to the station. He saw them settled into their compartment with their luggage. 'I hope to see Jerusha this weekend,' he mentioned.

'Tell her,' Emma said impulsively, 'to give you an answer, yes or no – time is precious, Chas—'

'I know, I know . . . You're right, Emma.' He smiled to show he was not offended.

TF sat quietly by the window, looking grey and drawn. The walk along the platform had left him breathless, with a pain in his chest. Five-year-old Tommy sat by his father. He was a serious boy, old for his years, his parents thought.

Emma sat opposite, holding on to Ernie, now an active toddler. Immi, eight, was in charge of her little sister Alice, who at three needed persuasion to sit quietly.

Alice said in her carrying voice, 'I has wet my drawers!'

'Shush!' Immi whispered, seeing the expression on the face of the other occupant of the carriage, an elderly woman, who'd looked disapproving when the children clambered onto their seats. 'You are not to worry Mother,' Immi added. 'Sit tight.' She gave Alice a sweet to suck.

Emma was uncomfortably aware that Ernie too needed a change, in his case a fresh napkin. She had come prepared with damp flannels, a small towel in a bag, but had hoped to only use these for washing hands and faces after they had eaten their packed lunches. She would have to wait to see to the baby when their travelling companion alighted further up the line. They were facing a three-and-a-half-hour journey via Ipswich to Norwich. She was glad when TF opened the carriage window for fresh air. You couldn't blame the children, she thought, they were over-excited at their first train journey. So am I, she realised. My first holiday since Brighton, and I'm actually going back to Wymondham!

It was late afternoon when they arrived at Norwich and there was William, waiting on the platform for the train to stop in a cloud of smoke, with a wicker bath chair for TF, along with a porter and his trolley to convey their luggage to the wagon outside, where they would be reunited with Sarah.

'Here you all are, then!' William hugged them in turn. He looked older, Emma realised with a start, with greying hair and beard, but prosperous too, wearing smart clothes and a stove pipe hat, not a cap. 'It be good to meet you at last,' he said to TF, offering a strong arm to assist him into the chair. 'There you are, my boy – will you tek the babe on your lap?' He lifted Alice on to his broad shoulder, and Immi blushed, thinking of the damp drawers. Emma pushed the chair, with Tommy beside her, while Immi held on tight to her brother's hand. 'Not far,' William assured them. 'See, there's your Aunt Sarah awavin' from the wagon!'

Emma thought, he called Tom, 'my boy', Emma thought. that's a real Norfolk compliment!

There were bales of straw in the back of the smart wagon and these had been covered with sheeting to make less prickly seating. The chair was lifted on with TF still seated in it and the baby handed to Emma. There was a canvas cover overhead and two smart horses out front. They were quite overawed. The lettering on the wagon sides was impressive too: *William Wright & Sons.*

Sarah joined the family in the back. 'Yes, dear Will hev his own business with our two eldest sons. He be the proud owner of two of the latest steam threshing machines! He do hire them out to the local farmers. The lads do the driving. The hard times is past, I'm glad to say.' She looked with concern at TF. 'Us will do all we can to see you git well. There is a room ready downstairs for you, Emma and the little ones. Tommy and Immi can share a room upstairs, eh?'

'You are so kind,' TF said gratefully. 'Thank you for making us so welcome.'

William and Sarah had a much larger house, with outbuildings including a forge and a barn where machinery was kept. Here a sign proclaimed *William Wright, Engineer, Blacksmith & Threshing Machine Owner.*

'Your dreams came true!' Emma cried. 'How wonderful!'

Sarah nodded. 'We pulled together. I worked in the village shop, and now we own that too!' She ushered them inside. 'This is your room. Maybe you would like to rest before the meal, Tom?'

'Ten minutes will do. Someone has cooked a splendid dinner, judging by the aroma!'

'Talking of aromas: Ernie and Alice need a change of underwear first,' Emma said ruefully.

They went through into the dining room, where they were greeted by Jane, as her mother placed the joint of beef on the long table, which Emma was delighted to see was the one from the farmhouse. She noted that Jane was obviously expecting again, 'Oh Jane, you were a little girl like Immi when I saw you last! I hear Will has a grandson named after him?'

'That he hev,' Jane said shyly. 'He be hiding under the table!' The tablecloth shifted and a little boy crawled out and clung to his mother's skirts.

Sarah put in, 'Jane takes after you for cooking, Emma! And Immi looks like you, when you were her age!'

'Wait till you see the lads,' William said proudly. 'My older sons are taller than me and young Jeremiah, well, he's fifteen and still at school.' The family hoped it would be Jeremiah who'd return to the family farm one day.

The month in Wymondham passed all too quickly and the improvement in TF's health was encouraging. Emma was able to introduce him to her youngest sister Rebecca and her brother Jonathan, who visited soon after their arrival. Rebecca had recently wed Richard, a friend of Jonathan's from Wymondham. He was a station porter and like Keturah and Harry when they lived in Yarmouth, they took in lodgers to boost their income. Rebecca confided to Emma that she missed Keturah now she had moved away. 'I cried for her when she lost her little son, as I know you must have done, too, but have just heard that the dear girl is now expecting another baby. When her time is near she will stay with her friend Liza in Newbottle. She'll look after her.' Then she smiled, and Emma exclaimed, 'Oh, you are still Rebecca as I have always remembered you – you were such a happy child! You always kept the family spirits up.'

Jonathan had served his apprenticeship as a boot and shoemaker in Wymondham and married his boss's daughter when he was in his early twenties. Not long before Emma and her family visited Wymondham, the older man retired through ill health and moved away, while Jonathan took over the business. His wife had gone to help her mother with her ailing father, taking their eldest daughter with her. This left Jonathan as a single parent to their three younger children, there being just three years between them. He had abiding memories of his time at Wicklewood and the night terrors his younger brother had suffered there, when Joseph used to creep out of his bed to be comforted by the boy whose name had been changed to Ebenezer.

William confided to Emma that he considered Jonathan as another son, and worried about what would happen in the future. 'He say he think of me as his dad, and I wish I could have spared him and his little brother their time in the workhouse. They were there longer than the gals, poor lads.'

'You did all you could,' Emma said, seeing a tear in his eye.

'He say he wish he was called William after me, but some folk still refer to him as Ebenezer. He hev a troubled soul and us must not judge his wife for going away. She was so young when she married and the babes come so quick. Us cannot take sides. He be a good father to his children, but little Ellie do miss her mother.'

When Emma and TF were nearing the end of their stay, the family had good news. Keturah and Harry had

had another little son, named Herbert. William said, as he always did at both joyful and sad times, 'All is well.' And this time, it was.

While they were there, the children walked with their mother to Wymondham Abbey and placed flowers on the family graves. Emma introduced her family to the Reverend Eden and they all were invited to visit the vicarage where his wife was eager to see her too. The youngsters also loved calling in at Sarah's shop, which sold everything for a rural community, from mousetraps and mothballs to hand-carved bacon and haberdashery. Of course, the main attraction was a row of glass jars full of boiled sweets, which Sarah poured into the pan on the brass scales, then into deftly fashioned poke bags. Outside the shop hung tin baths and pails, baskets of crockery in straw and bags of kindling. 'If you ask for it, 'tis likely us hev it,' said Sarah, cutting a length of rope for Immi and Tommy to use in turn to skip back home. Alice threw a tantrum and had to be allowed a try as well.

Out in the garden there was the delight of the currant bushes, long established, with their strings of glistening red and black berries and the more elusive white ones, which looked like tiny pearls. They were protected by old net curtains but that didn't prevent the small birds from pecking their share. 'All God's creatures,' Sarah observed with a wry smile. Sarah made red currant jelly for them to spread on teatime bread and butter, and of course they sampled many of the tiny currants, relishing their sharp taste on the tongue. William fixed up a swing and a plank of wood fastened to two tree stumps for 'Seesaw Marjory Daw'. They hunted butterflies with home-made nets, watched caterpillars nibbling leaves and saw rabbits in the vegetable patch. TF sat out in the garden, resting in the shade of a sycamore tree, watching his children at play. He was feeling the benefit of the fresh air and being more involved with his family.

TWENTY

It was a family holiday they would never forget, and after all the sunshine and fresh air, the family returned to Southwark Bridge Road and an uncertain future. But at least there was one piece of good news, as Chas and Jerusha were at last engaged! Chas made the announcement in the cab on the way home.

'I told her what you'd said, Emma, and she said she'd been thinking along the same lines, especially since she'd learned her family were moving away from Sydenham, so she'd marry me! Then she *kissed* me – in front of the children in the nursery and their mother came in to find out why they were all jumping about and excited. Jerusha told her there and then that she'd help find her replacement and train her if necessary.'

But the good times couldn't last . . . TF's sterling service with the LSC was about to end. His employers were both sympathetic and realistic. TF resumed his wharf inspections but was not allowed to attend fires. He continued these duties for the next six months, but in November

1874 it became obvious that things would have to change. The family were no longer entitled to live on the station, as the accommodation was specifically for officers who were available for service at fires.

In view of his past exemplary service TF was given a grant to find accommodation for his family elsewhere. But despite the support of the Committee, this was a serious set-back for TF and Emma. They would have to move from the place they had called home for eight years.

'How can we manage without the usual allowances?' Emma worried. She was also aware that TF's health was deteriorating, and that he often needed the assistance of the loyal Chas to cover for him when he was struggling to carry on with his duties. This could not continue for much longer.

Sacrifices would need to be made, she realised. She would have to part with her maid, as the cutbacks would need to include her wages, and she would have to leave the smaller children with Immi while she was out searching for somewhere to live. This was proving almost impossible: there were places within the budget, but not suitable for a family and in the wrong areas, reminding her of Marylebone Passage, and past traumas.

A month later, came the bad news that TF and Emma had been dreading. The surgeon said that the disease had increased, and that he could not recommend TF continuing his duties. Chas replaced TF as Inspector of Wharves and, at last, stepped out of the shadow of his great friend. The appointment was well deserved.

Emma was aware that she would have to take charge of family affairs from now on. She was determined to save her husband from further worries, and to be cheerful for his and the children's sake. She came to a quick decision. 'You were so much better in Wymondham, Tom. We won't wait until March but will move there now.'

'We can't impose on William and Sarah. Where will we live?'

'Will told me they recently bought their old cottage, where they started their married life. He has been tidying it up – and he suggests we might like to go there. It's nothing like this place – it has poky rooms I recall, but oh, Tom, just to be near family would be such a comfort – what do you think?'

'I think,' he said after a long moment, 'I have the most wonderful wife in the world, and I would follow her to the ends of the earth. When can we go?'

'Immi and I will start packing right away,' she said.

Will and Sarah, with help from their family, had transformed the old cottage. The walls and ceilings within were freshly whitewashed, the old range in the kitchen cleaned and black-leaded, new curtains hung at the sparkling clean windows, and with a little manoeuvring, their furniture, delivered the day they arrived, was fitted in place. A daybed provided by

William and Sarah was placed by the living room window, giving TF a view across the garden. Sarah had made a pretty cover for it, with matching feather-filled cushions, so it could double as a family sofa. Jeremiah offered to pump up the day's supply of water before he went to school each morning, and his brothers set to clearing the overgrown garden and promised to maintain the privy.

There were only two bedrooms and TF insisted that for the moment he could manage the stairs with support from Emma or Immi. The second room was shared by Immi and Alice, who had young Ernie in with them, while Tommy swung up a rope ladder into his bed in the loft. 'Climbing the top rigging, Tommy, eh?' TF joked. Emma smiled, too. She thought, Wymondham is working its magic already!

That first night, as they settled down in bed, watching the firelight flickering on the walls, TF said suddenly, 'Emma – when we are just on the pension, how will we manage? Your family have been so kind, but we can't stay here and pay no rent. I expect they intended to let the cottage before they offered it to us, didn't they?'

'Shush, don't worry about that. I have an idea. I always wanted to be a nurse when I was younger, and now could be the right time for me to train as a local midwife. Immi could look after the children when I'm called out – she's a good cook and very capable. Tommy is a responsible lad and will help when he is not at school. You could see that Immi keeps up her studies too. I'm sure it will all work well. It is important that you rest, keep cheerful and, well, be *here* for us.'

He gave a long drawn-out sigh. Then he held her close. 'Dear Emma, what would we do without you?'

She was wakeful a long time after he had fallen asleep. There was much to mull over. The doctor was calling in the morning to assess TF's condition – his swollen legs were a worry. Also Reverend Eden had promised to visit shortly. She disengaged herself gently from TF's arms. If she could bring herself to ask the doctor, she must find out if normal married relations were possible, though she would not wish for an unexpected pregnancy in these circumstances.

Emma was already aware what was involved in becoming a local midwife. There were no lying-in hospitals nearer than Norwich, and learning midwifery in the countryside was achieved by working with an experienced midwife, alongside some teaching sessions from the local doctor. Doctors attended the well-to-do patients and the local midwives saw to the mothers who could not afford hospital care.

After the doctor's first examination of TF upstairs, Emma was anxious to talk to him out of earshot. Immi brought cups of tea to them in the living room, and then took Alice and Ernie for a short walk along the common. They were well wrapped up against the cold.

Emma sat facing the doctor over the table. He said, 'Mrs Meehan, as you are aware, your husband is a very sick man.

However, I will endeavour to do all I can for him, and I think it would help if the excess fluid could be drained from his legs. There is a procedure for this, which I would like to try, with your permission.' He supped his tea while waiting for her reply.

'Is it painful?' Emma asked anxiously.

'We have to cause discomfort, I'm afraid, in order to achieve relief.'

'He isn't one to complain,' Emma said. Her hands were shaking and her cup rattled in the saucer, but she added resolutely, 'What must be done must be done.'

'I'm glad you agree. Now, what was the other matter you wished to ask me about?'

'I must be the breadwinner now, doctor. I have told Tom, and he agrees – I wish to train as a midwife. Would you be willing to assist me in this?'

'My dear Mrs Meehan, I would, but you must also speak to the local midwife. However, I believe she could do with another pair of capable hands. So go ahead, but bear in mind that life will become more difficult as your husband's disease progresses.'

The standard treatment for oedema of the lower legs – dropsy caused by build-up of fluid when the legs can become enormous – at this time, and for almost a century thereafter, was the insertion of Southey's tubes which drained the fluid.

Although the doctor would have preferred TF to have this procedure done in hospital, Emma was adamant that she wanted him to be at home, with her support. The treatment would take at least a day, possibly two. TF bore all this with his usual stoicism, and the relief was great after the initial sessions.

The doctor observed, 'You will make a good nurse, Emma.' He was already a friend to the family and she had invited him to call her by her first name. It was arranged that she would begin her midwifery training after Easter, when the children were settled in their new routine.

Reverend Eden called once a week and spent time talking to TF and Immi, and Tommy took Alice to Sunday school at his suggestion. Sarah was always 'dropping by' with welcome dishes – 'I made too much as usual and thought of you!' – and William appeared with baskets of vegetables in season and newly laid eggs from Sarah's pet bantams.

Immi's cat Tip soon took to the countryside, and stayed out all night, bringing not-so welcome gifts to the kitchen, like wriggling mice, which Immi rescued and released away from the cottage garden. 'They'll come back,' Emma reminded her gently. They did, and Tip pounced.

TWENTY-ONE

1875

The highlight of their first year in Wymondham was the marriage of Jerusha and Chas, in the Abbey church in March. Emma and her family had shown their support by hearing the banns read in church. It was all very exciting, for Alice was to be a bridesmaid along with Ellie, her Uncle Jonathan's small daughter. Ellie's mother had not returned home, in fact the poor young woman was in and out of hospital at this time with 'nervous problems'. Ellie, it seemed, could not come to terms with this.

TF was to be best man and William would give the bride away. Sarah and her daughter Jane were providing the wedding breakfast, which would be in William and Sarah's house. Jerusha and Chas arrived there on their wedding eve, a bitterly cold day, and overnight there was a fall of snow.

William took Chas over to the cottage early on, as the bridegroom was not allowed to see the bride again before they met in church. He brought Emma and Alice back with him and then went to fetch Ellie. Then he and Jeremiah got busy with shovels and brooms to clear the path before the bride emerged next morning.

There was a lovely fire warming the big bedroom, and Emma and Jerusha were there together, while the small girls were playing downstairs with Jane's children. As Sarah said, 'Best dress them at the last minute, eh?'

'I hope you're wearing something warm, Ru,' Emma said anxiously. 'I could have offered you my wedding gown, as I did Keturah. I've not worn it again – since my waistline expanded.'

Jerusha said, 'Open the box, I know you want to! To my surprise I was given twenty pounds when I left my position in Sydenham. For nearly ten years – can you believe it? – faithful service! Anyway, I asked Anna to accompany me to a couturier in London, because she has such good taste. I hope you will approve of our choice!'

Emma lifted the jacket and skirt from tissue wrappings. 'Oh Ru, it's perfect!'

'I chose blue because Chas says it's my colour, and velvet, like you, for warmth.'

Emma laid the outfit on the bed, and said, 'Sit by the mirror; I must do your hair now.' She removed the hairpins and, after sprinkling a little eau de cologne on the brush, began to sweep the long locks back and upwards to twist into a topknot. The heavy fringe softened the effect, together with ringlets teased out either side of her face. 'The fringe suits you and is very fashionable.'

It was time for Jerusha to divest herself of her flannel wrapper and to shiver in her undergarments, despite the fire, before Emma helped her into the underskirt and then the overskirt, with its extravagant tiers of ruffles at the back. The tight-fitting jacket flared over her hips and there were wide cuffs at the wrists, sparkling with diamanté, and a high collar similarly embellished. The tiny matching hat, which would perch on the topknot of hair, remained in its box for the moment.

'Ru, what made you change your mind?' asked Emma.

'I suppose it was because I realised I was coming up to thirty-two and I had kept dear Chas waiting far too long.' She paused. 'Also, he told me what you said to him, Emma, and how time is precious.'

'It certainly is. I don't know how much longer Tom and I will have together, Ru, but the most important thing is that we *are* together.'

The door burst open and the little bridesmaids rushed in to show off their own blue velvet dresses with matching bonnets and ribbons tied under the chin. They were well-matched for size, though Alice's fair curls contrasted with her cousin's braided dark hair. Jane appeared behind them. 'Are you ready? Father hev put the pony in the shafts – he is going to take TF and Chas to the church first, so they don't get their boots muddy. Can you watch the girls up here?

Mother needs me to put the finishing touches to the table. My Tom will be round to see to our little ones, they would cause too much disturbance in the church!'

'Nonsense!' Jerusha said firmly. 'You must all come, or I won't go myself!'

Just then Ellie burst into tears, sobbing, 'My mama in't coming, Auntie Ru—'

Jerusha scooped her up into her arms – this wasn't the time to worry about her lovely dress – and said, 'Well, *you* are, my darling girl – I need you and Alice to help me down the aisle!'

Back in the cottage, TF and Chas were talking of this and that, remembering all the good times when TF was fit and well, and of their friends in the fire brigade.

'I requested a week off for a honeymoon and to my surprise, it was granted!' Chas said.

'We will be brothers-in-law, now,' TF realised.

'I couldn't wish to join a nicer family. If only things could be different for you.'

'I know you and Jerusha will be there for Emma and the children, when—'

'I can promise you, we will.'

Before any more could be said, Immi appeared with Tom and Ernie in tow, in their best clothes. 'Uncle Will is here,' she said.

Chas helped TF to his feet, then wound a warm scarf round his mouth against the cold air, and passed him his stick. William supported him on one side and Chas the other as they assisted him up into the trap. 'Jeremiah will collect and bring all of you in the wagon very shortly,' William told Immi.

The bride and bridesmaids were the last to leave the house with William. Jerusha wore a lovely cloak of midnight blue over her wedding finery, a gift from the bridegroom. Ellie insisted on sitting on her lap. Jerusha had a sudden inspiration. She wouldn't say anything until after the wedding, she thought. How could she put it to her new husband? 'Shall we ask Jonathan if we may take Ellie away with us? A holiday is just what she needs . . .'

A chair was waiting for TF after his slow progress down the aisle with Chas. The pews were fast filling up, but they followed tradition by facing the altar until the organist alerted them to the arrival of the bride. Chas wore his uniform at Jerusha's request, but TF wore his best suit and retained his overcoat, because there was little heating in the church. Emma watched anxiously from the front pew, hoping that Alice and Ellie would remember what was expected of them, after all, they were only four years old. Tommy was with his mother and Immi, but the smaller children sat in a row between Sarah and Jane. Emma suddenly recalled when she and Jerusha had followed Sarah on her wedding day, wearing the white muslin frocks her mother had made. It was summer, she thought wistfully, and *I still miss dear Mother, but I hope I am the woman she wished I would become . . . Father, too, they will both be in my heart and prayers always.*

Heads turned as the music swelled and the bride in her beautiful wedding gown must have been aware of the gasps of appreciation. Behind came the little girls, catching up now and then with a skip or two.

The Maid's Head Hotel was close to the great cathedral in Norwich, and the railway station was conveniently close by. The original building dated from the thirteenth century and over the years had encompassed other buildings already on site. The impressive facade faced the intersection of Tombland, Wensum and Palace Streets. There were eighty-four bedrooms and several staircases within the hotel and it was rumoured that Queen Elizabeth had slept there in 1587.

'I hope her ghost doesn't walk at nights,' Jerusha murmured in Chas's ear, as she didn't want to frighten an already nervous child.

'Oh, she would be too regal for that. But,' he whispered in return, 'it said in the brochure I sent for that if you sense a smell of musty lavender, you won't see her, but a maid is passing by.'

'Auntie Ru, where will I sleep?' Ellie tugged at her sleeve. They were standing in their bedroom with its big carved oak bedstead and brocade curtains.

'On this couch. It is called a chaise longue. The maid has provided pillows and blankets for you, see?'

'I hope it weren't the maid who smells of lavender!' Ellie said. Jerusha and Chas looked at each other, then burst out laughing, and Ellie joined in.

Maybe it wasn't the honeymoon night they'd dreamed of, but as Chas told Jerusha, 'There is plenty of time for that – I'm just glad you agreed to marry me at last!'

They spent two days sightseeing in Norwich, which Chas had not visited before, then it was off to London after Jonathan had collected his daughter. Ellie clung to Jerusha. 'Can I come and stay with you again?'

Jerusha kissed her tearful face. 'Of course you can! But now your family are looking forward to having you back home! You must tell them the story of the maid and the scent of lavender, eh?'

'Not so many musty smells in London now, I hope,' Chas said. 'The main sewage system is at last complete.'

'Thank goodness for that!' Jerusha said with feeling. 'I'm glad we will be in the Southwark Bridge area. 'The only drawback is, London will lose some of its history.'

The newlyweds were not required to share their large house, as Chas rose swiftly up the ranks in the brigade, but it seemed they were not to be blessed with children of their own.

However, when Jonathan decided to move to Cambridgeshire to set up in business, Ellie was upset and said she wanted to stay with her Auntie Ru and Uncle Chas in London. Jonathan had hoped she would stay on with him, but he decided she be allowed to do so.

Jerusha and Chas regarded Ellie as their foster daughter. They were a happy threesome. However, as Emma wrote to Jerusha: *Wicklewood has much to answer for in the problems of this family. It breaks my heart.*

When Jonathan's in-laws moved near their widowed daughter, Susanna, a dressmaker in Battersea, Ellie was reunited with her brother John and later with her sister, Ivy, who joined Susanna and her family after a while. Susanna was a handsome woman with a flamboyant personality, whose skills at design and dressmaking afforded the family a comfortable living. She had a young daughter of her own, named after herself, known as Little Susie.

Jerusha wrote to Emma:

I take the children out and about, yes, to the Crystal Palace, of course! Susanna gets on with her sewing meanwhile! Chas comes with us when he can. I wish you were able to visit us though!

I am excited because dear Chas is taking me to Trial by Jury *tonight! It is a new comic opera by Gilbert and Sullivan – you must have heard of them? Susanna has made me a special gown to wear – I wish you were here to arrange my hair! Ellie is staying overnight with Susanna. She wanted to come too, but we felt she is too young to be in an evening audience and although it is a comedy, we think the law is not a subject she would appreciate.*

Emma, Jerusha and Rebecca were also glad to hear that Keturah and Harry not only had the support of their friends, Eliza and Francis, but were in touch with Jane in Amble, where they had been invited to visit when possible. Keturah's letters were full of her little son and her hopes for a daughter in due course. *Henry says a girl will be Keturah after me! So, dear Becca is expecting a baby soon – they took their time.*

If Jerusha felt a pang that she had no such news to impart, she kept it to herself, but Chas knew she regretted the fact that she couldn't have a baby of her own. He gave her a special present for her birthday: a gramophone. It had an elaborate horn, and it was a pleasure not only to them, but to young Ellie, who loved music and singing. Another favourite entertainment was the magic lantern, a Christmas treat which they never tired of, despite the jerky movements of the actors.

Jerusha had nice clothes to wear now, not hand-me-downs from her employers as in the past. She and Ellie wore the latest fashions, created for them by Susanna, sometimes matching outfits. If Chas sometimes thought privately that she was spoiling the little girl, he kept it to himself, for he adored the child, too.

That evening, Chas came home to get ready for the opera with a surprise for Jerusha. She was sitting at her dressing table, regarding herself in the mirror. He bent over her, and gently moved her hair to one side and then kissed the back of her neck.

She smiled: 'That tickles!' she told him.

'You know you like it! I gather that Ellie has already been collected by Susanna?' he asked.

'Yes. Susanna says young John will entertain them with his Magic Lantern Show!' She turned her head and smiled at him. 'I hope he has more slides than we have!'

'I must just get changed,' he said, 'out of my boots for a start and wear my new shoes! We will be eating at the restaurant before we go to the Opera, of course. I have a surprise for you—'

'Whatever can that be?' she exclaimed. 'Don't tell me it's a box of new slides!'

'You will shortly find out!' He smiled.

Chas fastened the emerald necklace round Jerusha's neck. 'It's not my birthday!' she exclaimed, for the gift was a surprise. 'Or even Christmas!'

'I know, but I knew when I saw it in the jewellers that I had to buy it for my beautiful wife—'

'Chas! How good you are to me—' She gazed again into the mirror. The filigree silver chain gleamed in the gas light, and the jewels sparkled.

'How lucky I am,' he said quietly, 'To have married you, Jerusha.' He kissed the nape of her neck again, cleared his throat. 'I guessed right, it is a perfect match for your frock. I'll fetch your cape. Your carriage awaits!'

'Just a minute,' she put out a hand to keep him beside her, as she rose from her chair. They embraced and she said breathlessly, 'I love you so much,' before they exchanged a long, lingering kiss.

Jerusha thought happily, this is the perfect way to begin our evening out.

TWENTY-TWO

Wymondham, September 1876

After three months of assisting the experienced midwives, Emma attended her first birth, and following a question and answer session with one of the three local doctors, known as surgeons, she passed the test to Dr Hughes's satisfaction. He was the father of two little daughters himself and he was also the doctor who looked after TF and the one who had encouraged her in this venture. The births, he reminded Emma, would not always be happy events, however, he believed that Emma, having experienced tragedy with her first baby, was someone who could console and help in similar sad situations.

And he was right, Emma made great efforts to help her patients and always kept her hands soft and supple with home-made lotion. Often she'd ask for a hairbrush and soothe her patients with rhythmical strokes, and the exhausted new mothers would close their eyes and relax. 'You are so gentle, nurse,' a grateful new mother who had endured a lengthy labour, told her.

One morning, Emma received a very unwelcome request when the doctor told her that the matron at the workhouse urgently needed help with a difficult patient who was having a protracted delivery. The workhouse in Wymondham was a place Emma had no wish to visit, because of the memories it evoked of her younger siblings being sent there when the children were orphaned, however she did not hesitate to say she would go. 'The regular nurse is with her, but has other patients to see to, of course,' Dr Hughes said.

The assistant matron met Emma at the door when she arrived, bag in hand. She was very pleasant, but obviously worried about the young woman in labour. 'I'll just put you in the picture, Mrs Meehan, before I take you to the infirmary, where the patient is in the isolation ward,' she said. 'This young woman was sleeping rough in a local barn, and the farmer's wife, seeing her condition, contacted us and we took her in, because it was obvious she would soon give birth. I can't even tell you her name, and it seems she is a vagrant. She must have been wandering for some time and is in a filthy condition, which is why she is isolated, as we follow Nurse Florence Nightingale's rules here regarding cleanliness. Our nurse here is very efficient but she is young and unmarried, and the patient, well, she struck out at her – nurse was very charitable and put it down to the pain. She tried to give her a bed bath, but the patient would not allow it.'

'Have you any of the old portable baths? And a basin for me to wash my hands frequently?' Emma asked. 'We will need gallons of hot water, Lysol, soap, washing cloths and some big towels, a nightgown and a bristle hairbrush for our patient, as no doubt her hair will be tangled. If you provide a screen, she can be bathed in privacy. Hopefully, a bath will provide some relief from the pain and will help the baby on its way.'

'Will you need the nurse's help?'

'Only if I call out for it. Nurse should make the bed ready for the birth, so the patient can be returned there after she is cleansed. The doctor will be calling later after completing his rounds.'

The young woman in the isolation ward turned her face to the pillow when she became aware that the midwife was looking down at her. Gently, Emma took hold of her left hand and felt her pulse. The patient said nothing, but she tensed up as another pain struck her swollen abdomen.

'You may call me Emma,' she said to her. 'Don't be afraid, my dear, I will be with you until after you have had your baby. Would you tell me your name? Trust me, I am your friend.'

'Thyrza,' she managed; she had a local accent.

'That's a lovely name, from the Bible, isn't it? My sisters all have names like that, but I – well I was first called Emily, but then my mother decided on Emma. Have you come a long way from home?'

The girl turned her face then and opened her eyes. Emma was still holding her hand. 'It seems like that, but

I got lost and I – I slept rough, and then I couldn't ask the way because folk pretended not to see me.'

'Where did you wish to go?'

'I – was trying to find the Bridewell.'

'Prison?' Emma prompted her. 'To visit someone there?'

'He – laboured on the farm where I was a scullery maid. My mistress threw me out when she guessed I was – in trouble – and she shouted that I was a slut and he was a thief. She'd heard he'd ended up *there*, and said it was the best place for him – and me.'

'Did he know you were expecting a child?'

'Course he did, that's why he went off one night and took the master's cash box with all the wages in it.' The girl was weeping now, and she was struggling to sit up.

'We'll find him,' Emma assured her. 'But now, will you allow me to bath you behind that screen? You can't bring a baby into the world unless you are clean, you know, and especially . . .' She hesitated. 'When the baby is born you could pass on any infection and endanger both the baby and yourself. Have you heard of childbed fever? Not many afflicted mothers survive that.'

Emma's mentors had stressed the need for constant washing of her own hands because in earlier times, puerperal fever was sometimes caused by nurses unaware of the importance of this practice during childbirth. The death rate was high. Three days after giving birth the mother would develop a high temperature, severe headaches, abdominal pain and vomiting, which inevitably led to peritonitis and septicaemia.

'I'm sorry – I haven't been able to wash for days,' Thyrza whispered. This was obvious, for the dirt had become ingrained in places on her body.

'We will have to burn your clothes and the linen from this bed. Nurse will disinfect the mattress and you will have a nightgown provided after the bath. Can you manage the few steps to the bath?

It may not smell too nice because we use Lysol to kill the germs.'

Emma helped the girl out of bed and supported her across the room. She was wearing a protective apron, her sleeves were rolled up, but her hands were bare, and she would scrub them well before she delivered the baby. She was concerned to discover, when the clothes were discarded and wrapped in newspaper for the porter to take away and incinerate, that her patient had bow legs, meaning she had suffered rickets as a child, as many from poor families did. This, Emma had learned during her training, often meant distortion of the pelvis in women and was probably the reason for the long labour.

Once in the hip bath, Thyrza's head was carefully positioned so that her hair could be washed with a solution of softened green soap and rinsed in a bowl of clean warm water, as it was believed that hair could harbour germs and must not be washed in the bath water. A small towel was wound round the damp hair. Emma mouthed to the nurse, 'Not lousy, thank goodness.' Then she helped Thyrza from the bath, while the nurse held out a big towel to wrap her in. They sat her on a chair, and this time the girl did not demur when the nurse aided in the drying process and helped her into a voluminous flannel nightgown. Then Emma applied the hairbrush to Thyrza's hair, now restored to its normal colour. She was fair-haired and blue-eyed like many Norfolk girls, though she lacked their rosy plump cheeks. 'Norfolk dumplings' was not used in a derogatory sense, but affectionately.

Thyrza's face contorted as they laid her back in the clean bed; the mattress was covered with brown paper to protect it during the birth.

'The pains are regular now,' Emma observed. She went to change her apron and scrub her hands yet again. It was now early evening, and she thought of her children coming in from school. Was she expecting too much of her eldest daughter? At least it was still light, and they could play in the garden until supper time. Immi could cope.

The screen was now round the bed and a familiar voice signalled the doctor's arrival. 'You have done well, Emma, as always,' he complimented her.

'Nurse was very helpful, and the patient has accepted her now,' Emma said.

The warm bath had done the trick and the doctor advised Emma as with gentle massage, she carefully manoeuvred the baby's position in the birth canal. The only relief on offer to the mother was ether – a few drops on a cloth, pressed to the nostrils was administered to dull the pain. Chloroform was not generally used, and only by doctors, as midwives were not permitted to do so. However, when Thyrza became agitated and cried, 'No – no!' Emma couldn't help recalling another mother who refused this help, saying, 'I was told we have to suffer pain, that God punishes us like this because Eve sinned in the Garden of Eden. Our minister do tell us the pain make you love your baby more.'

'*I can't do it!*' Poor Thyrza screamed. Suddenly the baby emerged and Emma caught it.

Emma cried, 'You have, Thyrza, you have! Your little daughter is here!'

Later, as the exhausted new mother cuddled her baby in her arms for the first time, she asked Emma, 'Can I call her after you?'

Emma's back was aching, she hadn't eaten since lunch-time, but she smiled happily and said, 'Oh, I would love you to do so!'

'I'll take you home, Emma,' the doctor offered. He looked at Thyrza with her tiny baby. 'I will make enquiries at Bridewell about – what was his name?'

'Reuben, I never knew his surname – oh, thank you, sir,' the girl said.

Emma wondered if she would see the girl and her baby again; she would not be calling in daily for two weeks after the delivery as she did with her local patients, because the staff at the workhouse would resume care of their charge. As they left the workhouse, Emma said to the doctor, 'The man responsible may deny he knew her, of course.' The workhouse seemed to be a better place than it was when her siblings had been there, but she wondered what would become of the young mother and her baby.

Later she related the story of her day to Sarah, as some of it was not for the ears of young daughters.

'I'm glad you are seeing the workhouse in a better light,' Sarah said. 'But some things haven't changed. The unmarried mothers have to earn their keep, like the rest of the residents, and she won't have long with her baby. Babies are separated from their mothers and are looked after in a nursery. Some of them will grow up there, and, like your sisters, they will be found positions once they are old enough.'

'I didn't realise that,' Emma said. 'It's not right to take a child from its mother . . .'

'Some of them, Emma, are very young and not capable of caring for their babies,' Sarah said sadly. 'At least the children are well-fed and go to school while they are at Wicklewood.'

A month later, Emma heard that the girl had vanished from the workhouse, leaving her baby behind. Enquiries at Bridewell revealed that Reuben had been released from prison around the same time. Whether they were reunited, Emma would never know. 'Perhaps,' TF said, trying to allay her fears for Thyrza's safety, 'she didn't want to leave her baby behind, but did it for the best. She knew the baby would be well-fed and cared for.'

Emma never forgot Thyrza and she said a little prayer for her most nights.

Several months after she had started midwifery, Emma decided to embark on a venture suggested by her husband. She intended to hold a monthly meeting for first-time expectant mothers to encourage them to learn about childbirth and how to care for their babies.

'Try the Quakers, they have a meeting hall and they would be likely to let you have meetings there,' Sarah advised. 'Would an hour be long enough? TF doesn't see enough of you as it is.'

'You are right to remind me of that,' Emma replied, 'But he supports me, I know.'

The first meeting was on a Wednesday afternoon. There were about two dozen expectant mothers, and a wide spectrum of ages, from fourteen to fifty years old. The older woman certainly was not a first-time mother, Emma knew, and she sensed she had come to make trouble. Sarah came along to take notes as Emma spoke to everyone present before she gave her lecture, which TF had helped her to prepare.

It was a shock to both Emma and Sarah to discover that these young girls were often servants in more affluent households and had been taken advantage of either by their mistress's husband or by a son of the house. Most of these girls had been summarily dismissed for 'bad behaviour', but as Emma would say indignantly later, 'It is obvious who is to blame, but nothing can be done, and nothing can be said.' However, most of the girls returned home to careworn mothers and were loved by their families, who would take on the babies also, when they arrived.

'Their mothers are partly to blame,' Sarah whispered to Emma, when they were getting ready for the lecture. 'They are not aware of the facts of life, despite coming from big families. Did your mother tell *you*?'

'I have to admit, she didn't, but we learned a lot from the Bible, didn't we – all that *begetting*, eh?' Emma murmured ruefully.

She began the lecture with a question and answer session. 'Who knows where babies come from?'

The mothers-to-be looked at each other, but only one spoke up. 'I know how you get to expect a baby, but, miss, I dussn't know where it comes out.'

Emma was spared the explanation, because the fifty-year-old mother of six grown children spoke up. 'Where it went in,' she said baldly. The girls sat in embarrassed silence.

'Thank you, Annie,' Emma said.

Annie was not to be silenced. 'And don't you believe drinking a bottle of gin while in a hot bath will get rid on it cos it didn't do that for me!'

Sarah saw Emma's shocked expression and stepped into the breach. 'We know that the young mothers-to-be here this afternoon wish to keep their babies and look after them well. Listen to Emma, she certainly won't recommend gin.' She turned to the older woman. 'Perhaps you would like to help me make the tea now, so we can all have a cup after Mrs Meehan has given her talk.'

The woman followed her reluctantly into the kitchen. 'I didn't mean—' she began.

'I don't think that's true, and you too need help and advice, Annie. Emma will not judge you, she never does, so listen when she speaks to you, please. Now, how many cups do we need?'

Later, Annie would confess that it had been a shock to her to realise she was pregnant again just when she believed she was 'past it'. She said, 'I've got four grandchildren, after all.'

'Are you sure you are expecting?' Emma asked. 'You need the doctor to confirm it.'

The woman gave a sigh. 'I know . . . and I know it ain't a good thing to have a baby late in life like this . . .' She sighed again. 'And I had an almighty hangover after drinking mother's ruin.'

When Emma relayed all this to TF later, he said, 'I always felt, well, guilty when you told me we were having another baby, Emma. I know we welcomed every single one of ours, after losing little Gussie, but one day someone will work out how to limit the number of children a mother bears.'

'I looked on our children as a blessing, not a burden, Tom.'

'So did I, but then a father doesn't go through all that, as a mother does.' He paused, and then said softly. 'Could you manage on your own, dear Emma?'

'Of course I could! I work now, don't I? And I have Immi—'

'Her health may let her down, Emma, you must realise that. I know my time with you is limited, and I regret that, but our love will always be part of us.' The children had gone to bed. He held out his arms to her. 'Time to stop talking and put the light out.' Every moment together was precious now, he knew.

Annie didn't appear at the meetings after that, but Emma kept in touch with her, and after she was allowed at last to examine her, she was perplexed for she could not discern a heartbeat from the baby. She encouraged Annie to attend the surgery and waited for her while she was with the doctor. The terrible truth was revealed: Annie was not expecting a baby at all; she had a large tumour in her abdomen. It was unlikely anything could be done, and Emma had to console her as best she could.

Just before Christmas, Annie was taken to the infirmary, and passed away shortly afterwards.

Emma was invited to the wake, but Sarah warned her that the widower had spent the insurance money his wife had saved for many years on several bottles of gin. Within a few months Annie's husband had taken up with a younger woman and moved away, and Emma realised that what had seemed an unlikely friendship was no more.

She remembered Annie's blunt answer to the question about where the baby would emerge, and what one of the young mothers had said when she attended her confinement. 'At least I know that the baby isn't coming out of my belly button, as most of us thought before Annie put us right!'

At the cottage, TF now slept on the daybed at night as well as during the day. If Emma arrived home late after attending a confinement, she shed her shoes and top clothes and joined him for a cuddle. This could lead to something more. It was not a passionate experience, as in the earlier days of their marriage, but a comfort to them both. After a precious half hour, she would reluctantly leave him and make her way up the steep stairs to the loneliness of what had been their shared room. Before she climbed into bed, she checked on the children. Immi would whisper, 'Are you all right, Mother?' and Emma kissed her beloved daughter and said softly, 'Yes, I am. See you in the morning.'

TWENTY-THREE

1878

A year after she began her work in Wymondham, Emma discovered that she would need a midwife herself in a few months' time.

Charles Edwin was named after their two good friends, but known as Ted. Emma worked right up to the day he was born, and it was a quick and easy birth as Ted was not as large as Tommy and Ernie were when they came into the world. Emma's colleague had been called to another patient, so it was a wide-eyed Immi who looked after her mother until her Aunt Sarah arrived. Immi was thirteen, but capable, as Emma had been at her age.

'He's so small, Mother,' Immi said, cradling the baby in her arms as Sarah made Emma comfortable.

'I'll take him downstairs – very carefully, I promise,' Sarah said, 'to show him to his dada.'

TF sat on the edge of the daybed. He was unable to climb the stairs, but he had listened for the call. 'It's a boy!'

Sarah said, as she laid the baby on the pillow beside him. 'He has your fair hair – see?'

He gently smoothed the baby's still damp flaxen head. 'Mine is more silver these days, as you will have noticed. Alice will be pleased he takes after her – is he smiling, or was that a grimace?'

The door burst open and Alice, Tommy and Ernie rushed in. 'Don't frighten the baby!' Sarah warned them. 'He's only one hour old!'

'Where's Mother?' Ernie demanded, his lower lip trembling. He was five years old and had just started school, and would rather have been at home with his parents and Immi.

'Mother is resting. Immi will be down to make your tea, and then you can see her.'

'What's the baby called?' Alice asked.

'Ted,' his smiling father replied. He lifted the baby, kissed the top of his head and passed him back to Sarah. 'Time to take him back to his mother. Tell her I love her and will see her soon. I wish I could get upstairs, but the doctor has forbidden it.'

'Ted has the same colour hair as me!' Alice cried triumphantly. 'He's not ginger like Ernie!'

Fortunately, Ernie didn't hear that, he was already on his way upstairs to see his mother. She welcomed him with outstretched arms. 'Oh, my dear boy – have you seen your little brother?'

He climbed into bed beside her, shoes and all, his little face as red as his hair. 'He in't big enough to play football with me,' Ernie said dolefully, tears rolling down his cheeks.

She gave him a kiss. 'He'll grow, you'll see,' she said, ruffling his wiry curls.

However, Ted would always be the 'little 'un' of the family, with a similar temperament to quiet, dependable Tommy, his older brother. Ernie would later be head and shoulders taller than both of them – big, bluff and hearty – but all the boys were fiercely protective of their mother as they grew up.

Six weeks later Emma was back on call as a relief midwife and Immi, with support from TF, was looking after her tiny brother and the older children. Emma came back at intervals to feed Ted. When she was putting down her bag in the hall one evening, she overheard a conversation between Immi and her father in the room beyond.

'If anything should happen to me,' TF said, 'I know you will look after your dear mother and comfort her, Immi.'

'I promise you, Dada, I will,' Immi replied.

Emma wiped her eyes and hoped they would not realise she had heard what was said. She plastered a smile on her face and opened the door, just as Ted woke and cried for her attention. Immi lifted him up and brought him to his mother.

She is our angel, Emma wrote to Jane in Amble later.

It was a shock when Immi experienced her first epileptic fit. Emma was out, but fortunately for TF, Billie Betts, an elderly neighbour who had worked at Browick Bottom Farm in the old days, was there. Billie enjoyed lively discussion of local and world affairs with TF. He could neither read nor write, but he had a thirst for knowledge and a dry wit, which TF appreciated. 'What's old Disraeli up to then?' Billie would enquire. The Liberals had been defeated in 1874 and East Anglia was a Liberal stronghold. When the fire smoked, he'd joke: 'Us dussn't send little boys up with a brush – that do let Tommy off.' He was referring to the Factory Act regarding child labour that was now in force, and soon all children would be entitled to a basic education. 'No more signing with a cross,' as the old man observed.

When Immi collapsed, Billie had just arrived, and he was able to deal with the situation, extracting the wailing Ted from her arms and passing him to his father, then moving things, so that Immi lay in a clear space, before he alerted the doctor, who came around as soon as he could. Billie said, 'I jest did what I allus did when a poor old cow collapse.' TF did not repeat that remark to Emma!

By the time the children came home from school, Immi was recovering from the fit. 'Why don't you take the young ones to Aunt Sarah's shop and buy some sweets,' TF suggested to Tommy. He kept a little bag of pennies under his pillow for that purpose. 'Then ask if you can go home with your aunt when she closes up. William will bring you back later.'

Emma was distraught when she heard what had happened. 'I should have been here for Immi!'

Immi, sitting by her father, was pale, but otherwise seemed normal and insisted, 'Mother, I'm all right, really I am. Doctor said so, didn't he, Dada?'

'He also said' – TF sounded anxious – 'we may be expecting too much of Immi, Emma.'

'Oh, Immi darling, do *you* feel that?' Emma asked. She sank down on the seat beside them.

'Mother,' Immi said firmly, 'doctor also said that apart from this, I am very fit, so don't worry!'

'Perhaps we could get Jane to look after Ted. Would that help?'

'Only if Jane came here and brought her little ones with her. When Tommy is home from school, he looks after Ernie and Alice. They've gone around to see Aunt Sarah and will be back later.'

'What a lovely family we have, Tom!' Emma said gratefully. 'Don't get up, Immi; I'll make the tea after I put Ted in his cot.' She thought, I must control my emotions, be cheerful, but I can't give up my job, we need the money. Immi really is our angel.

Despite her busy life these days, Emma still kept in regular touch with her family, who seemed to be far and wide, as she put it with a sigh, but a letter on the doormat from one or the other, gave her a good feeling as she opened it to learn their news. She didn't reveal her worries regarding TF for, she thought, most of them had problems of their own. When writing to Jane in Amble, she mentioned that her sister Keturah, who had recently had a new baby, wished she could manage a holiday with her husband and family. Jane responded to this by inviting Keturah, Harry and the children to spend a week with them in August: *The air is so clean here, and it is a lovely place to spend a holiday. Do come! You will be welcome – the girls would love to see you too!*

Keturah, 1879

Keturah was busy then making new clothes for Herbert and little Keturah for the holiday. When the family arrived in Amble, Jane, Rob's sister-in-law, who had trained as a dressmaker, was duly impressed by her efforts, examining the fine stitching and commenting, 'You have a real gift Keturah, especially as you cut patterns to your own designs.'

The house in Amble was near the sea, and there was plenty of room for the visitors. Rob was home for a couple of days and he and Harry immediately took to each other, and the two men went fishing off Coquet Point. Keturah and Jane relaxed on the beach with the baby, while Jane's nieces amused Herbert by building a sandcastle good enough for the queen, as Jane remarked, and read to him from a picture book.

Keturah and Harry had recently moved to Jarrow, and Keturah, breathing in the good sea air, remarked, 'How lucky you are to live in such a place, Jane.'

'I'll never leave here,' Jane said. 'I miss my sister still, and sometimes I regret that I never married and had children of my own, but I am so fortunate to have the girls with me. Rob leaves all the decisions to me, and I hope I am doing a good job.'

'Oh, you are, Jane! What would Rob have done without you?'

'He would have married again, perhaps. Oh, not to me – we get on well enough, but he gave his heart to my dear sister.' She changed the subject. 'I always hoped Emma would visit here one day, but I know that's not possible at present. How is TF?'

Keturah sighed. 'He is very frail. Emma is still doing her midwifery, and Immi is a wonderful daughter and does all she can to help.'

'It is strange, isn't it, that Emma's daughter and Margaret's both have epilepsy. These things seem to run in families, don't they?'

'I do hope not.' Keturah said a silent little prayer just in case, although she realised that it was unlikely as it must have come from Rob and TF's family.

'What can we use as a flag on the castle turret?' Lizzie asked, shaking sand from her skirt.

'How about this sweet paper?' Her aunt had collected the wrappers from the home-made fudge in her bag to take home as rubbish.

'It's sticky,' Lizzie said. 'But it'll do, thank you.'

Jane was busy sketching on a little pad she kept in her bag. She would send the picture in her next letter to Emma, she decided, so she could see how much her sister and her children were enjoying their holiday.

Emma, when she read this, decided immediately to find a small frame for the drawing. She thought wistfully again of how she wished she had met Margaret, Rob's wife, because they had a lot in common, but Jane had become a real friend, too.

TWENTY-FOUR

It was a shock to Emma to realise the following spring that she was pregnant again. She kept quiet about it for as long as she could, although of course she had to tell the doctor eventually. He could not persuade her to give up work, because as she told him, 'It is our only income! I know I will have to give up soon, because my husband is failing fast, but every little helps . . .'

In July 1879 Emma was in the seventh month of her pregnancy and still attending confinements. It had been a quiet day with just routine morning visits to new mothers and she was looking forward to an afternoon with TF, young Ted and Immi before welcoming Tom, Alice and Ernie home after school, and providing a tasty supper.

It was a sultry day and thunder crackled in the distance. It looked like there was going to be a summer storm so she closed the window.

'Sit down,' TF told her. 'Rest while you have the chance.'

There came an urgent rapping on the front door and Immi went to see who it was with Ted hanging on to her skirts.

'Tell Nurse to bring her bag – my lass hev need of her,' the man said. He had been shovelling manure in the farmyard when his wife told him to 'Git Emma – *now*!' Immi stepped back as the smell from the man's clothing and boots was overpowering.

Emma had heard the farmer's loud voice, and she came out into the hall with her bag, which was always packed ready for emergencies. 'It's all right, Simeon,' she said. She bestowed quick kisses on Immi's cheek and on Ted's blond head. 'Sorry, but I have to go.'

Emma got there just in time to deliver a tiny baby, but then, much to the young mother's surprise, a second, even smaller baby literally followed on 'her sister's heels' as Emma put it later.

It was a shock to Emma too. She braced herself for anxious hours ahead. Thank goodness it isn't winter, she thought, these twin babies have more of a chance in summer. She turned to the worried father. 'Will you fetch the doctor, Simeon? You should have his opinion, but the babies have good lungs it seems.'

The tiny girls were side by side in the crib, which their grandmother made ready even as they were born. As Emma swayed on her feet, the doctor arrived and came swiftly across the room to steady her. 'Emma, go home now, you look all in. When I have finished my examination here, I will ask the other midwife to take over.'

'Thank you, nurse,' the patient called, sitting up and looking proudly at her babies.

Emma arrived home after 10 p.m. that night and found Immi still up and talking to her father, while sponging his forehead with cool water. 'Dada felt feverish, Mother. I thought it might help. I propped up his poor swollen legs on a pillow. Do you want a cup of tea?'

'No thank you, dear, I just want to get to bed. You must get some sleep too.'

'I'll take the bowl away and get Dada some fresh drinking water first,' Immi said. 'Call me if you want me.'

Emma undressed, had a cursory wash, murmured a quick prayer, and climbed into bed. She was glad that William had moved the double bed down here from their bedroom; she wasn't up to going up those steep stairs herself. TF's eyes were closed; the cool sponging had sent him to sleep. She was so weary she soon succumbed to sleep herself.

She woke after half an hour, aware that her waters had broken. She stumbled out of bed and pulled the towel from the washstand rail to spread over the damp patch. The pains began – as one receded, another gripped her. She stumbled to the door, but it opened before she reached it, and Immi was there, with a lighted candle in its stick. 'Mother, let me help you back to bed—'

Emma managed to pull herself up by the door knob. 'No – I don't want to disturb Dada.'

'Shall I fetch Aunt Sarah? Is it the baby?'

'Don't . . . leave me.' Emma managed, clutching at Immi. Her daughter put the candlestick down.

'I must light the lantern, Mother. Then I'll try to make you comfortable – sit on here.' She guided her to the daybed, which was now used as the family sofa.

'Cover it with some of the newspapers I've been collecting, then go – to the linen press – and fetch all the towels.'

Tommy came downstairs, rubbing his eyes. 'What's up?' he asked his sister.

'Mother is about to have a baby—'

'What, another one?' Tommy had not been aware his mother was pregnant.

'Yes! Put your coat on over your nightshirt and get your boots from the scullery – you can't stop to clean all the mud off! Then run down to Aunt Sarah's and ask her to come, please! And try not to disturb the young ones; we don't want *them* coming downstairs!'

Sarah arrived with Tommy and told them that William had gone to the midwife's home and found she was out on another confinement. 'Us can manage – I hev delivered a baby before – when they come early, they usually come quick.'

She told Tommy to go back to bed and to listen out for the children upstairs and Immi that she would be glad of her assistance. Amazingly, TF slept on and they tiptoed about by the light of the lantern. 'Get the linen basket, use a flat cushion and flannel pieces for sheets,' whispered

Sarah. She poked the coals in the range and set a second kettle to boil.

The baby, another boy, did 'come quick' and Sarah quickly wrapped him, unwashed, in one of the flannel pieces. She swung him in her arms until he gave a faint cry, then a stronger one. 'Wipe his eyes and nose very gently with a bit of cotton waste,' she instructed Immi. Then she placed the swaddled baby in Emma's arms. 'I must see to your mother now. You can fetch me a bowl of warm water, a clean towel and a big basin.' The latter was to catch the afterbirth, which must be left attached to the umbilical cord, until the midwife or doctor arrived. By the light of the lantern, Sarah saw that Immi's lips were trembling. She was near to tears; it had all been too much for her. 'I can manage now; you must get some sleep, my dear. Ah, a knock on the door – let the midwife in before you go upstairs.'

The baby was examined, the cord was cut, and he was laid gently in his improvised bed. The midwife said quietly to Sarah, 'You hev done well. But I don't hold out much hope. He is very small.'

TF stirred and called out, 'Who is here? Where is Emma?'

Sarah went over to him and sat on the side of the bed, 'The baby hev come. It is a boy. Hev you a name?'

They both started as they heard Emma's voice. 'Frank . . . Herbert Frank.'

'Can Emma come to bed?'

'She should stay near the baby tonight and he must be kept warm by the stove,' Sarah said. She sighed. 'Shall us all have a nice cup of tea? Then I must get off home to my William.'

Somehow, the tiny baby clung to life. His skin was too delicate to wash, his finger and toenails were not yet properly grown, his hair sparse, his eyes hardly ever open. Emma had to clean him carefully with olive oil. He was still swaddled; the baby clothes she had sewn would have swamped him.

Emma had to express milk every two hours and try to get the baby to take it almost drop by drop from an apostle egg spoon. Then she laid him back gently in his cocoon in the basket close to the warmth of the range and sang him snatches of lullabies. TF, propped up by pillows in bed to help his breathing, tried one day to whistle a familiar tune, and as the sound faded when he became exhausted, Immi joined her mother on the sofa and encouraged her to sing 'If I were a Blackbird'. Little Frank opened his eyes fully for the first time and appeared to be listening.

TF closed his eyes and remembered those long-ago days at sea, when he nimbly climbed the top rigging for the first time. Emma rested her head on Immi's narrow shoulder. The girl was fourteen now, with responsibilities beyond her years, just as Emma had had herself, at that age. She was growing into a beautiful young woman, her mother thought. She sighed. With problems she didn't deserve.

'Frank is a fighter, Mother,' Immi observed. 'He'll be a hero like Dada.'

Emma was unable to return to her work. TF needed her to be at home, as much as the baby did. Sarah and William were there for them all, and Jane would mind the shop when Sarah was called on to help at the cottage. William and his boys cut wood for the fires which must be kept burning bright, especially when autumn turned into winter.

Billie Betts looked in on TF most days. Often he had a rabbit for the cooking pot, or a sack of potatoes which he had grown on his vegetable patch. One day, TF had something important to entrust his old friend with. It was coming up to Christmas and then it would be Emma's fortieth birthday in the January. He wanted to give her a special present. 'Emma must not know,' he whispered. 'I have a couple of guineas put by.'

'A ring, you say,' Billie paused for thought. 'Somethin' special. There in't a jewellery shop in Wymondham, but I could try old Perfitt's Fancy Repository on Town Green.'

'I thought he was a watchmaker,' TF said.

'That's so. But he hev a few things to tempt the womenfolk. Some of it was once in pawn. He always help them in need, they say.'

'I want something dear Emma can remember me by, Billie.'

'I'll see what I can do,' Billie promised.

Emma was not expecting a present at Christmas, or much of a celebration, but Sarah and William were determined to make sure they made it as good as they could for the children's sakes. They provided the Christmas dinner and there were wrapped parcels by every plate on the table set near TF's bed. He watched the excited youngsters opening their gifts and managed a smile, although he was unable to eat anything. He waited to see Emma open her parcels after the children had uncovered all theirs. William had made wooden toys for the little boys and Sarah had knitted woollen gloves and scarves for them all, as well as sewing pretty aprons for Immi and Alice.

Emma left the little box until last. When she opened the lid, she saw a ring nestling on a cushion of black velvet. TF had guessed well; the narrow gold band could be worn above her wedding ring. There were two lovely stones, turquoises, set round with tiny diamonds. The message inside read: *This Forget-me-not ring is for my beloved Emma, with all my love from Tom.*

TF died two weeks later, in January 1880. Billie Betts, his faithful companion, was by his side as Emma had gone to church for the first time since Frank's birth with the older children, while Sarah looked after the baby in her home.

'His poor old heart give up I reckon,' said Billie.

As Billie was the only person present, this was noted on the death certificate, naming him as 'informant'. TF was forty-two years old.

The family rallied round and he was buried in the grounds of Wymondham Abbey. The pall-bearers were led by William and his sons, along with Chas and Jonathan. Rob was unable to attend, but from his side of the family, there was his Irish Uncle Pat with his son from Woolwich and his Aunt Anna from Birkenhead. The railways had made such journeys possible, although Keturah and Harry were unable to come, as Keturah was heavily pregnant. They were all reminded of the old saying: *As one goes, another comes into the world.*

Emma was supported by Jerusha and Rebecca as well as Sarah and her daughter. Chas represented the LSC. Tributes were paid by family and friends. 'He was a courageous man – a good husband and father.'

There was one letter in particular which made Emma think of happier times, when she and TF met in Kensington and walked in the gardens with Anna, Frances and young Nan.

Frances wrote to say:

We are all sad to hear the news and are praying for you and your family, dear Emma. I often think how you befriended a rather lonely girl and how we walked in the gardens. I thought TF was so handsome and the perfect match for you – I was privileged to be your bridesmaid.

You will see that I have a new address: after my father moved to Chislehurst with Rosalie and Adelaide and me, he became semi-retired. My eldest brother is now a practising solicitor back in Kensington, and he and his wife, Jessie, have three children. My younger brother is also married and is a vicar, no less! He and Barbara have two children. Maria is still in China. Anna keeps in touch with us and Nan.

Yes, I am still a 'Miss' but if someone comes along . . .

Your loving friend,

Frances.

Why is it always January and bitterly cold at these times? Emma thought, as they walked to the graveside. William had his strong arm round her shoulders, which was a comfort. The children had remained in the church with Jane and her young ones. Suddenly, as they stood round the grave and Reverend Eden began his committal speech, a shaft of winter sunlight haloed the small crowd of mourners. Emma said to herself, Tom can rest in peace here.

Later, Emma received 'under £200' in his will, and used this money for a striking memorial stone erected over his grave. On this was engraved an entwined spray of forget-me-nots. Perhaps some saw it as a happy release from his suffering, and the end of a love story, but Emma would perpetuate his memory in family stories to the end of her own long life. She packed away the precious mementoes of TF's life into his mother, Isabella's, trunk, along with the out-dated clothes and the pink woollen bootees Frances had made long ago for little Gussie. His certificates, naval log books, his references from the fire brigade, family pictures, his Crimean War medals, his gold watch and Albert chain.

A letter from the Reverend Robert Eden of Wymondham, was read to the LSC committee . . .

> *. . . asking on behalf of Mrs Meehan, who is left with six children, for a continuance of the pension which ended on 31st January, granted to her husband Mr Foreman Meehan who died on the 10th of January. Resolved that Mrs Meehan be granted the allowance given to her husband for the period of six months from the present time.*

The LSC were greatly supportive, and the pension continued for the six months. As Emma said proudly, they recognised her husband's qualities and he was privileged to have worked for them.

Kind William had an idea and acted upon it. He told Emma, 'Immi has always wanted a dog, and now her old cat is gone, us would like to give her one. It will be company for her in the house when you feel you must return to your work.'

So, the first of a line of pug dogs joined the family and Immi immediately named him Puglet, which is what pug pups are called. This was an expensive present, for it was a popular breed among the upper classes.

Puglet had a comical face and was an intelligent little fellow; he made the small, sad children laugh at his antics and was included in all their games. Emma thought that he was capable of guarding them if they were out walking and were approached by an unsavoury character, though this was unlikely in this friendly place. Puglet was Immi's dog, they all knew that, and he developed an awareness of when she was about to have a fit. He would bark to alert the family, and then stay beside his mistress until help arrived. The little dog was a comfort to Emma too, and she 'confided' in him when she returned from a night call after the children were in bed, just as she had whispered to her much loved spaniel, Fly, when a child herself. 'Oh, Puglet, I miss my Tom so much, but at least I have you to greet me when I come home.'

After some thought, Emma discussed her situation with her family and Reverend Eden and decided on their advice to begin a new way of life in Beccles as the landlady of a boarding house. Reverend Eden had a suitable large property in mind, in the centre of the main thoroughfare, which had been the home of friends in the ministry who had been tragically killed in a train crash. The house had been empty for some years, but was available for rent, complete with furnishings. It was the spur Emma needed to become independent once more and to be able to provide a good home for her children.

She would be sad to leave William and Sarah, as they had looked after her family so well, but she felt she was a burden to them, though they insisted she was not. They were also bringing up their grandson, young William, since their daughter Jane had been widowed, but remarried a friend of her late husband, and had started a new family. William was considering turning over the threshing machine business to his elder sons, and while waiting for an opportunity to arise for a new tenant at Browick Bottom Farm, he intended to help Sarah in her shop. He continued to be listed in local trade directories as 'Engineer and Shopkeeper'. Ten years later this would be amended to Farmer, Machine Owner and Shopkeeper. Jeremiah was engaged to be married and was learning the ropes on a friend's farm in preparation for the time when there would be Wrights again at Browick Bottom Farm.

Emma, if she seized this opportunity, would be near Rebecca, whose husband Richard was well-established as a railway porter at Beccles Station. They were a happy couple who doted on their daughters, Beatrice, Bertha and baby Bella.

Emma twisted the turquoise forget-me-not ring on her finger. Tom would say do it! she thought. Her lower lip trembled, but she was resolute. Now it is just me and the children. I am both a mother and midwife, and my work will help us all survive.

TWENTY-FIVE

Hungate, Beccles, 1881

Rebecca was waiting for them inside the three-storied house in Hungate, Beccles, when they arrived. She lived just around the corner and her warm greeting was uplifting.

'You and Aunt Becca look like twins,' Immi commented. Emma was flattered by this, as she was six years older than her sister. But it was true: they were both small in stature, dark-haired, and had inherited their mother's high cheekbones, as well as Sophia's quick intelligence. Rebecca, despite spending part of her childhood in the workhouse, was always cheerful and positive. Emma had been the same until her tragic loss, and now she determined to be so again, for TF's precious legacy to her was her six children.

A century or more ago Hungate had been a modest lane, but since the advent of the railway it had developed into a busy thoroughfare with a mixture of ancient, picturesque properties and newer business premises. It was now known as London Road. It seemed very noisy to the new residents after the country lanes around Wymondham.

The cavalcade of horse-drawn carriages which passed constantly along the road to Norwich, Lowestoft or en route to London, just over a hundred miles distant, were well catered for by the local blacksmiths and coachbuilders, and travellers often broke their journey at one of the boarding houses and inns along Hungate. Emma's intention was to provide accommodation here.

Beccles, a market town on the edge of the Norfolk Broads, had the river Waveney at its heart. From Saxon times herring fishing had flourished there, but was now in decline. The residents were proud of the magnificent St Michael's Church, overlooking the river. An imposing tower had been built on the 'wrong' side of the church, as it was considered unsafe to position such a large structure on the far side because of the proximity to the cliff. The church was linked with famous names – Horatio Nelson's parents were married there in 1749, and during the same era the Suffolk poet George Crabbe wed his wife there. Another name connected with Beccles was Sir John Leman, a Lord Mayor of London in the seventeenth century, who had once been a tradesman in the town and had a big influence on its prosperity.

Emma and her family were not far from the congregational church with its new school room, where the late Reverend Stacey had been pastor. The Reverend Eden at

Wymondham had warmly recommended Reverend Stacey's successor, Jonathan Calvert, so Emma decided to attend this church with her family.

After the cottage in Wymondham, where they had lived for five years, the sight of the cavernous rooms in their new home, where greying dust sheets disguised what lurked beneath, made Emma's heart sink. She looked up at the cobwebs, which festooned the rafters, and sighed, but Rebecca tackled them with a broom until the carter arrived and unloaded all Emma's furniture higgledy-piggledy into one of the sitting rooms.

Emma lamented, 'I had been looking forward to living in a big house again but, oh, Becca, not somewhere as neglected as this! Where are the furnishings they promised?' She warmed her hands at the fire, which Rebecca's husband had lit first thing before going to work. 'I'm grateful to Richard for sweeping the chimney though,' she added.

Rebecca uncovered a faded tapestry chair. 'You should have seen the soot . . . two sacks full. Sit down. You look worn out already, Emma. This motley collection was donated by the good folk of the local church. I was told that the Reverend Stacey and his wife auctioned their belongings before they left the house six years ago for the mission field, but perished soon after in that awful train crash at Thorpe.'

'I tried not to think of that when we boarded the train this morning. It was good to see Richard waiting on the platform at the other end. Three rooms downstairs, besides kitchen and scullery; five bedrooms and five attic rooms. How on earth can we manage to make a home here? Let alone take in boarders.' Emma sighed. 'You mustn't overdo it either, Becca, you're a nursing mother, remember.'

Rebecca blushed. 'It won't stop me doing my bit. Richard's mother enjoys looking after the baby, the girls are at school all day, and I will be glad to come in and help for as long as you need me. I can always pop home to feed little Bella. We get on well, don't we? I know you can't afford to pay me at the moment, and of course, I don't expect it, but when you are looking for permanent help, well, put my name at the top of your list, eh? And with regard to the house, there's a good kitchen for a start. The stove is hot and Immi is making a large pot of tea. Gas lighting, no smelly oil lamps and wicks to trim. Tom is taking the little 'uns for a grand tour – can't you hear the thumps from overhead?'

Emma managed a smile. 'There are the beds still to carry upstairs.'

'Richard and his mates will be along after work, they said leave the heavy stuff to them. Tom will need to get busy at the pump in the yard. You have a right of way to that and to take water. It belongs to your neighbour.'

'I hope we don't get snow or the pump is bound to freeze. Tom should fill all the pails under the sink tonight, just in case.' Emma heaved a sigh. 'Why did we choose *January* to move?'

Immi came into the room. She looked quite grown-up at fifteen, with her hair piled high and one of her mother's white aprons wrapped round her slender frame. Emma accepted the steaming tea gratefully, warming her cold hands round the cup. Puglet waited for his saucer of tea and then lapped it eagerly.

'Make sure he goes out in the yard after that, we don't want any puddles,' Emma reminded her daughter. This was likely to happen when the little dog was excited.

'The kitchen is well equipped, Mother,' Immi said. 'We needn't unpack our boxes yet. Thank you for the scones you made, Aunt Becca. I called the children – they must be hungry by now. We had breakfast so early.'

'Thank you, dear. I must go after the tea – I have to meet the girls from school and get something from the grocers for their supper,' Rebecca said as the children rushed into the room.

'Guess what we found,' Tom said to his mother. He was twelve and had decided to be known as Tom, not Tommy, after his father died.

'Spiders?' she suggested.

'No! A four-poster bed with curtains all round it.'

'No one inside, I hope?'

'Of course not! We pulled the curtains and they were so rotten they tore a bit – don't be cross, will you?' Alice interrupted. She wouldn't tell tales about her little brothers jumping up and down on the sagging mattress. At ten she was supposed to be sensible like her older sister, or serious like Tom, but she was more like Rebecca had been at that age – jolly and high-spirited. Her aunt winked at her.

Ginger-haired Ernie dusted his grubby hands on the back of his trousers before Alice, handing round the scones, would permit him to put his hand in the tin.

'Can us boys sleep in that bed tonight, Mother?' Ernie asked Emma, prodding his small brothers, Ted and Frank, to agree. Ernie was seven and the boys were two and a half and eighteen months old.

'Certainly not! Your own clean beds will be ready later. You three boys will have the room next to me and the girls on the first floor. The other bedrooms will be for the boarders – when we find them. We will sweep the attic through, but not furnish that at present. That will make a good play area for the children. The family will use this big sitting room and the other will accommodate travellers in need of overnight accommodation. The regular boarders will have their meals with family in the dining room. Thank goodness the washstands and chamber pots were left in the bedrooms, there's a heap of good linen in the cupboard, and dear William gave us two extra single beds.' She paused for breath.

'What about me? 'Tom asked.

'You'll be a working lad soon, Tom. You deserve a room of your own. There is the small bedroom at the end of the corridor. And you must keep up your studies, your uncle says, if he is to recommend you for a position in the station office when you are a little older. Now, will you go into the yard and pump enough water for the next couple of days, please? Ernie, you can pass the empty buckets to him to fill. Then you can go along with Aunt Becca to the grocer's and introduce yourselves – say that I shall need a delivery tomorrow. I've written an order, oh, and an advertisement for his window.' She took the papers from her purse. At least she didn't have to worry about money this week. William had made sure of that.

Rebecca, Tom and Ernie walked along the street to the grocery store. Signs outside proclaimed: *General Grocer, Tea Dealer, Cheesemonger.* There was also a crate containing glass, earthenware and china in straw. Like Aunt Sarah's little shop, it sold a variety of goods. Under the overlap of the long counter were stacked the containers of biscuits, sacks of sugar, flour, and potatoes, and boxes of giant carrots, onions, swedes and winter greens.

Tom, who was already a head taller than his aunt, bent down to read the labels on the biscuit barrels. '*Garibaldi* – I'd like to try those but Mother makes all our biscuits and cakes.'

Rebecca reminded him, 'Give the grocer your list. I don't make my own bread nowadays, the loaves here are always fresh – Jim, the grocer, gets them daily from the baker's shop at number 4 – and bread is so much cheaper than it was. The children will like Miss Money's little front room shop, too. She's a dear old lady – such tempting cakes and jars of sweets. I don't suppose Emma buys margarine instead of butter? Or canned food?'

Tom shook his head. 'Dada always said Mother has a passion for cooking – they had the best food in the big house in Kensington.'

'You all look well fed, I must say. I made the scones with margarine; I don't suppose you could tell the difference? May I have a dozen eggs, please,' Rebecca asked the smiling girl behind the counter, while her father, Jim, in his spotless white apron, carved bacon from a flitch. 'I got a nice piece of haddock from the fishmonger when he called yesterday and the family like a poached egg with that,' she added.

'Sausages,' Jim said, when he perused the list Tom passed to him. 'Now, lad, you can't do better than go down the road a bit to the pork butcher, old George – he hev fresh sausages every day. He hev his own slaughterhouse in his yard.'

'Poor pigs!' said Ernie.

'That reminds me, I'll come with you, Richard likes his chaps,' Rebecca said.

'What are *chaps*?' Ernie wanted to know.

'Pork cheeks my dear, cheaper than chops and meatier too. Don't you like pig's trotters?'

'No! Only Dada ate those.' Ernie gave a shudder.

'Ernie's squeamish,' Tom told Rebecca.

'Afore you goo, boy,' Jim told Tom, 'tell Mrs Meehan I will deliver the goods tomorrow morning. What's this other piece of paper? Oh ho, I see she's looking for gentlemen lodgers. Might be able to help her there, I hev a young journeyman who need a home from home. I'll tell him to wait a day or two. He hev a friend who is a cooper at the local brewery, he was asking me if I could recommend a good place. I don't suppose *you* want a part-time job, do you?' He looked Tom up and down approvingly. 'You look a strong young man, and smart with it. I need an errand boy.'

'I'll have to ask my mother, but I think she'll say yes!' Tom said.

A loud knocking on the front door of number 10 heralded the arrival of Richard and two friends. Richard was a short, stocky man with a smiling face, an impressive sandy moustache and twinkling blue eyes. 'Reinforcements!' Richard told Emma, and Immi went to brew more tea for the workers while they carried the beds one by one up the main staircase to the respective bedrooms. Alice was asked to take the smaller children up to the attic to play while the older children were helping Emma. 'But come down when I call,' she reminded Alice. 'And see they have a good wash before going to bed.'

'I've thought up a good game,' Alice said – she had a vivid imagination. 'The old bed up here can be a ship, and we can tie the curtains up to look like sails. I can use my hair ribbon. We'll be sailors like Dada was when he was young. You can jump on the mattress as much as you like, because it will be rocking on the high seas.'

Tom wasn't staying for childish antics. 'I'm off to help with the beds,' he said.

It was past midnight when Emma, Immi and Tom finally crawled into their own beds, exhausted, but all was quiet now on the home front. Puglet snored in his box beside the bed Immi shared with Alice, and Emma pulled the old purple eiderdown up round her neck after she'd closed her bible and said her prayers. Wasn't it a blessing, she thought, that they had discovered the pair of copper warming pans hanging by their long handles on the hall wall. They were tarnished, but Immi had given them a quick rub-up and then filled them with red-hot cinders from the fire, so they had been able to heat the beds with them in turn.

Now that most things were in place, particularly in this room, including her mother-in-law Isabella's trunk, and the tulip-patterned washstand from the Summers' house, she felt at peace. She thought to herself, The mourning period is over, and this is our new life, here in this house which I am determined to make into a real home. I am going to work hard to be successful for my children's sake. Immi, Rebecca and I will make a good team, I think, and Tom is growing up fast and will become the man of the house.

TWENTY-SIX

They awoke that first Sunday morning to a snowy world and the younger children wrapped up well and dashed out into the yard to throw a snowball or two, while Puglet stepped delicately on the thick carpet of white with a very aggrieved expression on his face. 'Just like the old queen,' Alice said with a grin. Then they rushed indoors to steaming bowls of porridge, thickened in its pot overnight on the stove, with plenty of brown sugar. 'For energy,' Immi said. 'Not that they need more of that.'

'Hurry up, or we'll be late for church. Good job it's not far to go,' Emma said.

Tom came in with an empty bucket. 'You were right, Mother, the pump is frozen, but Mr Neal is pouring boiling water over the spout to free it up.'

'Your nose is running, Tom,' Ernie observed.

'It's not surprising, is it,' he returned. 'Made the tea yet, Immi?'

'Give me a chance,' she said, as she lifted the big kettle with both hands.

Later, 'washed and brushed' as TF always described it when Emma took her children to church on Sundays, they walked along to the Congregational Chapel. This, they had learned, had been erected to replace a more primitive building in 1812, during the ministry of an inspiring preacher, Isaac Sloper. The building was extended in 1833, with a fine new facade and galleries within. The interior was panelled with pitch pine, an improvement on stark white walls. Some years later, a substantial two-storey extension was built to accommodate a vestry and a Sunday school room. Only last year a school hall was provided alongside the building and there had been further additions inside the church: a high pulpit, new pews, a balustrade and arched apse for a splendid new organ, recently acquired after much fundraising through musical events at the popular Assembly Hall. Handel and Mendelssohn were much appreciated by the audience but 'The Last Rose of Summer' was something everyone knew and could sing.

Joyous music pealed forth now as they joined the large congregation. They were welcomed by those already ensconced there into a side pew with warm smiles and handshakes. They looked up at the gallery. This too was packed with people.

'I like this church,' Alice said loudly, and there was no need to shush her for the minister, waiting to begin the service, looked up from his notes and gave her a little wave of approval.

As they emerged after the service, Emma became aware of two young men waiting to one side of the path to the gate who were doffing their hats to greet her as the family approached. She paused, and the little cavalcade halted behind her.

'Excuse me, but I believe you are Mrs Meehan?' the taller of the two enquired.

'I am.'

'My name is Walter Vincent and I am employed by Mr Ecclestone, the grocer. My friend and I are looking for lodgings in Hungate and he said we might ask you if you could help.'

'I didn't expect to hear from you so soon,' Emma said, hanging on to her hat in the bitter wind.

'I apologise, but we were told you were likely to be in church this morning, and as we are not going home because of the weather – they say there are snow drifts on the railway line – we thought we'd come along.'

The second young man put in, 'I am Frederick Curtis, cooper's journeyman.'

'It's too cold to stand out here talking,' Emma said impulsively. She smiled at them. TF would have approved of them, she thought, for they were polite young men. 'Come back with us now and we will discuss the matter.

They were ushered into the kitchen. 'The warmest room in the house,' Emma said appreciatively. Immi divested herself of her cloak, tucked her hair, which had become loose when they were bowled home by the wind, behind her ears and busied herself with making tea for the unexpected visitors. Her mother noticed the tips of her ears were pink, which meant her daughter was blushing.

Frederick sniffed the air appreciatively. 'Something smells good,' he remarked with a disarming grin. He was the younger of the two, and shorter and stockier than his friend.

'Our Sunday roast,' Emma replied. Thanks to Rebecca, she thought, telling the pork butcher about us. He had come around with a joint of meat to welcome them 'to the best town I know of, Beccles.'

'Reminds me of home,' Walter said. 'Thank you.' He took the proffered cup and saucer from Immi. 'You make a good strong cup.'

'My father liked it like that,' she said primly. 'He called it naval tea.'

'Sugar?' Alice asked. 'How many lumps?' She liked using the silver tongs but was not as domesticated as Immi had been at her age. The only thing she concentrated on was sewing, at which she excelled.

'You are very efficient for a little girl,' Walter told her.

'I'm eleven,' she said firmly, 'and if you're wondering, my sister is fifteen.'

Walter smiled. Emma had seen the admiring glances directed at Immi.

'Tom should have gingered up the sitting room fire by now,' she said, rising. 'Shall we go and discuss business in private? Immi, get the children busy preparing the vegetables, please.'

'I'll make the pastry,' Alice offered unexpectedly. 'I promise not to roll it too hard.' Her last attempt had been candidly described by Tom as 'heavy as lead'.

'As you will see,' Emma told her prospective boarders, 'We are not settled in properly yet – I hope to make the place more like home shortly. I think it would be better, if you decide to come, to arrive next weekend. My terms are four shillings a week, full board and lodging. Meals with the family. I am going to the auction house as soon as I can to hopefully acquire a bigger table and more chairs, with a sideboard. My daughter Isabella and I do all the cooking between us and my sister is going to help generally. You would have separate bedrooms and the private use of the other sitting room across the hall when required, but that room will also be used by travellers who require overnight accommodation. Tom has painted a sign, perhaps Walter, as you are taller, you would put it up over the front door? You are welcome to have friends call but they should leave by ten o'clock in the evening. Baths – once a week in the scullery. I won't charge you for bathing if you fill the bath yourself and empty it afterwards down the drain in the yard. There are washstands in each bedroom and Tom will bring up jugs of hot water in the mornings. If you require your laundry to be done by me, there will be a small charge.'

'It all sounds very nice,' the young men agreed. 'We accept your terms, thank you.'

Frederick added. 'We bathe in the river in the summer months – most people do. There is a changing hut, and men and women have their own bathing places.'

'The river is iced over at the moment, and there will be skating, tell the children,' Walter said.

'Oh, I couldn't allow them to go there unsupervised,' Emma said.

'We would be happy to oblige in that respect,' Frederick offered. 'I am sure our employers would tell you we are trustworthy. We both have brothers and sisters in Lowestoft, though we only manage a monthly visit home.'

'We'll see.' Emma smiled at them. 'I can expect you next Saturday, then? I am sure we will all get on. Will you come up to see the rooms now?'

As she showed them out later, she thought, I must have a tactful word with Immi. Emma worried that although she looked like any other pretty young girl of her age, she wasn't, and marriage and motherhood may not be possible for the future – it was sad, but a fact of life.

Alice, Ernie and Ted were enrolled at the board school in Peddars Lane, a short walk from their new home. They took a reluctant Ted along to the infants' class where he was whisked inside by Miss Chastney.

'I hope he won't get *chastised*!' Alice said to Ernie. Fortunately, Ted didn't comprehend her meaning.

The board school had been built on the site of an old silk mill, a dwindling industry, and had previously been named the British School when it was founded by the dissenters, though at that time it was not intended for the poor of the parish. Now that education was compulsory for all children it still wasn't possible for some impoverished families, for it was not free. Copperplate handwriting was demanded of every child and the headmaster was a great believer in the three Rs. One look from him was enough to quell a noisy class.

Emma insisted on further study at home, and they were also enrolled in the Sunday school. Tom, who was now errand boy for the grocer's and becoming very superior in manner to his siblings, reminded them, 'It costs Mother a penny a day to educate each of you and I am contributing to that!' His wages were one shilling and sixpence a week and he was allowed to pocket any coppers given him by customers.

'He push that old handcart so fast, sparks do fly from the wheels!' Jim the grocer told Emma. 'You can be proud of your Tom.'

The children were glad to put their books aside the following Saturday afternoon when the new boarders, Wally and Fred arrived, and to their great excitement, Alice, Ernie and Ted were allowed to go with 'the lads', as the family referred to them, to watch the skating on the frozen river. Tom went with them, and Ted clung to his big brother's hand.

Immi stayed at home with Emma and young Frank. '*He* is too adventurous by half,' Emma said.

'Now they are out of the way, Mother, I'll polish up the furniture in the Traveller's Rest,' Immi offered. Rebecca had suggested the name, and they all agreed it was fitting. The furniture had arrived from the auction house the previous day. It was of good quality, but old-fashioned and cumbersome, so Emma and Rebecca had been successful with modest bids.

'And I'll make one of my special fruit cakes for tea,' Emma said.

'I'll lick round the bowl,' Ted offered eagerly.

'You'll do no such thing, you'll scrape round the bowl with a spoon!' Emma reproved him.

Later, when the cake was in the oven, Emma sat at the kitchen table and opened the writing slope that TF had given her on that Christmas long ago. There were her weekly letters to write before the children rushed in, hungry for their tea.

The first letter must be to Jerusha in London, in answer to the one she had sent wishing them happiness in Number 10. Chas was now the London Salvage Corps Municipal Officer.

Dearest Jerusha,

We are settling in well, despite the bad weather. I am becoming used to all the space after our little cottage. We even have two boarders who arrived this morning! Nice young men. They asked permission to take the younger children to watch the skating on the frozen river this afternoon. Immi stayed to look after Frank, she is telling him stories by the fire at this moment. His favourite is 'Three Little Kittens Have Lost their Mittens'.

Next week, now the children are at school, I will make myself known to the local doctor, as if I could resume my midwifery this would greatly help our finances. Immi is very capable in the house, thank goodness, and Rebecca will be helping and keeping an eye on her in case she has a turn, but thank God she has been well these past months. I sometimes wonder if I expect too much of Immi and Tom.

Emma paused, writing about Immi reminded her about Rob's daughter Isabella in Amble, and she hoped she had also remained well. She finished her letter to Jerusha, and took out a fresh sheet of notepaper, intending to write to Keturah in Jarrow, who had recently set up as a dressmaker. *I must tell her that Alice aspires to follow fashion too,* Emma thought.

As she began to write, she was fortunately unaware that at the same moment, her sober, responsible Tom was strapping a pair of borrowed skates onto his feet, eager to join his new friends on the ice. Alice, with Ted clinging to her skirts, revealing her flannel petticoat, jumped up and down excitedly on the bank, shouting encouragement. She didn't notice immediately that Ernie, bored because he was being ignored, had wandered off towards some boys kicking a ball. They immediately spotted his red hair and began to tease him: 'Ginger nut!' He went dashing after the ball, tears in his eyes: he had to put up with this during playtime at school, too.

Wally and Fred were hanging on to Tom's arms and propelling him along the ice. He quickly got the hang of it and shrugged them off, but within seconds he was out of control, his feet splayed, and he landed on his bottom, winded – but the worst thing was, his clean trousers were soaked. A passing lady helped him to his feet, which was highly embarrassing. Other pairs of skaters continued on their way, effortlessly it seemed, silver skates glinting in the pale sunlight across the glassy stretch of ice.

The big lads exchanged glances. Time to go back. 'Maybe his pants will dry out in the wind,' Fred said hopefully. He unbuckled his skates, and then dealt with Tom's borrowed pair.

'I'm cold,' Alice realised. 'Ted is shivering, and oh no, where's Ernie?'

Ernie's companions were tussling over the ball and had landed on top of the little boy, obscuring him from view. Ernie, sturdy child that he was, was intent on wriggling out from under the scrum. Wally ran up to help free him and brought him back, hanging firmly on to his collar. He said to Fred, 'We got some explaining to do to Mrs Meehan – come on!'

When they stamped their feet on the doormat, Tom hared upstairs to his room for a quick change of trousers. He didn't want to get his new friends into trouble and Alice put a finger to her lips. She didn't wish anything said about Ernie, either.

The lodgers enjoyed their slice of cake, but then excused themselves. 'We usually meet some friends on Saturday night.' They didn't add, 'At the Barley Mow.'

'Front door is locked at ten,' Emma reminded them, but she was relieved they would have the evening to themselves. 'Cocoa in the jug in the kitchen if you want a nightcap.'

The children were ready for an early night after the afternoon's excitement, but Tom and Immi kept their mother company by the sitting room fire. Emma and Immi were tackling the darning of socks and stockings, which had been put aside during their moving-in, while Tom studied the train timetable given to him by his uncle. He wanted to be as knowledgeable about the railways as he could before his hoped-for interview with the stationmaster. The trouble was, this evening he found it hard to concentrate; his conscience was troubling him. Emma and TF had instilled in them all that they should always tell the truth. When Emma asked on their return, 'Did you enjoy watching the skaters on the ice?' Tom had replied. 'Yes. I wished I could do it.'

'Perhaps we can buy you some skates next year,' she said.

Now, she looked up from her sewing and regarded him thoughtfully. 'Tom, is there something you wish to tell me?'

Tears welled in his eyes. 'Mother, I'm sorry, but I borrowed some skates from Fred's friend and – and I went out on the ice, and I know you thought I was just watching – but I had a go at skating and – I fell over.'

'Did you hurt yourself?' she exclaimed, her expression betraying her concern.

'No – just winded – but my trousers were soaked and I changed them when I got home, so you wouldn't scold me.'

'My dear boy, I'm not cross, it's natural to want to accept a challenge – it's how a boy becomes a man. Your father was at sea when he wasn't much older than you, climbing the rigging, fighting for his country even in the Crimean War. You are bound to make mistakes, but never lose your sense of adventure! Just think before you act. And never do anything you know is not right.'

'I'll try not to,' Tom said humbly. He put his studies to one side. 'I'll get another bucket of coal in –then I'll go to bed. Goodnight, Mother; goodnight, Immi.'

TWENTY-SEVEN

Shortly after Emma and her family moved to Beccles, the large house next door was taken over by two middle-aged sisters who ran a dressmaking establishment which employed six local women. They soon had a good clientele as word spread of the superior garments, which they made on the latest sewing machines.

Alice was curious to find out more, and to meet the misses Janet and Sarah. Emma had taught her to sew by hand and she had practiced with a wide range of stitches on a sampler. However, she preferred to draw and colour her own bold designs, which Emma admired, but told her gently they were impractical. Emma had given up fancy frocks when her family grew, and now she was a matron, she wore plain black or grey garments and starched white pinafores, very like the uniform she had worn in her days as a cook-housekeeper, so her simple patterns were not the latest fashion. When Alice helped her mother to hang clothes in her closet after the move, she had spotted the cherished red velvet wedding dress. This was much more to her taste, and she thought, *Perhaps I will wear it one day, too.* Emma had looked at it briefly as Alice admired it and said, 'I should have made something from that for you girls, but, well, I didn't.'

The most exciting thing for Alice that winter had been going with the lodgers and her brother Tom to watch a donkey and cart being driven under the stone bridge on the frozen river. Bets were taken by men in the crowd about whether the ice would hold and hats were thrown in the air when it did.

Now it was spring, the river flowed freely once more, so she looked forward to the summer bathing, though she wasn't sure Mother would allow her to participate. She had also enjoyed a family visit, along with Aunt Becca and her cousins, to Mrs Jolly's Waxworks at the Assembly Rooms; the figures were eerily lifelike. She dared to touch the face of the look-alike Princess Alexandra after whom, of course, she had been named, and to finger the fine silk of her exquisite gown before she was reprimanded by a stern Mrs Jolly, who didn't appear to live up to *her* name.

One morning, Aunt Becca was in charge because Emma had been called to a confinement as the regular midwife was unwell. 'My big chance to show what I can do!' she'd cried happily, while Immi fetched down her big black bag so they could check the contents were all ready for use. It was a Saturday so there was no school and Alice was bored. Immi was cooking a late breakfast for a young couple who'd stayed overnight, while Rebecca was sorting through the linen in the cupboard on the landing and tossing superfluous items into a pile on the floor. She carried these downstairs and told Alice, 'Here you are, some of these can be cut up for cushion covers. Make yourself useful, eh?'

Alice found something of interest, a single green velvet curtain which she recalled had kept out the draughts from the Wymondham cottage kitchen door. It had originated from the farmhouse and Emma had regarded this relic sentimentally. Now, Alice folded and tucked the curtain under her arm to conceal it as she passed by Immi in the kitchen, went out into the yard, ostensibly to the privy, and then disappeared smartly round the back to emerge in the street.

Miss Janet responded to the knock on the door. She was a tall lady with a coronet of unlikely red hair and piercing dark eyes under thick brows, and she stooped to regard the golden-haired child on her front step. 'You are one of the children from number 10, I believe?' she enquired.

Alice gave her a dazzling smile. 'Yes, miss.'

'You have a message for me?'

Alice hesitated for a moment. She hadn't thought up a reason for her impromptu visit. Then she said impulsively, because Miss Janet was regarding her in a friendly way, 'I want to be a dressmaker myself one day, and I was wondering—'

'You were wondering if I would invite you in, so you can see what we do here.'

'Oh, yes, please!'

'Your name is?'

'Emma Alexandra, but I am always called Alice.'

'Well, I am Jane, but I am always called Janet! Follow me, Alice.'

A door was opened, and Alice followed Miss Janet into the large workroom. The seamstresses sat in rows at two long tables, each with a shiny new sewing machine before her, guiding pieces of material under the darting needle with one hand while turning the handle of the machine with the other. At another table, two women were pinning paper patterns to cloth and then cutting out the various shapes with sharp scissors. They didn't speak, for concentration was important, and the whirr of the machines and clatter of the shuttles was constant.

'We have the latest sewing machines, the Jones Cat-Back model – in London they call it the Serpentine because of the graceful shape – see? We like to support British industry – these machines are made in Manchester.'

Alice revealed her secret with some relief. 'I know this is just a curtain, but I think it might make a nice skirt for my mother – what do you think?'

Miss Janet took the curtain from her and shook it out, holding it up to the light to look for worn patches or small holes. 'It's a good colour still, a little faded here – but you needn't use that part. You want this to be a gift, a surprise?' Alice nodded. 'Come through into the next room, and we will discuss it.'

This was a smaller room with a desk and cabinets and in a corner a dressmaker's dummy with a gauzy dress displayed on it. 'I am expecting an important customer to call for a fitting in half an hour. Now, Alice, tell me why you want to make this skirt for your mother?'

'My mother wears black all the time since my father passed away and we came here. She used to wear smart clothes, or so my sister tells me, but she is a midwife as well as a boarding-house keeper now and thinks she has to dress accordingly! I think it would cheer her up to have an outfit which will make her feel younger and smarter!'

'Well, Alice, I think this is an excellent idea. First, you must take your chance when she is not around, to measure a garment which you know fits her now – waist, hips and length. When you have these measurements, come back and we will decide on a pattern and style. A slight bustle at the back, I fancy, but nothing elaborate for a busy mother. Leave the material with me, and I will show you how to use a sewing machine. Now, I think you should go home in case your family are wondering where you are. I will see you soon.' As she showed Alice out of the front door, she added, 'My sister is out ordering new materials today, but I know she'll want to meet you too.'

As soon as Alice returned to her house, Rebecca exclaimed, 'Where on earth have you been? Poor Immi had one of her turns, and Emma hasn't arrived back yet – fortunately the guests have gone – you had better see what the young ones are up to in the attic, and then get them some lunch. Tom will be back from his deliveries any minute now. I must go home and feed *my* family.'

'Sorry, Aunt Becca – I'll do it right away,' Alice said. She was relieved not to be questioned further, or to be asked to sit with her sister. Tom was the best one for that job. She sighed; the two of them were hard to live up to. She and Ernie were the mischievous ones and the less studious members of the family too. Ted was obviously going to be a second Tom, and Frank was the family favourite. *I was Dada's pet*, she thought, blinking away a tear; *he never scolded me . . .*

Emma certainly did when she returned to hear what had happened in her absence. 'You mustn't just disappear without telling someone where you're going, Alice. That is a selfish attitude.'

Alice thought resentfully, *It isn't fair; I was only planning a surprise for you.* However, she thought it prudent to tell Emma or Immi in future when she was visiting her new friends.

Immi was resting on the old daybed, with the protective Puglet curled up beside her. The tremors had ceased since Rebecca gave her the dose of bromide recommended by their new doctor. The drawback to this medicine was it could make her depressed. She managed a smile when she saw Emma and Alice. 'How did it all go, Mother?'

'It was not straightforward, but all was well in the end. A large baby boy,' Emma said. 'Alice, any chance of a nice cup of tea?'

'Yes,' said Alice, 'but can I tell you where I've been first? I went to see Miss Janet next door. I want to learn all I can about dressmaking, then perhaps I'll get an apprenticeship, and you'll be proud of me!'

'You still have more schooling to accomplish first,' Emma reminded her. 'When you are fourteen, well, we'll see, but London is the place for high fashion.'

'That's where I intend to go!' Alice said confidently.

Emma sighed. *If only I could afford to buy my daughter a sewing machine*, she thought. But the business was not proving as profitable as she'd expected because although the boarders were not much trouble, they did have hearty appetites.

The green velvet skirt was taking shape. There was ample material and the fashion now was for much narrower skirts with light padding judiciously placed for just the hint of a bustle lower down at the back, not prominent as in the past. It took several hours to tack the parts together.

When it was finished, Miss Sarah, who was just as nice as her sister, Alice decided, wrapped the finished garment in new tissue paper and tied the parcel with a white satin ribbon.

'There, now you can present it to your mother. Do let us know what she thinks of it!'

When Emma saw it, she cried, 'Oh, did you really make this all by yourself Alice?'

'Yes,' Alice said proudly. 'I know how to use a sewing machine now, too.'

'I shall wear the skirt to church tomorrow, with my new white blouse,' Emma decided. She hugged her. 'You have a gift, Alice. Make the most of it!'

In June, a new bathing place at the river was opened to the public, and Alice begged her mother to allow her to go there. Emma, who had never learned to swim herself, had a few reservations.

Tom and Ernie had already been taught how to swim a few strokes by Wally and Fred, but Alice had to wait for a chaperone. Rebecca offered to take her with her two young daughters, now six and seven. Bella, the toddler, could be with Emma and the younger boys for company, Becca suggested.

'Alice will need a swimming costume, Emma. Perhaps she could make it herself. I made the girls' costumes from white calico – a simple tunic top and short pantaloons – I saw one displayed in a window and they were simple to sew . . .'

'Calico is cheap enough from the market,' Emma said. 'Alice is growing apace at the moment, so it's not worth going to a lot of expense.'

Alice didn't think too much of Rebecca's idea of a home-made costume because she had always admired the display of women's fashionable swimming attire in the high-class dress show. However, her friends agreed to help her, and promised her the costume would be comparable to the ones she had admired.

Immi looked pensive after Alice went off with her aunt and cousins. 'I expect you would have liked to join them, Immi?' Emma said, putting an arm round her daughter's hunched shoulders as she bent over a book she was reading.

'No, Mother, I know you would worry I would have a turn and make an exhibition of myself.'

This response was unexpected. Emma's eyes filled with tears. She hugged her daughter tight. 'Oh, Immi, I don't mean to make you feel different.'

'But I am, Mother. You protect me because you love me, I know that – but even though Uncle Rob's Isabella has the same trouble, *she* is training to be a pupil teacher. I haven't even been to school.'

'I'm sorry Immi, I thought I was acting for the best.'

'Don't cry, Mother. Please.' Immi said. She kissed Emma's damp cheek. 'You look after me, and I love you, too.'

The water in the pool was cold, and due to the numbers of people who had already flocked to the new place since it had officially opened, it already looked murky. It was an overcast morning, and the sun was not yet up. It was a time reserved for the ladies, and they were complaining and shivering. The young cousins were soon asking to come out of the water, and Alice didn't like the wet pantaloons clinging to her legs. She had only waded in up to her waist and it wasn't long before she heaved herself out and dripped her way to the changing hut. The swimming season was over, and she decided she would wait for the winter skating.

She didn't wear the new costume again, and by the next summer it no longer fitted. Alice was on the threshold of womanhood. There were rules to follow: no baths or hair-washing allowed at certain times of the month, and certainly no swimming. She became closer to Immi, who understood and sympathised with how she felt in her adolescence, because she had gone through it herself. However, Alice remained single-minded about her future career.

The popularity of the new swimming place soon waned. It wasn't big enough for a large number of bathers and serious swimmers preferred the old place. Weeds hidden in the depths continued to be a problem there, but some clearing was achieved. There was still the occasional sad drowning and brave rescues, but the water in the new pool grew murkier and 'lewd behaviour' (skinny dipping?) was rumoured to carry on.

TWENTY-EIGHT

Beccles, 1882

When the family had been established in Beccles for more than a year, Tom had progressed from errand boy to grocer's assistant, and his employer, Jim Ecclestone, asked him if he would like to be considered for an apprenticeship. Tom politely declined, explaining that his Uncle Richard felt he was old enough now to apply to become a railway clerk. Jim assured Tom that he would be happy to give him an excellent reference and wished him luck with his coming interview. Reverend Eden of Wymondham, on learning of Tom's aspirations, also highly recommended him.

Being nominated by a respected member of the railway staff was always helpful but Tom was aware that he would have to pass a written examination to prove that he was both literate and numerate and had reached the required standard of education. Spelling was important, also handwriting, but most importantly applicants must be of good character. Tom had continued his studies diligently after leaving school and learned a lot about the origin of the railways and in particular about the local station from his uncle.

'You will have more chance of promotion as a rail clerk, good pay and a job for life, if you want it,' Richard said. 'Porters like me, signalmen, cleaners, or even drivers, however long they have been with the company, know they can be dismissed with a week's notice. There was some revolt against the rules, but they got nowhere. But if you work hard, boy, you can rise up to be a stationmaster in years to come.' Tom was suitably impressed.

His uncle accompanied him to the main station – a red-brick building with gothic windows which was permeated with the powerful smell from the maltings next door – for his interview, but departed before Tom knocked on the door. When Tom entered the stationmaster's office, his knees were knocking with nervousness – he was glad they were covered up by his first full-length trousers, which he had saved to buy.

The stationmaster, who was wearing gold pince-nez and sitting behind an impressive desk, regarded him solemnly and held out a large, warm hand for him to shake. 'Sit down, Meehan. Now, tell me why you want to join the clerical staff here.'

For a nightmarish moment Tom could not recall a word of the introduction he had so carefully rehearsed and presented to Emma and Immi the evening before. But then, responding to an encouraging smile from the large man, he said, 'I want to be a small part of a wonderful organisation, sir.' Then, gathering confidence, he let the rest spill out.

Later, he dipped his pen in the inkwell provided and sat at a desk in a room where clerks perched on high stools were busy writing to do his written test. The majority appeared not to notice him, but a junior clerk raised his head and gave him a friendly nod. Tom was determined to do well and read the questions carefully before he began to write, and his confidence grew with every pen-stroke.

Tom was already aware that clerical workers were expected to stay at the long counters until their allotted task was finished, and it might be necessary to take work home at times. The day for them began at 9.15 a.m. but rarely did staff leave at 6 p.m. No overtime was paid. The rule book decreed they were to be on duty whenever required, even on a Sunday. They really earned every penny of their starting salary of £35 per annum, which seemed like a fortune to young Tom, even though he would have to work a month before he was paid.

Beccles was an important station from its inception. There were branch lines to Lowestoft and the original Waveney Valley Railway and a main line from Great Yarmouth to London. Facilities included a turntable, four platforms, station buildings and lofty goods sheds. There was also stabling for the majestic Suffolk Punches, which provided 'horse power' to haul disconnected engines along the track to the turntable or engine shed. The handsome chestnut horses could move up to three times their own weight and also carted any goods that arrived by train. There were sidings, signal boxes, many uniformed staff, cleaners and mechanics. Those crossing by the footbridge had an amazing view of luxuriant pasture land down the line.

A few weeks later, the family celebrated the news that Tom had passed his interview with credit and jolly Uncle Richard predicted, 'The boy will do well.' But later, when Tom wished his mother goodnight before he climbed the stairs to bed, he mentioned something that worried him.

'Immi didn't say much, Mother.'

'She's happy for you, Tom, as we all are, but I guess she thinks this is the parting of the ways for you both,' she said softly.

'I – I don't understand.'

'Oh, Tom, it must seem to her that you won't be in and out like you are at present, but away all day – she'll miss your support.'

'Mother, I'll *always* look after Immi, I promise you!' he said.

Ted was already determined to follow in his hero's footsteps, but Ernie, who was now almost nine years old, had different ideas. He was a bright boy, Emma sighed, but not academic, and he was intending to leave school as soon as he could to 'work with his hands'. He made a start by asking the friendly local butcher for a part-time job. He was soon earning six-pence a week for sweeping up the soiled straw on the floor each evening after the shop was closed, and replenishing it with fresh straw ready for the following day. He still felt sorry for the squealing pigs housed in the yard, knowing their fate to come, but he was overcoming his squeamishness in that respect, and was proud of taking home a parcel of meaty bones, given to him by his boss, with which Emma would make good soup and stock. Like Tom, he was contributing to the family, but in his own way.

'He's the most religious of the children,' Emma said fondly to Rebecca when she shared her bounty with her sister. 'Unlike school, he never has to be pushed to go to Sunday school. The teacher there speaks highly of him. He loves to sing and has joined the choir. His dada always said our Ernie takes after his father, Irish Tom. He was always happy and smiling as well. He liked to think of him like that, but the poor man didn't recover from losing his wife.'

'The children must have suffered, too,' Rebecca observed. She looked pensive suddenly, recalling her years in the workhouse.

Emma sighed. 'Yes, but d'you know, they were stronger for it, and TF and his brother both did well in the years after they left home.'

'Would you think of marrying again one day?'

Emma shook her head. 'No. My children are my life now.'

Rebecca said impulsively, 'Surely you must miss – you know . . .' She saw Emma's face flush and added, 'I'm sorry, I shouldn't have said that.'

'Oh, Becca, of course I miss that side of my marriage. I have so many happy memories of when TF and I first fell in love, but I can't imagine that with another man.'

'I wish sometimes you would remember you're still quite young, Emma. And, well, I recall the way you were on the farm. You kept us all going. We owe you so much.'

'Now I feel in *your* debt because you help me so much and I can only pay you pennies for all your hard work.'

Emma was worried that she hadn't heard from her beloved sister Jerusha in London for several weeks. She suspected that she might be unwell, so she decided to write out of turn – she had an excuse, she thought, with the news about Tom's job. She hoped to persuade her sister and young Ellie to visit them in Beccles for a short holiday. *The Traveller's Rest awaits you!* she wrote. *This may be town life, but we are surrounded by lovely countryside and the Waveney is cleaner than the old Thames!*

A reply came by return of post, but the envelope was not addressed in Jerusha's handwriting. Emma opened it in sudden trepidation.

My dear Emma,

We were pleased to receive your letter and to know all is well with you. Regretfully, we are unable to accept your kind invitation to visit at this time, as Jerusha has been unwell these past few weeks. She is resting in bed and has a nurse who attends her daily, a kind woman highly recommended by her doctor. She asks that you do not worry too much, but she has been feverish and bronchial.

Sadly, we had to come to the decision to send young Ellie to her mother to avoid infection. Naturally, we both miss her very much, but Ellie's mother is now in better health and is living with her elder sister and brother-in-law in the country.

I hope to be able to give you more encouraging news of Jerusha's recovery in due course. She sends her fondest love to you all, as do I.

Chas.

Emma put the letter down. She was sitting at the breakfast table by herself, Tom having gone to work earlier and the children to school. Immi was washing up the dishes in the kitchen and Frank was playing ball in the yard with the dog. Emma lifted the hem of her apron and buried her face in it, trying to stem her tears.

Immi touched her shoulder gently: 'Have you had bad news, Mother?' she asked tentatively.

Emma nodded. 'Read the letter, Immi. I knew something was not right when Ru didn't write as usual.'

'Aunt Becca has arrived, I can hear her in the kitchen. Shall I show her this?'

'Yes, please.' Emma smoothed her apron down and dabbed her cheeks with her handkerchief. 'We'll make up a parcel for Ru today, things to tempt her appetite.'

'You have another letter here, Mother,' Immi said, passing it to her. 'Uncle Chas seems to think things can only get better – Aunt Jerusha has been ill before and recovered, take comfort from that.'

The second letter was from Frances Summers. The family were now living in Brighton as Mr Summers had finally retired. Frances wrote:

Papa and I have decided to spend a few days in Great Yarmouth next week while the weather is good, and wonder if you would be able to visit us at the Royal Hotel for lunch? Suggest Tuesday, if convenient to you. It seems so long since we met up.

'Good news this time, Mother?' Immi asked hopefully.

'Yes, it is indeed! You've heard about the Summers family many times, I know, and the happy years I spent in their lovely home in Kensington, before I met your dada, and young Frances whom our dear Anna and I took under our wing? Frances must be in her thirties now and is still at home with her father and two of her aunts. Her Aunt Maria went to be a missionary in China. Oh, I would love to see Frances and her papa again! But I'm not sure I can go. What about the children – young Frank, especially.'

'No excuses, Mother! I'm sure Aunt Becca will help out, and Frank is my shadow anyway!'

'It's time you had a new frock – what did you wear last time you met your friends?' Rebecca asked, riffling through Emma's wardrobe. 'All this black!' she exclaimed.

'I wore a mauve silk dress and carried a parasol,' Emma remembered.

'What happened to the dress?'

'I unpicked it later to make party frocks for my girls.'

'We'll go down to the market today, Emma, and buy some pretty material – you, Alice and I can make a new outfit for you between us! I'll bring round my sewing machine. Alice has been wheedling to use it!'

It was nearing the end of September breezy weather so cotton won the day over silk or georgette. The latest floral prints were the height of fashion, Rebecca assured her sister. 'You just need a new straw bonnet, with a curvy brim and long gloves, as Alice has decreed elbow-length sleeves. Miss Janet is kindly lending her a pattern.'

They couldn't resist the stallholder's offer of an extra length of the chosen material, as it was the end of the bolt of cloth.

'Immi and Alice will have something new to wear, too!' Emma said. She also purchased a bright red rubber ball for Frank. 'Seeing as Puglet has punctured the ball you bounce in the yard.' She looked round for her small son. As usual, he was petting the stallholder's donkey – he wasn't nervous of any animal, even great carthorses; he had an affinity with them.

Alice cut the dress pieces from the pattern under Miss Janet's supervision after school that evening, then hurried home to tack them into shape before Rebecca brought the sewing machine the following day.

There was much discussion of what difference a corset would make worn under the frock, and despite Emma's protests, her little store of saved pennies diminished when Rebecca accompanied her to the corsetieres in London Road.

'Your bosom is your best feature, madam,' enthused the assistant. She tightened the lacing to emphasise Emma's waist, and Emma could hardly believe the transformation she viewed in the long mirror. Her breasts rested in 'cups' at the top of the corset and appeared much more prominent. She had begun to think she must resign herself to middle-aged spread, but had to admit the constriction was worth it. She now had a figure to match the illustrations in the ladies' journals!

She said faintly, 'I'm not sure I could wear the corset every day.'

'Keep your head up!' Alice cried impatiently. She and Rebecca had insisted on accompanying her for the corset-fitting. She demonstrated the action herself. 'A swan-like neck, see.'

'That makes me look as if I am getting above myself,' Emma said doubtfully.

A few days later she was squeezed into the corset and then Alice slipped the dress over her head. 'Now sit down, Mother, while I do your hair.'

'Nothing fancy,' Emma hoped.

Alice was not particularly gentle with the hairbrush. She damped down the irrepressible curls and swept Emma's hair back into a low knot at the nape of her neck. The style was softened by the fringe at the front, which Rebecca, at Emma's request, had trimmed. Alice would have cut it shorter, she thought. Then it was time for the hat to be placed on her head.

'I'm off to school now,' Alice said reluctantly. 'But I wish I was going with you to Yarmouth. Don't move from the chair until it's time for you to leave for the train, will you? I'll tell Immi the boys can come in now and see how grand you look.'

Emma hugged them in turn. 'I'll bring you back a little surprise,' she promised.

Rebecca, Immi and Frank accompanied Emma to the station. Richard was hovering on the platform, relieved to see Emma arrive before the train. The sun was shining on a cloudless late September morning, as they waved her off on her journey.

She sat down carefully, because of the low bustle at the back of her dress, and the rigidity of the corset. Well, she thought, after all I am off to the Royal Hotel. She knew that Charles Dickens had stayed there while he was writing *David Copperfield*. And that when Lillie Langtry was performing at the Queens Theatre in Great Yarmouth a few years before she had stayed there too. It was rumoured that the Prince of Wales had been with her. Thinking about this, Emma smiled to herself. She doubted very much that she would be greeted by the stationmaster, a guard of honour and a military band when *she* arrived at the South Town station. Nor would there be church bells pealing, and sightseers climbing on to nearby terrace roofs. But even so, she *felt* like royalty today!

Her hosts were waiting to escort her to the hotel. Mr Summers no longer sported Dundreary whiskers, but a neat grey beard, which matched his hair. He wore a Norfolk jacket, correct country wear, and carried a silver-knobbed stick.

'My dear Emma.' He raised her gloved hand to his lips. 'It is good to see you after so long.'

Frances was plumper, but she really didn't look much older, Emma thought. She must have given the same impression herself, thanks to Alice and Rebecca, as Frances exclaimed, 'Oh, Emma, what a delightful gown! You are just the same as you always were!' She linked arms with her friend. 'We have so much news to catch up on, haven't we?'

The Royal Hotel was very grand indeed. It had been called The Victoria at the end of the eighteenth century, Frances told Emma, and she confirmed that Charles Dickens had stayed there with his friend Mark Lemon, who founded the popular satirical magazine *Punch*. 'He wrote to his wife that Yarmouth was *the most wondrous sight I have ever beheld,*' she said. 'And characters in *David Copperfield* are said to be based on local folk.'

They sat at a table by the window, with views of the seascape beyond, and the menu was perused. The choice was unanimous: asparagus soup, followed by chicken breasts wrapped in strips of bacon, with roast and boiled potatoes, onion gravy and buttered parsnips. For dessert there was ice cream and fresh fruit for the ladies, and cheese and biscuits for Mr Summers. Bitter coffee with cream was served in tiny cups.

Later they strolled along the golden sands, where the sea rolled back with the tide, and talked of old times. 'You young ladies go ahead,' Mr Summers said after a time. 'I'll make for the nearest seat and read the paper. I'm sure you have a lot to say to one another.'

'Papa has rheumatic knees,' Frances confided as they walked on. 'He is feeling his age, I suppose.'

'Well, I am wishing I could dispose of the wretched corset my sister and youngest daughter persuaded me I needed today!' Emma replied ruefully.

'Oh, Emma, I was thinking how lucky you were to possess such a splendid figure after having all your children!'

'Well, I imagine you feel a good deal more comfortable than I do!'

'Yes, but I am unlikely to marry and sometimes I feel as old as my aunts,' Frances said. She looked at Emma. 'You know I used to pray that Papa would ask you to marry him, Emma.'

'It wouldn't have been – seemly,' Emma said quietly. 'But you have always been like a younger sister to me, Frances. Don't give up hope, the right man could still come along, perhaps when you least expect it.'

Frances squeezed her arm. 'Thank you, Emma. We'd better turn around now, I think. Time to go back to the hotel for tea and cakes before you have to catch the train home to your family.'

'Can we call at that little gift shop along the parade? I promised the children some small surprises.'

'I should like to help you choose those,' Frances said.

When she returned home, the family crowded round Emma to receive their gifts and to hear about her day. Although there were things she kept to herself. She wasn't sure why she had felt a pang or two when she saw Mr Summers looking elderly and not so sprightly, but then, she realised, he must also have noticed the difference in her. It made her realise that now she had been able to put aside the way TF looked in his final years, she had the comfort of recalling him as he was in his prime. He will be forever young, while I will not. But, she said to herself, age is all in the mind, I must be content with how I am, except I really must do something about those grey hairs I noticed.

TWENTY-NINE

1884

Emma opened the small envelope, knowing what it must contain. It was a few days after her forty-fourth birthday, which was on 23 January. There had been no family celebrations this year, for they were waiting anxiously for news from London. They were aware that the end was near for Jerusha. The family curse had struck yet again – she had succumbed to phthisis and bronchitis.

The card was black bordered, the message simple but poignant.

In Affectionate Remembrance of
JERUSHA,
The Dearly Beloved Wife of
CHARLES HOLMES
Who departed this life January 27th, 1884
Interred in Lower Norwood Cemetery

....

'Blessed are the pure in heart, for they shall see God.'

Later, they would learn that Jerusha had requested a simple, private burial, and 'no mourning, please'. She was laid to rest near the Crystal Palace, which had a special place in her affections, as it was where she had first acknowledged her feelings for Chas.

William arrived to offer comfort to his sisters. His and Sarah's youngest son, Jeremiah, was about to be married to his long-time sweetheart Emily in Wymondham in February. 'Chas wrote to me just last week that Jerusha wished the young couple to carry on with their plans. She was so happy to hear Jeremiah was taking over Browick Bottom Farm too.'

'I'm glad she knew that,' Emma said. 'This is thanks to all you and Sarah have done to make that possible, Will.'

'I will be helping out on the farm – I hev turned my business and big house over to our other two boys, and Sarah and I will soon be living over the shop. 'Twill be a slower pace of life, but us do look forward to it.'

'Do the rest of the family know about Jerusha?' Rebecca asked.

'Chas hev written to Martha, Lizzie, Keturah and Jonathan – I am to let Sophie know,' William said. 'I make sure to keep in touch with her and her life in Norwich. She hev her troubles, poor gal, her little lad hev become deaf after he took a fever. 'Tis how this news affects young Ellie, worries us.'

Emma said tremulously, 'We feel the same. I hope she is happy with her mother, but she hardly knew her, after all. She was *Jerusha's* little girl.'

Later, after William had departed, Rebecca confided a secret to Emma. 'You know the saying, Emma, as one goes, another comes into the world. Well, I have told no one yet, apart from Richard, of course, but I am expecting again in August.'

Emma hugged her sister. 'Dear Becca, I hope you have a little son this time.'

'So do I. But it means as time goes on, I won't be able to help you as much. Also, now Richard's mother is gone, his father will need us more.'

'Don't worry about us! I have been wondering if there something I could do, other than running a boarding house! The older children are not so dependent on me now; it's the two youngest boys I have to consider. Ernie is impatient to leave school and to begin training for a job. The boarders are both engaged to be married and will be leaving here soon; the travellers by coach are becoming less frequent, since most people now take the train. Alice is set on getting an apprenticeship later this year and Immi needs more in her life than drudgery. Her cousin Izzy in Amble is teaching at elementary school now, despite having the same disability.'

'I'm sure Immi doesn't think of it like that, Emma. After all, we were employed in the same way at her age, and before that, you were housekeeping on the farm.'

'At least I escaped the workhouse, unlike you, Becca.'

'I put that behind me when I wed my Richard, but Keturah took it very hard.'

'Our young brothers did, too.'

'One never grew up, and the other . . .' Rebecca sighed. 'It has tortured him ever since.'

'We should write to Reverend Eden, he will say prayers for Jerusha at the Abbey.'

Back in Wymondham, the weather was milder than was usual in February, which was perfect for the wedding. The family were reunited with some members they had not seen for years, including Martha and Lizzie. However, Keturah was unable to come from Jarrow, which disappointed her sisters. Chas, too, was not present because of his bereavement, and Jonathan did not acknowledge his invitation.

It was a shock to Emma when she realised that the grey-haired, thin woman who followed her tall, elegant half-sister Lizzie into the church was her sister Martha.

Lizzie had no trace of a Norfolk accent – she had lived in London for many years and achieved success through hard work. She was housekeeper in a foreign embassy, but she kept in touch with her extended family and offered help in hard times.

Martha's six children were not in evidence. They were older than Emma's, and Elijah, whom her family considered a restless spirit as he changed jobs and uprooted his family so often, had not accompanied his wife. To Emma, Martha looked sad and unwell. I should have written to her more often, even though she rarely replies to my letters.

She has never said, but I don't imagine she has had much love or luck in her life, she thought.

Emma was proud to show off her family, minus Tom, who had to work that Saturday. She and Immi sat either end of the pew, with the three boys, warned to be on their best behaviour, and Alice in between.

Rebecca was not the only expectant mother there, for the bridegroom had 'jumped the gun', as William put it, and there would be the blessing of a new baby that September at Browick Bottom Farm. The bride was unaware that the congregation knew this fact, but none were censorious, it was a very natural state of affairs after all. Emily was a smiling bride, with her little sisters following her down the aisle.

After the service they walked in a triumphant procession to the farm they had been forced to leave all those years ago. Sarah and her family had cleaned and polished every corner of the house, and Jeremiah's brothers had lit the fires to warm the rooms where they gathered. The long pine table was restored to the cosy kitchen and was laden with good food, prepared by Sarah and her daughter. Emma and Rebecca had contributed the wedding cake, which was dark and full of fruit, glistening with icing, on a silver plate.

William stood at the head of the table to make his speech and raised his glass of Sarah's elderberry wine. He cleared his throat, as the company looked at him expectantly.

'Us hev come home, at last,' he said, and then sat down abruptly, tears coursing down his seamed cheeks.

Sarah stepped into the breach. 'Us should toast the bride and groom – Jeremiah and Emily!' She took a tiny sip from her glass, as although she had brewed the wine, she did not usually imbibe herself. Then she bent to console her husband. Her arms went around him and she cradled his head against her comfortable bosom. For a moment the guests were silent, then there was a chorus of 'The Bride and Groom!' and they remained standing to applaud the patriarch of the family, who had made their return home possible.

'Just think, I was born here in this house,' Emma whispered to young Frank.

'Was it a hundred years ago?' he whispered back.

'Not quite, but I'm not telling you how old I am!' she returned. The house was full of memories, of whispers. She remembered kneading the bread dough on this table, with Martha scolding her and her little sisters playing with the dog on the rag rug in front of the range. She thought of her mother, Sophia, and how she cared for them all, and taught them from the Bible. Her father, unlacing his heavy boots as he sat in his chair, after working from dawn to dusk each day, responsible for so many of them. Long gone but not forgotten. She thought too of the small Jerusha and the special bond between them.

The words inside inside a condolence card came back to her:

She is not lost! She lives, she lives for aye;
To those rent hearts, this healing hope is given
When from our sight, our loved ones pass away,
All that seems lost to earth is found in heaven . . .

Emma said to herself, '*Amen*, so let it be.'

A new phrase entered the English Language – *Roller Coaster*. The first one of these amazing, hair-raising fairground rides appeared in 1884, but the whole year was a roller coaster of events for Emma and her family. It began sadly with the loss of a loved sister, but there were happier times ahead.

In August, Emma was with her sister Rebecca when she delivered a healthy baby boy. His parents named him Albert Gordon, his second name in honour of the general fighting in the Sudan, but this young man would always be known as Bertie, one of the 'four bees', as his family called them, which pleased his sisters, Beatrice, now ten, Bertha, eight, and little Bella who was three.

For the first time, Rebecca and Richard were able to put a painful memory to rest, for their first baby had been a boy, born prematurely some months after their marriage, and had only survived a few weeks.

Shortly after this, there was a new baby at Browick Bottom Farm, when Minnie was born to Jeremiah and Emily.

'All is well,' William said proudly. Although supposedly semi-retired, he worked as hard as ever, labouring on the farm, passing on his skills and knowledge to his son, and helping out his dear Sarah in her shop.

'There will be another baby,' Sarah predicted, 'things always goo in threes.' She was proved right when they heard from Keturah in Jarrow that she had added to her family too, with a son, Horace.

THIRTY

When Alice confided in her friend Miss Janet that she had ambitions to go to London and become an apprentice in a fashionable dressmaking establishment, Miss Janet went to see Emma and suggested how she might help.

'An old school friend of mine and my sister now lives in Ealing and has set up a dressmaking school and academy alongside her business. Mrs Norton already has an exclusive clientele, including members of the aristocracy, and she mentioned in a recent letter to us that she was looking to take on another apprentice and would be placing an advertisement in *The Lady*. Why not get the magazine and see what you think? We would be delighted to put Alice's name forward for her approval!'

Immi, coming into the sitting room with a tray of tea and shortbread biscuits, overheard this and bit her lip. She and Alice clashed at times, but she was the elder sister and sometimes it seemed unfair that Alice had far more freedom than she herself, while she led a sheltered existence. She was eighteen years old, and yet she felt she was unlikely ever to leave home.

Alice, of course, was overjoyed at the news, and promised her mother, 'I'll work hard and one day I'll be famous, you'll see!'

Tom put her in her place. 'You'll need a bigger hat, Alice, to cover a swollen head, that's certain, anyway!'

However, they all knew they would miss lively Alice, even though she was aggravating at times.

Ealing, that green, leafy village had, since the advent of the railway, grown rapidly – and by now was referred to as 'the Queen of the Suburbs'. The parks and horse chestnut trees, which lined the streets, the lovely old houses, including Ashton House, retained the rural atmosphere, but the High Street now extended to the Broadway, exclusive shops appeared along its length and the wide roads made access easy.

Mrs Emmeline Norton had left an established business in Devon to further her ambitions, but her husband, an ostler, remained there with their two older children, while her youngest son accompanied his mother. He was now fifteen and an apprentice pianoforte finisher.

Oxford Road was a short walk from the station and the Broadway and Emma and Alice arrived there on a crisp, autumn day, in good time for their appointment with

Mrs Norton at 3 p.m. They surveyed the grand residence with awe and some trepidation from across the road. They noted that the house was five-storeys high with steps up to the massive front door, and more steps down to the railed basement area. 'Like the Summers' South Kensington house,' Emma said, 'except it's much bigger.'

Alice, her golden hair fanning out under her tam-o'-shanter, tugged her arm impatiently. 'Mother, they can probably see us from one of the windows!'

A nearby church clock chimed the hour, so Emma shifted her valise to her left hand and held on to Alice firmly as they crossed the road. She allowed Alice to lift the heavy knocker on the door, which was answered promptly by a maid.

'Mrs and Miss Meehan? Please follow me.' They went up the staircase to the first-floor room where Mrs Norton was waiting for them. Alice was impressed by her purple gown and the thick, black upswept hair, but later she would realise that it was one of a range of immaculate wigs. Mrs Norton's complexion was pale, perhaps due to the fact that she rarely went outside, avoiding direct sunlight, and her face was well-powdered. There was an almost over-powering smell of expensive perfume – she must be quite old, Alice imagined, maybe fifty, but she certainly hadn't dabbed on lavender water like Emma.

Mrs Norton appeared rather aloof, regarding Alice through a monocle, which hung round her neck on a silver chain. 'You will have gathered, I hope, that this is a superior dressmaking establishment, not a sweatshop where the workers are exploited, and that I only take on young girls of good character, decently educated, who have the skill to hand-finish expensive garments. The business is constantly expanding, and at present I have three other apprentices of a similar age to Alice who are supervised at work by my niece, Lucy, who is a few years older, but has successfully completed her apprenticeship with myself. There are a number of skilled dressmakers in the main workroom, who will take it in turn to instruct you in the academy. I also employ two mantle-makers, who carry out special commissions, like ceremonial cloaks, and they work with the most sumptuous materials. They also repair precious old mantles and are superb at embroidery and embellishment. Now, Alice, if you and your mother will follow me, I will show you the workrooms, the classroom, the showroom, where clients are received, and your living quarters on the top floor.'

Sewing machines whirred in the largest workroom, and Alice took in the atmosphere; the seamstresses concentrated on their work, not seeming to notice the interruption. They tiptoed out of the room and Alice was asked to comment on what she had seen. She could only manage to say, 'I can't wait to use one of those beautiful machines.'

'You have a lot to learn first,' Mrs Norton said drily.

In the classroom, the apprentices were handling swatches of cloth, feeling the texture, deciding which fabric was suitable for which purpose, and learning where the material had been made and how it had been printed or dyed. Lucy greeted her in a friendly manner and introduced her to each of the girls. 'Take a seat, Alice, and join in the discussion,' Lucy continued. 'Purple dye has been the most popular colour since the third century, when it was so expensive it was said to be worth its weight in gold. Can any of you tell me how the dye was originally made?'

Observing the class from the back of the room, Emma saw Alice's hand shoot up. Oh dear, she thought, is she going to embarrass me?

But Alice had been well primed by Miss Janet. 'Purple dye was made in those early days from the crushed shells of a mollusc, but now aniline dyes are used,' she said.

Mrs Norton put in, 'Can you explain how aniline dyes are made, Alice, please?'

Alice answered, 'They are extracted from coal tar – mauve was the first dye in 1856, then other colours, but some of them faded in sunlight.'

'However, you must agree, Alice, that aniline dyes, in particular royal purple, have been improved to a high standard nowadays?'

'Yes, Mrs Norton,' Alice agreed.

'You can complete the tour with our new apprentice after class, Lucy. Meanwhile, I will discuss business with Mrs Meehan,' her aunt decided. She turned to Emma. 'I expect you intend to travel home tonight?' Mrs Norton led the way back to the reception room where they had met.

Emma's throat felt dry. It was the first time she had been invited to speak, she thought wryly. 'I am staying with relatives tonight in Commercial Road and returning home tomorrow. My eldest daughter is holding the fort, not so much to do now the younger children are all at school.' She thought it prudent to say 'with relatives' not, 'with my brother-in-law' as that would lead to more explanations.

'I think Alice will fit in well here,' Mrs Norton said unexpectedly, with a glimmer of a smile. 'Now, we have some papers to sign.'

It was only when she knocked on Chas's door later that Emma realised she hadn't said goodbye to Alice or wished her well. She said to herself, *I must write to her the minute I get home.*

Chas opened the door to Emma. He was still in uniform, though had removed his boots, and had just come off duty. His face was gaunt, and he had obviously lost weight, but he ushered her in, and said, 'It's so good to see you, Emma. I just wish . . .'

'I know,' she told him. 'I know, and I feel the same, Chas.' She looked at him with concern. 'You need a good, square meal, my dear, and I am willing to cook for you this evening, so let's talk in the kitchen, shall we?'

'Allow me to escort you to your room first, and while you are unpacking your bag, I will get changed, if you don't mind. I had thought I could fetch some fish and chips for our supper. I've let the cupboard run low. I haven't had much appetite, I'm afraid.'

'Fish and chips sounds just what we both need tonight,' Emma said. 'We've both had a long and tiring day, I imagine.'

They ate their meal at the kitchen table, with a big pot of strong tea to wash it down. 'Not much washing up – I'll tackle it,' Emma said firmly. 'I'll join you in the sitting room in a few minutes.'

'I've got a little cat for company, she'll be outside the back door. It's time for her supper too. Give Kitty the fishy bits, eh?'

The sitting room looked rather neglected. Emma guessed the reason why.

'I spent most of my time when I was home sitting with Jerusha. She never complained, Emma, and accepted the inevitable. She was back in her childhood those last few days. Talking of her mother and father and her special sister – you. I was so fortunate to marry her and so proud of my wonderful wife. The years we spent together have been the best of my life.'

'How has little Ellie taken her loss?' Emma asked gently.

'Hard. Very hard. I would love to have her home, but it's not possible for me to care for a child on my own because of my profession. My hours of duty are unpredictable; she could not be left in the house on her own. I understand that her Aunt Susannah in Battersea, who already cares for Ellie's sister, has offered to have her live with them, the mother being not so well again, so at least I will see Ellie from time to time, and can contribute to her keep, which is what Jerusha would have wished.'

'Jonathan's children are still being moved from pillar to post,' Emma said sadly.

Glancing round the room she saw the basket of sewing open on the small table by the fire, untouched since Jerusha's final illness. There was the gramophone, which Chas had bought his wife, in a cabinet with a pile of records. From a bureau drawer, Chas took out a velvet-covered box.

'Jerusha said this was for you, Emma. Have a look inside.'

Emma recognised immediately the emerald necklace that Chas had given Jerusha on the evening they went to the opera as she'd told her about it in such detail. 'I'm not sure I can accept this,' she faltered.

'Of course you can! You must, because it was her wish.'

Emma said tremulously, 'I will treasure it.' But she didn't think she'd ever be able to wear it without getting tearful, and decided to give it to Immi when she was twenty-one.

Alice, at nine o'clock that same evening, was already in her narrow, single bed in the dormitory under the eaves. The room was shared by the young apprentices and was modestly furnished; the beds had identical quilts and feather-filled pillows. The bathroom along the corridor was a cavernous room with a deep, mahogany-surrounded bath tub, and a row of basins with shining taps from which gushed hot water – what luxury to most of the girls! There was a list of rules and bathing times. In the WC, a separate cubicle, they were reminded *One pull of the chain is sufficient.* However, there was no ban on conversation, which suited Alice. No mother to call, 'Go to sleep, Alice, you're keeping us all awake!'

Emma missed her daughter's chattering that night. My first fledgling to fly the nest, she thought. I hope she won't be homesick.

Alice was, in fact, relishing every moment of her new life. She was an independent young lady, although not yet fifteen years of age, and Lucy, Mrs Norton's niece, discussing the new recruit with her aunt that evening, predicted, 'Alice will do well, you'll see, Aunt Emmeline.'

THIRTY-ONE

1885

Emma's family were spreading their wings. Alice was the first to leave home, while Tom was a railway clerk at Beccles, but still living with his mother, and Immi and Rebecca were helping Emma to run the boarding house. Ernie was eager to become a working lad and only Ted and Frank were still at school.

In September 1885, Emma told Rebecca, 'Tom has been offered one of the new railway houses in Ravensmeer now he is a senior clerk and will be moving out shortly. I'll miss him and the support he gives us. We really can't make ends meet, I feel, without his money coming in. Although I am called out to confinements when the main midwives are busy, that income is not predictable. It seems to me this is a good time to seek a permanent position as a housekeeper, somewhere I can take the boys – Ernie is ready to begin work but wants to remain near me, I know. However, Ted is doing well with his studies here and I'm afraid he won't want to change schools: he has been promised a job later as a railway clerk if he does well in his studies. Frank, of course, is confident enough to take a move in his stride.'

'What about Immi?' Rebecca asked. Immi was out of earshot, wheeling little Bertie in his perambulator up the street, to induce him to have a morning nap.

'I have discussed the matter with Immi, and she would like to take up Tom's suggestion and keep house for him—'

'That sounds the perfect solution, Emma,' Rebecca agreed. She was relieved, for now it would be easier to tell Emma that *they* may be moving to Docking, as Richard hoped to be transferred there so they could keep an eye on his father, who was becoming more forgetful.

Emma studied the advertisements in *The Lady* and finally she came across something she knew instinctively would suit her.

> Bedford Lodge, Newmarket. Applications are invited for the post of housekeeper to the residents of the stables cottages, including stablemen/grooms, tack men and several apprentices aged between twelve and fifteen years. The housekeeper will be assisted by a live-in cook and housemaid, and she must be prepared to help the housekeeper in the main house when necessary. A cottage on site will be provided and there is no objection to one or two children of

school age interested in working in the stables part-time.

The successful applicant will be a mature woman, intelligent and discreet. Letters should be addressed to Mr Gurry, the racecourse trainer who is in charge of the stables.

Excellent references are required.

'How old is mature?' Emma asked Immi. 'The references aren't a problem!'

'About forty, I think – you are a matron, aren't you?' Immi said innocently. She was excited at the thought of a more independent role herself.

'I'm forty-six – but I don't look it – or do I? I could pass for forty if I do something about my hair!'

'Ask Aunt Becca about that. She doesn't seem to have any grey hairs!'

Tom had a word with his mother on Ted's behalf. 'Mother, Ted has asked if he can stay on in Beccles with me and Immi. He doesn't want to go to Newmarket if you get the job. He wants to become a clerk on the railway. I promise you we would care for him, and see he attends school until it is time to leave.'

'I know I can trust you both to do so, but it hurts a bit he that he doesn't want to be with me,' Emma said, her bottom lip trembling. Was she doing the right thing – dividing the family?

'He loves you as we all do, you can be sure of that,' Tom assured her.

Shortly after she'd sent her application, and much to her excitement, Emma received an invitation to come to Newmarket for an interview. Rebecca was called upon to give advice on improving her appearance. Emma had, after all, given her age in her letter as forty!

'How do you cover the grey in your hair, Becca?' she asked bluntly.

'Well, I'm not so worried about that yet,' her sister replied cheerfully. 'I use some of Richard's pomade; he darkens his moustache with that. But you need a safe dye – how about henna?'

'I don't want to turn into a redhead!'

'I believe you can use henna first and then indigo for black hair – or the chemist, I've heard, mixes up something in a blue bottle—'

'That means it's poisonous!'

'Only if you drink it, Emma. A friend of mine recommends tincture of iron, mixed with red wine—'

'We don't have any wine, red or otherwise,' Emma said flatly.

'The grocer will oblige, I'm sure. Some use it in cooking. You wash your hair and rinse it well, then while it's still damp, apply the solution with a fine-tooth comb from the roots. You need to protect your face, ears and neck from splashes. When your hair is dry, my friend says, oil your scalp and brush as usual.'

'I'll try that,' Emma decided.

'You can always drink any wine that's left over.' Rebecca winked.

The hair colouring was successful, and then Emma was persuaded to rub a little rouge on her cheeks and lips. 'The dark hair makes you appear pale,' Immi said.

On the morning of her appointment, Emma wore her best black dress. 'I want to look like a housekeeper, not a lady of leisure,' she said, rejecting the floral dress she'd worn to Yarmouth.

She didn't find rail travel daunting nowadays, and it was a pleasant journey, which she whiled away by reading her well-worn copy of *Mrs Beeton*. Tiring of this, she tucked it away in her reticule. I know I'm a capable housekeeper, she thought to herself, and I guess I look the part now I'm older. She gazed out of the window at the rolling countryside and on the horizon saw a string of horses being galloped. Frank will be excited to be near the stables if I'm successful and secure the position, she thought.

She was met by a groom, who tipped his cap respectfully and assisted her into a gig. A flick of the reins. and they were off at a trot to the estate.

The Lodge was an impressive edifice with an adjacent group of outbuildings, surrounded by extensive grounds.

The groom pointed to a new building, 'That's the squire's boxing saloon; us grooms never get a look-in. He got left a fortune when he was a young boy and money runs through his fingers like water, they say,' he said laconically, but seeing Emma's reaction, omitted to tell her about the cock-fighting and gambling. There were two cottages nearby. 'The butler lives there with his family,' the groom told her, 'and the other one is the gardener's house. Beyond are the stables. they look like a horseshoe, don't you think?'

Emma had already learned that the squire was George Alexander Baird, whose exploits, both in the racing world and romantically, were often in the newspapers. She felt apprehensive. Now she knew why *discretion* was required.

'You won't have too much to do with *him*,' the groom said cheerfully, reading her thoughts. 'However, you'll have a lot to do with the staff who live in at the Lodge but you'll find them all easy to get on with. Here we are, this is the stable block. Mr Gurry is waiting to greet you.' He added, 'He and the squire fall out regular so don't be surprised if another trainer gets to take over.' Emma's unease increased.

Mr Gurry was in his office talking to a wiry man wearing breeches and boots – there was an aroma in the air that Emma immediately identified, for it reminded her of the farm and her father after working with the horse all day.

Mr Gurry rose to greet her and introduced Emma to his companion. 'Mrs Meehan, this is Fred Archer, the champion jockey, he came along this morning to observe the exercising of our string of horses, one in particular, on Bury Side. That's our nearest gallop. The squire rode out with us as usual, too, but he is off to Paris today, so he left this side of things to me.' He turned to his companion, who was about to leave. 'Well, Fred, I'll see you later, no doubt?'

Fred Archer nodded. He was very tall for a jockey, Emma thought, and he had a sad face. She recalled that she'd read in the paper of the tragic loss of his wife in childbirth. 'I must get back to my own stables at Falmouth Lodge; nice to meet you, Mrs Meehan.' He shook her hand before leaving. Emma was unsure after whether his parting words were addressed to her or not: 'Good Luck.'

'Do sit down,' Mr Gurry said to Emma, indicating a chair. 'I must say we were impressed with your letter, and your references are excellent. The butler was looking forward to meeting you this morning. He sends his apologies. The squire requires his services before he leaves, but there is also a houseful of guests who arrived last night for a party. Now, we can discuss the matter of your employment and what the job entails, please ask as many questions as you like.'

They were soon talking like old friends, and Emma was reassured it would be a rewarding position, both financially and personally, as she planned to send money home to help with Ted's keep.

'You have a motherly look,' Mr Gurry said, 'and I'm sure you can handle spirited lads of this age group – they are a good bunch, but they need guidance at times.'

Emma thought ruefully, Motherly . . . so much for dyed hair and a tight corset! 'My younger son, Frank, will enjoy life here, I know. He is passionate about horses.'

'I understand your older boy will be looking for work? He might be employed here in some capacity, perhaps as a stable lad, but we are not looking for another apprentice at the moment.'

'I would be most grateful,' Emma said. 'His name is Ernest.'

'As for young Frank, he could work here part-time as kitchen boy – he has to have a title, to earn a small wage.'

'Thank you.' She added impulsively, 'Please call me Emma, everyone does!'

Mr Gurry smiled. 'Now, follow me and I will show you where the stable staff are housed. The first cottage, which is fully furnished, you will share with Dorcas, our cook. I'm sure you will get on splendidly – she will take you to the kitchen and mess hall to introduce you to the daily staff. Dorcas will also inform you about the tradesmen who call, and the daily records of expenditure.'

'Does that mean I have the job?' Emma had to know.

'Yes, Emma, it does,' he smiled. 'If possible, we would like you to commence your duties in a month's time.'

Emma helped Tom furnish his new home with furniture she had collected before she came to Beccles. 'I know Immi will keep it polished,' she said. 'Those particular things hold sentimental value for me. The furnishings we bought in the auction rooms can go back there to be sold. The money won't be much but should pay for the move.'

Immi was to be custodian of her grandmother Isabella's trunk, which also held memorabilia from her father. 'I bequeath you my purple eiderdown, too,' Emma told her. 'I must travel as light as possible to Newmarket, though there will be a trunk full of our clothes for the three of us.'

There was good news about the lease of the Beccles boarding house, for the house and business already had a new tenant waiting to take over.

Emma had been there with her family for almost five years: Time to move on, she thought. However, first, she was looking forward to a fortnight back in Wymondham, with her younger boys. William had written *Come home and have a well-earned rest! Friends ask after you. All is well, Love Will and Sarah.*

EPILOGUE

Wymondham, Autumn 1885

'We're home, boys!' Emma exclaimed excitedly as the train arrived at Norwich Station. They would soon be back at Wymondham and Browick Bottom Farm, where they would stay at the farmhouse with William and his family; it would be her first time back there since Jeremiah's wedding some eighteen months before. She reached up to the rack and took down a bulging bag – this was TF's old naval sack, as he'd referred to it. It was nice to have something of Tom's to bring back with them to Wymondham and she was glad she hadn't discarded it when they'd left Hungate. *He'd probably smile and say, 'You're sentimental, Emma, about my old sack, but I suppose I kept it for the same reason,'* she thought with a sad smile.

Jeremiah was waiting on the platform and took them round to board the farm cart, for the smart wagon William had owned years ago had been given to his elder sons when they took over his business.

When they arrived, the boys were given a tour. There were some changes to the farm, of course. There was a fine new cowshed, and one of the barns was now a repository for all the machinery. There was no big shire horse to pull the plough, though. No pigs either, and the hens now had a large secure pen – no more searching for eggs hidden in hedgerow nests – and there were ducks swimming in an enlarged pond, as their eggs were popular when sold at the market.

'Where are the cats?' Frank asked.

'Some in the barn, but they are not domesticated, Frank,' Jeremiah said. 'Indoors, us hev a pet kitten, a ginger one, so that's a tomcat, and us do call him Ginger, too.'

'Like Ernie – they call *him* Ginger at school!' Frank said, earning a poke from his brother in return.

Then they went into the dairy to see William busy churning the butter. 'The gals do like a chatter when folk come, so I be doing my bit,' he said. 'Who would like to turn the handle?'

'Me!' cried the boys in unison.

'One at a time,' William said, hoisting Frank on to a three-legged stool.

Inside the big kitchen, still with its black-leaded range and singing kettle, Emma sat down at the old pine table, and said reflectively to Sarah and Emily, Jeremiah's wife, 'Do you still make bread and use the oven in the wall?' She looked round the room, thinking, It doesn't seem the same without all of us who once lived here.

'We do,' Sarah said with a smile. She was bustling about as usual, making cups of tea and putting hot griddle scones on a plate, with a dish of farm butter beside them. Minnie, who was shy at first with visitors, was strapped in her little chair. She was toddling now at a year old, but not in the kitchen when cooking was going on. Emily was adding dumplings to the simmering salt beef in the big pot on the stove, for dinner later. She turned and asked, 'I'll call them in, shall I? Lucky it's not raining, the boys would hev muddy shoes.'

The little ginger cat suddenly jumped up onto Emma's lap. She stroked him and he purred loudly. 'You make a lot of noise for a little 'un,' she told him, tickling him behind his ears.

Ernie and Frank came in, and Sarah told them to wash their hands in the scullery first, before eating the scones. Frank was eager to tell his mother what they had been doing outside but followed his brother reluctantly. He was back in a couple of minutes. 'I made some butter in a big churn, it rolled over and over but William made it do that – I wasn't big enough, he said.'

'Uncle William,' Emma reminded him.

'Oh, I'm Will or William to all of 'em.' William said, smiling.

'I didn't see a horse. You haven't got one now, have you, William?' Frank piped up.

'No, I'm an engineer you see, us don't need one now, but I miss our old hoss too,' William said.

'And they haven't got a spaniel called Fly any more, like the one you told us about, Mother.' Ernie had arrived. He held up his clean hands to show his mother, and she nodded. '*He* only dipped his in the water, not washed them,' Ernie said.

'Don't tell tales,' Emma said firmly. 'He's younger than you, so it's allowed.'

'Pass the scones round, Ernie,' Sarah suggested. She smiled at Emma. 'Boys don't change, do they? Just like mine used to be . . .'

That evening, after the boys had gone to their beds in the room Emma's brothers had slept in years ago, and Emily and Jeremiah had retired, Emma, William and Sarah sat round the fire talking of old times and remembering life as it was here thirty or more years ago. Then Emma enquired after old friends. 'Do you remember – the day Frank was born?'

'I certainly do,' Sarah said, sipping her bedtime cocoa.

'I delivered those twins, I recall, and then went home to be delivered myself – by you, Sarah!'

'Those twins, who were so small,' Sarah said, 'are big girls now and today they can wrestle any lad to the ground who teases them. Where do the years go to, Emma?'

Emma shook her head. 'Don't ask me, but I am glad I am back home again, even if it's for a short time. Sarah, I have a favour to ask of you. Would you mind if I go by myself to the Abbey – could the boys stay here with you – I need to say goodbye to my husband and tell him I will be away and not able to visit him for some time.'

Sarah leaned over: 'Go there whenever you feel the need, my dear, us understand.'

Emma stood looking at the impressive headstone over TF's grave. She had gone early to the Abbey graveyard, while the mist was clearing and the stone gleamed white; it was obvious her brother and sister-in-law had cleaned it regularly. Emma traced the outline of the forget-me-nots carved above her husband's name with her finger. She spoke in a whisper, although there was no one about: 'My darling Tom, I have to go away for a while, but I had to say goodbye to you. My love for you is as strong as ever, and I will think of you every day, I promise. Our wonderful family are growing up fast, and I have to let them go, but they all love you too. You would be so proud of what they have achieved.'

She looked up; the sky was still streaked with red, but the mist was gone. There was the promise of a lovely day ahead.

ACKNOWLEDGEMENTS

The support and enthusiasm of Glenys, Nell's daughter is much appreciated. Glenys, a dedicated nurse/tutor, helped with recalling times and places and advised on medical matters of the era. I am grateful to Pam Kempton for her painstaking research concerning TF, his family, as a boy sailor in the Crimean War, service in the original London fire service (LFEE) and the London Salvage Company. The information from the LFB museum was most helpful. Various letters come from my late mother Bella's box; Bella perpetuated Emma's stories in the Uggeshall Book and Nell too shared fond memories of their grandma. Myrtle's daughter, Sandra, is also thanked for her warm support. My dear husband John as always helped in my research. Thanks too, to Lynne in Canada for sharing memories of her intrepid great-grandfather Frank.

All Emma and TF's children were very special in their own way, and the youngest, Frank, was heroic like his father. There is one character, previously unknown to me, who was an unsung hero, Emma's half-brother, William, who looked out for every single one of his extended family.

I hope I have captured the essence of Emma. I was very young at the end of her long life, but I still see her in my mind's eye, and now I have given her a voice I hope others can see her too. I have followed in Emma's footsteps it seems, for she was a great storyteller and certainly used her imagination . . . and I believe she would have approved of my interpretation of her love story.

I would like to thank both Claire and Gillian for their skilful editing and for not changing 'my voice' or the storyline. I really must pull my socks up and not capitalise so freely! My apologies for those slip ups! This was a very special story to write, and I hope I might be asked for more . . .

NB: The names of minor characters in the story have been changed, as they appear briefly in the story and were not relevant to research. Some friends come and go during a long life. Too many characters called Thomas on both sides of the family could cause confusion, so Emma's father, the most prominent of these, is now Tobias!

Welcome to the world of *Sheila Newberry*!

Keep reading for more from Sheila Newberry, to discover a recipe that features in this novel and to find out more about what Sheila is doing next . . .

We'd also like to introduce you to MEMORY LANE, our special community for the very best of saga writing from authors you know and love and new ones we simply can't wait for you to meet. Read on and join our club!

www.MemoryLane.club

MEMORY LANE

Meet Sheila Newberry

I've been writing since I was three years old, and even told myself stories in my cot. So it came as a shock when I was whacked round the head by my volatile kindergarten teacher for daydreaming about stories when I was supposed to be chanting the phonetic alphabet. My mother received a letter from my teacher saying, 'Sheila will not speak. Why?' Mum told her that it was because I was scared stiff in class. I was immediately moved up two classes. Here I was given the task of encouraging the slow readers. This was something I was good at but still felt that I didn't fit in. Later, I learned that another teacher had saved all my compositions saying they inspired many children in later years.

I had scarlet fever in the spring of 1939, and when I returned to our home near Croydon, I saw changes which puzzled me – sandbags, shelters in back gardens, camouflaged by moss and daisies, and windows reinforced with criss-crossed tape. Children had iron rations in Oxo tins – we ate the contents during rehearsals for air-raids – and gas masks were given out. I especially recall the stifling rubber. We spent the summer holiday, as usual, in Suffolk and I remember being puzzled when my father left us there, as the Admiralty staff was moving to Bath. 'War' was not mentioned but we were now officially evacuees, living with relatives in a small cottage in a sleepy village.

On and off, we returned to London at the wrong times. We were bombed out in 1940 and dodging doodlebugs in 1943. I thought of Suffolk as my home. I was still writing – on flyleaves of books cut out by friends – and every Friday I told stories about Black-eyed Bill the Pirate to the whole school in the village hut. I wrote my first pantomime at nine years old, and was awarded the part of Puss in Boots. I wore a costume made from blackout curtains. We were back in our patched-up London home to celebrate VE night and dancing in the street. Lights blazed – it was very exciting.

I had a moment of glory when I won an essay competition that 3000 schoolchildren had entered. The subject was waste paper, which we all collected avidly! At my new school, I was encouraged by my teachers to concentrate on English Literature and Language, History and Art, and I did well in my final exams. I wanted to be a writer, but was told there was a shortage of paper! True. I wrote stories all the time and read many books. I was useless at games like netball as I was so short-sighted – I didn't see the ball until it hit me. I still loved acting, and my favourite Shakespearian parts were Shylock and Lady Macbeth.

MEMORY LANE

When I left school, I worked in London at an academic publisher. I had wanted to be a reporter, but I couldn't ride a bike! Two years after school, I met my husband John. We had nine children and lived on a smallholding in Kent with many pets (and pests). I wrote the whole time. The children did, too, but they were also artistic like John. We were all very happy. I acquired a typewriter and wrote short stories for children, articles on family life and romance for magazines. I received wonderful feedback. I soon graduated to writing novels and joined the Romantic Novelists' Association. I have had many books published over the years and am over the moon to see my books out in the world once again.

MEMORY LANE

Dear reader,

This latest book is something a little bit different for me as rather than purely fiction, which my previous books have been, *The Forget-Me-Not Girl is* a saga based on the life of a very special family member, my great-grandmother, Emma. It is not a biography, but rather inspired by the events of her life and the love for her husband and family.

Writing this book was certainly a labour of love and must have taken me more than seven years. I originally envisaged it as a three book project. Before I started writing, a lot of research was required, which mainly involved talking to those family and friends who knew and remembered Emma and TF, or those who had stories passed down through the family. Gradually I could piece together the story of Emma's life and form a fuller picture of the wonderful woman she was.

I was very young at the end of Emma's long life, but I still 'see' her in my mind's eye, and have loved giving her a voice, which I hope others enjoy reading. Of course this is a novel, but I do feel I have captured Emma's essence. I think she would have approved of my interpretation of her life and love for TF and her children.

One of my fondest, and only, memories of Emma – she died when I was just four-years-old – was at Swan

House. She took me down the long garden to see if there were any walnuts on the tree, ready to pickle or to store for Christmas. It's a memory I really treasure. It seems I have followed in Emma's footsteps, as she was a great story teller and certainly used her imagination.

As a family we have a few photos of Emma throughout her life and when I saw the cover design for *The Forget-Me-Not Girl* it brought tears to my eyes. The girl looks just like my great-grandmother at her age and seems beautiful, but sad. Now that you have read the book you will realise that Emma certainly had some very hard times in her life, of heartbreak and loss, times when she was almost overwhelmed by events. She was a real survivor, the forget-me-not girl.

I hope you enjoyed reading *The Forget-Me-Not Girl* as much as I enjoyed writing it. If you did, please do share your thoughts on the Memory Lane Facebook page MemoryLaneClub.

Best wishes,

Sheila

A Recipe for Norfolk Dumplings

You can't imagine anything more 'Norfick' as the locals say, than a Norfolk Dumpling (aka Swimmers and Floaters)! Emma considered them a staple in her diet, and her family followed suit.

11 ounces of plain flour
2 teaspoons of baking powder
1 teaspoon of salt
1 egg
Half a pint of milk
1 ounce of butter
A little water if needed

1. In a large bowl mix together all of the ingredients.
2. Add a little water if the mixture seems too dry.
3. Season to your liking.
4. Take a teaspoon of the mixture and drop it into a bubbling stew, soup or mince.
5. The dumplings should float to the surface (hence the name) and cook in the stew.

Should you prefer bigger dumplings, you can stuff them and boil in gravy. They will swell like puff balls!

Don't miss Sheila Newberry's next book,
coming November 2019 . . .

A WINTER HOPE

All they want for Christmas is a new home

Number five Kitchener Avenue heralds the start of a new life for the Hope family. For pregnant Miriam it is a warm, safe environment to bring up her child. For her sister, fourteen-year-old Barbara, it means independence . . . and boys. And for Fred it means the security he craves for his young family.

In the lead up to Christmas, the Hopes settle in, and start to make happy memories in their new home. But World War II is round the corner, and this carefree life can't last.

Soon the family are split up. Bar, wanting to do her bit for the war effort, joins the ATS, while Miriam and her children are evacuated to the countryside and away from her husband.

As the country is thrown into turmoil, can the Hope family come back together and find the happiness they crave?

Sign up to MEMORY LANE to find out more

Tales from Memory Lane

Discover new stories from the best saga authors

Available now